PARDON ME,
YOU'RE STEPPING
ON MY
EYEBALL!

Other Books by Paul Zindel

THE PIGMAN

MY DARLING,
MY HAMBURGER

I NEVER LOVED YOUR MIND

THE EFFECT OF GAMMA
RAYS ON MAN-IN-THE-MOON
MARIGOLDS

LET ME HEAR YOU WHISPER

I LOVE MY MOTHER

a novel by
Paul Zindel /

PARDON ME, YOU'RE STEPPING ON MY EYEBALL!

#7249

HARPER & ROW, PUBLISHERS
New York / Hagerstown / San Francisco / London

Library of Congress Cataloging in Publication Data
Zindel, Paul.
    Pardon me, you're stepping on my eyeball!

    SUMMARY: Two alienated teenagers learn to cope
with their personal problems by being honest with
each other.
    I. Title.
PZ7.Z647Par3   [Fic]   75–25410
ISBN 0–06–026837–9
ISBN 0–06–026838–7 lib. bdg.

To John Foster

PARDON ME,
  YOU'RE STEPPING
  ON MY
  EYEBALL!

Chapter 1 /

"Marsh" Mellow was fifteen years old and hated almost everything about Curtis Lee High School. Sometimes, when he was in class, he'd just lounge at his desk making lists of the ten things he hated most on that particular day. His list for today ran like this: (1) I hate the school cafeteria because the daily special smells like steamed sneakers smothered in sautéed fleas. (2) I hate Mrs. Zucker who's teaching this class because she wears crooked eyebrows and talks like she's using reality as a crutch. (3) I hate the boy sitting in front of me because he looks like a duck and has RING-AROUND-THE-COLLAR. (4) I hate the sky because I don't know where it ends, and I hate people who call me Louis instead of Marsh. (5) I hate my mother because she's schizo and drinks diet beer while she chews cashew nuts. (6) I hate the principal of Curtis Lee High School because he caught me dropping a bag of Maxwell House coffee grinds mixed with Limburger cheese on the cheerleader squad. (7) I hate Marmaduke Jones because he was just elected Junior Class President, and sucks Tic Tacs. (8) I hate that my father is 3,000 miles away in Los Angeles, and I know he's in trouble. (9) I hate Mr. Meizner, the school psychologist, because he looks like the Good-year Blimp and keeps giving me tests to see how nuts I am. (10) I hate hating.

Marsh really hated the fact that it usually took him only five minutes of a period to make up ten new things he hated, so he'd try to kill the rest of the class making up a list of ten things he loved.

His list for this period went like this: (1) I love red ants. (2) I love octopi and Turkish Taffy. (3) I love the ball-point pen in my hand because when I press the thingamajig on top it makes a clicking sound that's driving Mrs. Zucker off her bean. (4) I love the letter my father sent me yesterday. I read it over and over and over, that's how much I love it. (5) I love it when my mother passes out after the seven o'clock news every night so I can start watching what I want on the television. (6) I love hairy spiders, especially when they eat other bugs besides red ants and praying mantises. (7) I love the moon because it makes were-wolves and vampires, and thereby is an effective weapon against overpopulation. (8) I love the school psychologist, Mr. Meizner, because he keeps sending for me during class so it gets me out of a lot of wasted mumbo jumbo, especially lousy Applied Chemistry. (9) I love money, and I wish I had enough of it so I could just hit the road and get out there and help my father. I'd spring him and we could go diving off the Galápagos Islands where wild birds come and land right on your shoulder because they don't know they're supposed to be afraid of human beings. (10) I love the school cafeteria during fifth period because there's a girl in there with long, straight, black hair whose name is Edna Shinglebox, and she looks as freaky and depressed as I am. I think it's a hoot that her family never changed its name from Shinglebox even though they probably got stuck with it because a couple of thousand years ago some weirdo ancestor of theirs probably went around carrying shingles in a box.

Marsh still had five minutes left of the period so he took out his father's letter again. Marsh knew he was the only one in the world besides his father who could know what it meant. *Dear Marsh,* his father had written. *We have only one life to live, and remember, this is no dress rehearsal. Whatever you do, and no matter what happens to me, don't let them step on your eyeball.* And it was simply signed *Love from Dad.*

Chapter 2 /

"Maybe high school is just one more place I won't have to face the world. I don't know, it's so complicated," Edna mumbled, sinking deeper into the plush Leatherette chair. The sunlight streamed into the windows of the office right into the faces of her mother and father and that strange, overweight Mr. Meizner who was just scribbling away into a notebook like *he* was the one that was nuts. Mr. Meizner was the only school psychologist Edna had ever seen who was less than five feet tall and weighed over three hundred pounds. She'd heard that the school psychologist at McGee Vocational High was an alcoholic, and that the one at Jefferson High looked like his mother had locked him up in a cupboard for thirty years. But she figured no matter what they were like, this Mr. Meizner had to take the cake.

"It's something deficient in us, Jack," she heard her mother whining, holding on to her stomach like she just swallowed marbles or something. "Maybe we should have sent her to private school. We should have spent the money. Maybe we were too cheap about it. They have cleaner boys in private schools, you know that. Edna, did you tell Mr. Meizner how boys throw things at you?"

Edna sighed, "It was only one boy, and all he threw was one pear, Mom. You don't have to make a federal case out of it."

Mrs. Shinglebox glared at her daughter. "Well tell him! Tell the shrink how you break down crying all the time."

"Mom, I don't break down crying all the time. I cry once in a while. I cry easy, that's all."

Mr. Meizner cleared his voice. "Edna, what do you do when a boy throws a pear at you?"

"I duck."

Mrs. Shinglebox took in a deep breath of air as though she were swelling herself prior to doing battle. "Now look, Mr. Meizner, I want you to know I sent Edna for posture lessons when she was seven years old. She used to look like a monkey when she went down the street. Don't think I didn't know about it. And one of the first things we ever did with her was to fix her lisp. I knew what her teeth looked like. She used to look like a woodchuck. You should have seen her. Now she's gorgeous. But I mean, that kind of thing took a lot of money. Anything that looked freaky about her we tried to fix. If the ears were off a little, we made sure they were pinned back closer to the head. We always encouraged her. That's why she's so unusual today. She has an unusual kind of beauty. But for some reason, boys don't seem to like her."

"Mom, you did the best you could. You and Papa are wonderful. I already told Mr. Meizner that," Edna stated firmly. "Anything that's the matter with me now, it's my own fault, my own personality defect. I'm a self-made yo-yo."

"You're not a yo-yo. You're a doll," her father spoke up strongly. "The only defect around here is this school. Did you see all the fags with beards running around the halls? All the pot smokers and Jesus freaks? And that's only the teachers. The students all look like twerps."

Mrs. Shinglebox put out her arm as though to stop her husband from popping out of his seat. "Mr. Meizner, ever since we've come into this office you've been staring at us as though we're crazy," Mrs. Shinglebox stated.

Mr. Shinglebox shot forward in his seat and whirled his head to look his wife right in the eye. "He's not staring at us. He hasn't even looked at us since we came in the room. If you ask me, he's crazier than we are."

Edna blocked out all their voices and just took in the sight of her parents. Her mother was wearing her best red dress with a white derby and shaggy Guatemalan shawl, and her father had on a pair of his best $9.95-Korvettes slacks with a shirt, tie and jacket that looked like the whole ensemble had been color-coordinated by a kiwi bird. And just the thought of the kiwi bird made her think of Mr. Meizner because she knew he had to have an appetite of a kiwi which is supposed to eat its own weight every day in worms. Edna really loved both her parents anyway, even though they were weird. Each of them was one of a kind. And the most remarkable thing was that they hadn't killed each other after so many years of marital bliss. The only thing she could find that they had in common was that they both loved watching horror movies.

Her mother's voice rose above the sounds of classes changing out in the hall. First there had been a bell and then there were these noises as though a couple of thousand elephants were rampaging beyond the door. "All right," Mrs. Shinglebox said. "A year ago I told Edna she shouldn't hang around with minority boys. Now we've changed our minds. We don't care if she hangs around with Attila the Hun. We don't care what it is as long as it wears pants and has the potential to grow whiskers. What we want is for Edna to join the living. I never knew a fifteen-year-old girl who hadn't once been out on a real date. The woman next door to us has a teenage daughter that's the ugliest little thing you ever saw and she goes out all the time."

Edna cleared her throat. "I'm sorry, Mom. I do the best I can, that's all I can say. I do the best I can. If it's not good enough, tough."

"Girls hate her too," her mother babbled on. "What have I done? Created Miss Super-Loser? Look, if it's my fault, just tell me. Maybe I'm trying so hard I'm just laying my trip on her. Just crushing out what little personality the poor thing has."

"Shut up," Mr. Shinglebox told his wife.

Mrs. Shinglebox waved her hand at him and only raised her voice. "Look, Mr. Meizner, I made her take courses in this school that no other girl in her right mind would take. I made sure she had maximum exposure to boys. She was the only girl in Advanced Woodwork. She made a beautiful table. You should have seen it. She's got chemistry, calculus, discus throwing and cooking."

"Cooking?" Mr. Meizner inquired, peering over his glasses and stomach.

"Yeah, cooking. I didn't want to throw her completely out of whack," Mrs. Shinglebox grunted. "My daughter is a very pretty girl, and she's very talented. I made her take nine years of ballet and she would have had a magnificent career on the stage, but we found out that she has a tendency to keel over."

"Mom. . . ."

"We gave her every opportunity to be a normal girl."

"That's true, we really did," Mr. Shinglebox added. "We let her do everything she wanted to do. She wanted to go with the Spanish Club to an expensive Mexican restaurant last year, and I gave her the money. I don't want you to think that we don't give her any money to go places."

Mrs. Shinglebox's eyes sparked as she remembered. "It was some restaurant, let me tell you. That was the night that a lot of her girlfriends in the Spanish Club found romance. But you know what Edna found? She found amoebic dysentery."

"You're embarrassing her," Mr. Shinglebox reprimanded his wife.

Edna was going to say something but her mother put her hand up to silence her. "I arranged for Edna to do a joint chemistry project with Joey Kapinolli who's on the football team and lives on our block. They were supposed to test the toxicity of local fungi, but she ended up poisoning him."

Edna protested. "It was an accident! I put the wrong label on the wrong mushrooms."

"I'm not so sure about that," Mrs. Shinglebox commented.

"Janet, will you just shut up," Mr. Shinglebox growled at his wife.

"I will not! It was horrible. Joey Kapinolli had a body that turned purple for two days."

"My wife has problems of her own, Mr. Meizner."

"I don't have any problems."

"Yes, you do."

"You and Edna are my only big problems."

Mrs. Shinglebox stood up, straightened her girdle and paced to the window. "My daughter's a sad sack, Mr. Meizner. She feels left out. In the forest of romance, she's a desert. If I had a hatchet I'd slit my wrists and write on the wall with my blood how sorry I am I made her into such a klutz. No matter what she does, she screws it up. She went to a picnic and came back with a tick in her ear. I take her to Macy's and her hair gets caught in the escalators. Do you want me on my knees, Doctor? Is that what you want? Just tell Jack and me, we'll do anything for our daughter, we beg you! Edna whimpers in her room at night. I hear her. Her bedroom's right next to mine. We were watching *The Blob* last week and all we could hear was Edna crying. Please, Mr. Meizner, can't you use psychology to help Edna get her hands on a boy?"

Chapter 3 /

It had been almost a year since Marsh had given his parents their nicknames. He called his mother Schizo Suzy and his father Paranoid Pete. Marsh really only hated Schizo Suzy when she was schizo, but he loved his father all the time, and especially when he was Paranoid Pete. Marsh decided that his mother, during the last year since Pete was gone, had come to look very much like Lady Macbeth with half a load on. All she seemed to do was run around the house all day in her polka-dot nightgown, with her long, graying hair flowing down her back, and watch news reports while sipping her diet beer and opening cans of sardines. Marsh figured she could make a fortune endorsing shampoos by saying how, whenever she used a certain shampoo her hair felt alive, and then they could just show a shot of her and everyone would think it was Medusa. Once in a while she did manage to get it all together. That was usually only once a month. She'd wash and get dressed and go buy food with her welfare check. Then she'd throw a dinner party. But the only people she'd invite would be the old couple next door because they were lushes too. It was kind of like a joy-juice jamboree. Mrs. Spooner, the wife

next door, looked like a gorilla that use
Ringling Bros. Circus. The gorilla was kn
The Kissless Bride, and the only thing i
didn't do that Mrs. Spooner did do, was to
portraits of hard-boiled eggs. Sometimes
Spooner would paint a single egg against a mag
background. Sometimes she'd do a couple of eg
together, like they were just rolling over the edge of
a hill. And sometimes she'd paint three and a half
eggs. Mr. Spooner, her husband, looked like a Bowery
reject, and he said he used to work at the Metropolitan
Opera checking hats, but that his primary position in
the world was as author of two plays, one of which
was called *What The Hell Am I Doing In The Middle
Of The Brooklyn Battery Tunnel During Rush
Hour!* Of course, nobody ever bought any of Mrs.
Spooner's egg portraits, and no one ever produced
Mr. Spooner's *What The Hell Am I Doing In The
Middle Of The Brooklyn Battery Tunnel During
Rush Hour!* So it ended up that Schizo Suzy and the
Spooners were the only families on the lower section
of Richmond Avenue who looked like white trash.

It would be just the four of them at one of Schizo
Suzy's dinner parties: Schizo Suzy, Mr. and Mrs.
Spooner, and Marsh. And usually halfway through
dinner, everybody except Marsh would be potted, and
that's when Schizo Suzy would do her thing. It was
like when she had just that little bit too much that a
buzzer would go off in her head and she'd become
another person. Her voice would go up three octaves
and she'd start talking like she needed an exorcist.
Then she'd turn on Marsh and start tearing him up

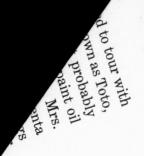

tongue until finally even the
rag Schizo Suzy away and
water glass of Drambuie.
n't you think I know what
ut at night?" Then she'd
uld flash like she'd stuck
by mistake. It used to
r try to keep artichoke
moking pot and being
chizo Suzy would say.
e loaded," Marsh would answer qui-

"Sex on your brain all the time, just like your filthy father."

When she said things like that, that was when Marsh felt like dumping a bowl of vegetables on her head. The only way he'd learned to deal with her was to keep his mouth shut and remember that she used to be a pretty good sport, and just because she was a little strung out now because of what happened to Paranoid Pete, Marsh didn't really have to hate her. Granted, his mother and father had some problems, but Marsh felt sorry for them and he also had a sneaking suspicion that the problems were a little bit too complicated and maybe he'd have to grow up a little before he'd understand them. He didn't know the reason why his father used to always walk around the house saying things like "J. Edgar Hoover used to sleep with a night-light."

Mr. Spooner used to be the only one that would stick up for him at the dinner table. "Don't pick on him," Mr. Spooner would say. But nothing would stop Schizo Suzy. "Our house is a crap palace and you don't care!" she'd yell at Marsh. "I know what you do when you're out all night. I know what you do with my Mazda. You think I don't look at the speedometer? You're a rotting, disgusting, revolting little son! And if you ask me, I should have had an abortion. That's what I think every time I look at you, Louis."

"My name is Marsh, not Louis."

"Your name is Mud, you little snot," she'd shoot back at him. "You're a sneak just like your father was. I hear you sneaking up the stairs. I hear the car pull into the driveway. You think I'm passed out, you little dope."

"Suzy, you're ruining the dinner," Mrs. Spooner groaned. "If you're not a good little girl, we'll have to put you to bed."

"Oh, go paint an egg!" Schizo Suzy screamed. Then there would be silence for a few minutes, but then it would start all over again. It was always the same splattering of accusations. According to Schizo Suzy, Marsh was either a sneak, a pothead or a sex maniac. It was always the same set of charges. She never even varied them. And it was the same set of charges she'd thrown against Paranoid Pete which used to make him take off once in a while. He'd tell Schizo Suzy he was going down to the corner for a pack of cigarettes and he'd go to Alaska or Venezuela. Marsh felt he and his father weren't sneaks. Neither of them smoked any pot. And they weren't sex maniacs. There was only one thing that Marsh knew he was, and that was this thing Schizo Suzy never even accused him of, at least not directly. Marsh was an out-and-out liar; a specialized liar.

Marsh would always lie about two things, mainly. Usually about girls, and about his father. If some kid in school happened to start up a conversation, Marsh would start bragging about what new trip his father took him on, and all the glamorous female companions they met on the journey. Marsh had a compulsion to tell everyone what lady-killers he and his father were. He'd tell the school-bus driver, he'd tell his Bio teacher, he'd tell Mr. Petrie, the garbage man. He'd tell the Spooners, Mr. Meizner, the Principal, Mrs. Zucker. He didn't know why he was unable to keep his mouth shut. They were huge lies. He told Mr. Foote, his Economics teacher, that he was dating an exotic dancer from a topless bar in Brooklyn, and that he had fixed his father up with a lady piano player. He told his Bio teacher that his father had taught him all there was to know about anatomy, and then he gave him a great big wink. He told Mr. Slazinski who ran the delicatessen on the corner of Richmond and Forest Avenues that his ambition in life was to become a garbage man, making pickups at high-rise apartments because there were lots of loose chicks running around the halls. He told Mrs. Spooner that if she ever wanted to switch from eggs to nudes, he knew seven of the top teenage fashion models in the Big Apple. He told Mr. Meizner and the Principal that he didn't care if they liked his libido or his Limburger cheese, because any day now, he was going to be married to a congressman's curvaceous daughter and would be leaving school anyway. He told Mrs. Zucker he and his father were dating hookers. And the bitter truth he knew oh-so-well. Marsh Mellow didn't have a friend in the world. He'd go around writing on walls "Electra loves Daddy" and "Double your pleasure, double your fun—Xerox your paychecks." But somehow, he couldn't seem to communicate directly with anybody. The only pal he had was Paranoid Pete, and that's why he thought maybe if he could get enough courage he could talk to Edna Shinglebox, and maybe something would come out of that. Marsh found himself lying so much, he used to pray "Oh, Lord, help my words to be gracious and tender today, for tomorrow I may have to eat them."

Chapter 4 /

Edna was busy working on headlines in the *Crow's Nest* office. The *Crow's Nest* was the school newspaper and it came out once a month, and all Edna did was write headlines and captions under the pictures. For example, the issue she was trying to put together today had a picture of Miss Cummingdinger who used to teach Home Economics at Curtis Lee High for three years, but had suddenly quit her job and joined an ice show at Madison Square Garden. The picture showed Miss Cummingdinger in a pair of sequined tights doing an aerial split through a hoop of fire. The caption Edna thought would be pretty good for the picture was "Out of the frying pan and into the fire."

Edna was in the dingy office alone with Jacqueline Potts, a sort of mysterious and intense senior who Edna knew lived in a glass house on the top of Emerson Hill and had a family that was sort of rich. Edna was only a junior, so she felt a little flattered whenever Jacqueline would talk to her because Jacqueline was a senior. Jacqueline wrote the gossip column for the *Crow's Nest*. It was called "Yaketty Yak." It wasn't that Jacqueline herself was a gossipy girl, but that happened to be the assignment that Miss Conlin, the faculty advisor, had given her. Actually, all Jacqueline had to do was empty the gossip box which was a box nailed on the wall outside the *Crow's Nest* office, and then she'd sort through all the contributions and string together different things that kids had written and try to get a ten-inch double column of juicy, unobscene bits with lots of kids' names in it so everybody would read the newspaper. The column would read like this: "Lucy S. and David P. were seen eating slices at the Tower of Pizza and is B. M., a certain brunette cheerleader furious!" Or, "There's a rumor that Shakespeare eats Bacon, but I know it can't be Donne."

The windows of the office overlooked the athletic field, and by now it was no secret that Jacqueline Potts had fallen in love with Butch Ontock, who was the best-looking guy on the football team.

"It must be very nice," Edna said as she continued to rework the caption beneath the picture of Miss Cummingdinger. She was glad to see Jacqueline smile because sometimes Jacqueline looked like she was ready to commit suicide. Sometimes she looked worse than even Edna did.

Jacqueline got up from her desk to look out the window and check the athletic field. "I never once thought I was going to end up with a guy like Butch. I wasn't having any luck with boys. They used to take me out, but I felt like they were using me and I used to get all uptight about it. I was so desperate last summer, my father had a shotgun and I was going to stick the barrel in my mouth and blow my head off."

"You're kidding," Edna laughed, nervously. But

one look at Jacqueline Potts, and she knew she wasn't kidding.

"I gave it a lot of thought and I decided I probably wasn't enough of a human being to attract a boy," Jacqueline said softly, still staring out the window. "It was going to be either the shotgun or an overdose of my mother's Valiums. But then I went to this witch."

"What witch?" Edna asked.

"The one on Richmond Avenue near Willow Brook Road. She's got this ten-foot sign out on her front lawn in the shape of a hand, and it says 'Palmist, Reader and Advisor.'"

Edna thought a moment. "Oh, yes. I see it all the time. I was wondering what it was."

"Well, I'll tell you. She's a terrific witch. And for only five dollars she told me not to kill myself, that I was going to meet a boy, and then two days later, sure enough there was this boy at my lunch table talking to me about how much he hated his father because his father only gives him twenty dollars a week allowance. And then I said something that made him laugh at himself, and before you know it, we were going out. We went to the movies, we went parking, a week later he gave me his Varsity jacket. And I keep thinking, maybe I'm going to wake up tomorrow and it won't be real. But, I'll tell you, that witch had something to do with it. I just felt she knew what she was talking about, and I really believe in her. She's a terrific witch. You ought to go see her some time."

Edna tried to concentrate on another headline she had to write for a picture of the Bowling Club. She

deliberately didn't want to look at Jacqueline anymore because Jacqueline might have seen in her eyes
what Edna had heard about Butch Ontock. Oh, he was
good-looking, that much was true. But Edna had
heard a whole lot of other things about him too, how
he was always being nice to girls that had a little loot.
He was like some kind of teenaged extortionist. And
she heard the only one Butch Ontock ever really fell
in love with was himself.

"I wouldn't want to depend on a witch," Edna said
as though trying to make a joke.

"No, you've got it wrong. This witch really knows
what she's doing. I heard about her from Mary Louise
Carter who went to the witch to find out where her
brother had run away to, and it was the witch that
told her her brother had died from an OD, which is,
as you know, the way it turned out," Jacqueline said.
But she added, "I haven't worn Butch's jacket to
school yet though."

"Why not?"

"Well, I'm afraid. I haven't told anybody about me
and Butch and I'm a little scared the kids might try
to ruin the whole thing. Maybe they don't think I'm
good enough for him. Or think I have too big a nose."

"You don't have too big a nose."

"Well, I think it's a little big," Jacqueline insisted.
"They see me with his jacket on, they'll start telling
him he's dating old eagle-beak or something. I mean,
I don't know, I don't think my nose is too big, but
there must be something wrong with me. All the boys
that ever took me out never really wanted to get
serious. They liked coming over to my house all the

time and eating, and using the trampoline and the pool, but I don't think any of them were ever really interested in me."

Edna looked straight at Jacqueline. "You're a very pretty girl," Edna said. "Don't put yourself down." The words had no sooner popped out of her mouth than she thought she sounded just like something her father would have said to her.

"Well, just cross your fingers for me, kid," Jacqueline said. "Because I'll tell you one thing, if this works out for me, something's going to work out for you some day."

Edna smiled and went back to the picture of Miss Cummingdinger just in time. She thought it was a little presumptuous of Jacqueline to imply that Edna was lonely, even if it was true. She felt the tears starting to roll down on her cheek. She didn't like people talking about falling in love, or that some day she herself would fall in love. She didn't go for all those promises that she didn't really believe were ever going to come true anyway. Maybe she should go see the witch, she thought, looking down at the palms of her hands. She never really noticed the lines in her palms, but they looked so crisscrossed she decided it was probably just as well not to know the future. Besides, there was no such thing as witches or palmists or astrologists who could tell you anything that was really going to be.

Fifth period, Edna went to the lunchroom alone as usual. It was always a madhouse, and Edna hated having to tackle the ice-cream line. Besides, a lot of boys were sitting around with their girlfriends, and that always made her feel more alone. The way half of them carried on you'd think they were lounging poolside at the Bogotá Hilton instead of being policed in the horrible cafeteria.

"What's the hot plate?" some kid yelled out at the end of her table.

"Maggots à la cockroaches," someone bellowed back.

One boy with fantastic blond hair was kissing a girl named Norma Jean Stapleton in a corner near where Mr. Fettman was patrolling. Mr. Fettman was the teacher assigned to keep control of fifth-period lunch, but he was too busy trying to figure out which kids were throwing grapes at him. Besides, every day somebody was kissing Norma Jean Stapleton in some corner or other. That sight began to look like a pop sculpture that simply got moved from spot to spot in the school. One time Edna saw Norma Jean being kissed right outside the Principal's office. But what was the big deal? Actually everybody seemed to be with someone, talking, having a good time; duets, quartets, eating sandwiches, laughing. A group from the football team came and sat down at the table where Edna was eating, and she could feel they were looking at her.

One boy was wearing a psychedelic T-shirt that said "Lower the age of puberty" on it. And another one had rolled up a copy of *Science World* as though it was a megaphone. He turned it towards Edna and yelled into it.

"Hi, honey," he boomed right at Edna. His friends all laughed as they munched away on their lunches.

"Say, where'd you get those gorgeous coconuts?" he asked.

"The A&P," Edna said, gathering her stuff up and scooting away from the table.

That night Edna finally got through dinner and safely into her room. Her mother and father had been particularly considerate and had kept the conversation limited to how much they had enjoyed *The Creature from the Black Lagoon*, which had been on the late show the night before. Edna put on her pajamas which ironically were white with red hearts all over them, and she began to do her presleep beauty treatment which consisted of a lot of oils and a good dose of Noxzema. She put the television on and there was some bearded man being interviewed by a nasty-looking lady hostess. Edna had already washed her face and decided to start with a little honey cream around the eyes. She was only fifteen years old and she could see she was already getting a wrinkle in her brow.

"I think we have to define loneliness before we can have a sensible discussion of it," some pompous-looking lady was saying on the television. "In fact, I think loneliness is a lack of sex."

"That's stupid," the man said, and the whole audience applauded. Edna wanted to applaud too, but she had already smeared her hands with Oil of Olay.

"Loneliness is when there is a quiet voice whispering inside of you, telling you that you need the touch and caress of another human being," the man continued. "Loneliness is a feeling of despair. A feeling like you're wrapped up in cellophane and no one sees you. It's a secret we're ashamed to admit even to our

closest friends. A pervading sense that we are un-
worthy, that something about us is despicable, that
we'd rather be dead."

"You are a male-chauvinist-pig sentimentalist," the
nasty hostess said, and then added, "Thank God we're
cutting to a commercial. Anything would be better
than listening to you."

Edna was Vaselining her lips and watching a Gravy
Train commercial when her mother came in with a
glass of milk and a banana.

"I thought you might be hungry," her mother said,
setting the food on Edna's bedstand.

"Thanks."

"We know how you love to eat."

"Right, Mom."

"Edna," Mrs. Shinglebox said, sitting on the edge
of the bed, "I was thinking about our visit with your
school's shrink, and I want you to know your father
and I are very sorry if we've made any mistakes in the
way we brought you up. We want you to know we
never wanted to do anything bad to you deliberately.
We only loved you and we didn't want to hurt you."

"I know, Mom."

"We think you're very beautiful, Edna. The butcher
down the street thinks you are too. He always tells me
what a wonderful, sensitive daughter I have."

Chapter 5 /

"Marsh, why do you walk around school with a baby raccoon in your coat pocket?" Mr. Meizner asked, sitting with his monstrous belly pressed smack against his office desk.

Marsh considered the question for a moment and swore to himself he would tell the truth. "I like it."

"I see," Mr. Meizner grunted. "Does the raccoon have a name?"

"Yes."

"What is it?"

"Raccoon."

"Raccoon?"

"Raccoon!" Marsh repeated with stress. "See, that's its name, Raccoon."

"Isn't that a strange name?" Mr. Meizner asked.

"What's strange about it? What do you think I should call him? Kangaroo?"

Mr. Meizner grunted again and began jotting wildly in his notebook. "You know the reason you carry the raccoon around with you, don't you Marsh?" he whispered as though he were passing an atomic secret.

"Of course."

"Good," Mr. Meizner said, a twinkle coming into his eyes. "Sometimes when we miss our father and have no friends we get lonely and need substitutes."

"What are you talking about?"

Mr. Meizner looked directly into Marsh's eyes and spoke as compassionately as he could. "Raccoon is your father, Marsh."

Marsh pulled the raccoon out of his pocket and took a good look at it. "Nah—my father isn't this small and he's not this hairy."

Mr. Meizner spoke calculatedly. "Marsh, I didn't mean the raccoon is *literally* your father. The raccoon is your father *symbolically*. Or, the raccoon could be your friend, symbolically."

"My friends don't have tails."

"Marsh, you don't have any friends. You told me that last week."

"I did not!" Marsh banged his hand on the side of his chair for emphasis and the baby raccoon recoiled with fright. Marsh petted the raccoon until he was calm again and then put him back into his warm pocket. No matter how Mr. Meizner provoked him, he swore he was not going to start telling fibs like he usually did. He could say that the raccoon was whatever he wanted to think it was, and he wouldn't even argue anymore. The main thing Marsh had to do was to just tell the truth. Not a single fib. "I have a lot of friends. And so does my father."

"Like who?" Mr. Meizner inquired.

"Like the gorgeous girl from the circus." Marsh felt like ripping his tongue out because already he was telling a big lie. "The girl who gave me Raccoon,"

Marsh added, feeling even more terrible as the lie was growing. He wondered why he couldn't just come right out and say that he found the baby raccoon on Todt Hill Road a couple of minutes after its mother had been knocked off by a yellow, hit-and-run, VW minibus. I mean, there the mother was, all squashed out like an old fur hat, gooey and oozing, and this poor little baby was standing on the side of the road and Marsh felt sorry for it and figured he'd better take it home before a muskrat or something would eat the poor baby raccoon. "And my father's dating the Tiger Lady," Marsh felt slip out of his mouth.

Mr. Meizner looked slightly skeptical. "What gorgeous girl from the circus are you talking about? And what tiger lady?"

Marsh felt his tongue warming up just from the tone of Meizner's voice. "Well, you see, there was this circus in Mariner's Harbor last week, and a woman trapeze artist fell in love with me at first sight and wanted to give me a job as the lion trainer because Ralph the Great had been maimed something awful the night before under the Big Top. Now, I know you're going to laugh, and I knew she was only kidding, but we went out after the show for a few drinks, and let me tell you, she wasn't kidding then. Ha, ha, ha. And my father came along, and he fixed himself up with Tessie, The Tiger Lady, which is the lady I was just talking about. Then, the whole bunch of us all went to this great bash out at the Fat Woman's estate right on Long Island Sound. And the circus gang just went berserk, having a ball, and running all around the place; midgets, neon-tube swallowers, the girl with alligator skin. And then there were three dwarfs, and a man who could dance on one finger, and that was when this girl trapeze artist started coming on strong with me. Now, don't think there weren't a lot of kids my age there, because there were. You know, you never stop to think of it, but freaks have kids too. And Tessie was teaching my father how to ride a unicycle while I got rapping with the son of the strong man who was billed as Mike, The Mule Face Boy. And we ended up singing "Let Me Call You Sweetheart" with the band, and everybody really thought I was terrific. A lot of the girls tried to kiss me, and my father ended up with about ten ladies just dying to marry him, and serving him things like shrimp with lobster sauce and Moo Goo Gai Pan and Hostess cupcakes. When my father goes to a party, or goes anywhere, I'll tell you, people love him. He's the tops. Mr. Cool. Sir Wingding. And everybody loved me too. And if my father ever heard you going around saying I had no friends, let me tell you, he'd sock you right in your face."

Mr. Meizner's eyes were as wide as balloons. He sat mesmerized for a full minute while Marsh pulled the raccoon out of his pocket and started tickling him. Then Mr. Meizner wrote on a slip of paper and handed it to Marsh. "You give this to your grade advisor, because I want your program changed to make sure you're free fourth period every day. I'm having some kids like you put into a special class!"

"Oh, some kind of a club?" Marsh asked.

"You might say that," Mr. Meizner said, "and then again, you might not."

Chapter 6 /

Once again Edna was in Mr. Meizner's office, only this time her parents hadn't been invited. The sunlight streamed through the windows illuminating the faces of seven other kids. And there was no beating around the bush; Edna was outraged that Meizner was starting group-therapy sessions at the high school. It was bad enough talking about her problems shut up with just her and the three-hundred-pound psychologist, but now she was expected to confess in front of this mob of weirdos.

All the kids in the group session looked like kooks, Edna decided, except herself. The way Edna had it figured out was that the group consisted of one mama's boy, two bed wetters, one boyish girl, one girlish boy, one unknown quantity, and she already knew Jacqueline Potts from the *Crow's Nest*. Edna figured Jacqueline's only problem was that she was a sucker for Butch Ontock. The unknown quantity was a boy who arrived at the first session with a live, baby raccoon in his raincoat pocket, and Edna thought that was really far-out. She also thought the boy had a very strange name. She figured you would have to be slightly mentally deranged to agree to go through life being called Marsh Mellow.

"What can I tell you?" Marsh was saying in front of the whole group. "Before I could stop her, she just threw herself right at me and my father."

Edna had to admit he was the smoothest talker she had ever heard. He was the only one in the group who seemed to really be able to tell what happened to him. She figured he was a real nebbish until he opened his mouth.

"Girls just plead with me and my father to give them a chance at romance," Marsh continued. "Love me, Pete! Love me, Marsh! That's what they say. And let me tell you, this one girl that was after me the night of the bazaar was no exception because she started to scream, 'Oh Marsh, Pete, I'm yours to do with as you will!' "

Edna sat on the edge of her chair, waiting for his next words.

"I said, 'Look young lady, you've got to control yourself. We just met at Baskin-Robbins.' " Marsh then let out a strange wheezing sound and sat back in his seat. "It was no use. She came on stronger and stronger, and finally she had her way with us. Afterwards, I kind of just wanted to get down on my knees and ask Cupid why does he send all his crazy little girls to me and my father?"

The bell rang, and a minute later Edna was rushing down the stairs to the cafeteria. She was very much aware of the fact that the boy called Marsh seemed to be pacing himself so he was right next to her in the stairwell. They were both moving fast with the crowd. And some of the kids were making baboon sounds and banging the walls, so it was all a little confusing and she couldn't be sure that he was tagging along. Most of the time Edna was in the halls of Curtis Lee High, she didn't know whether she was enrolled in a school or a monkey sanatorium. And on top of that, to have this emotionally disturbed guy tailing her made everything seem especially nutty. Suddenly she heard him speak.

"We ought to all chip in and send Meizner to Weight Watchers," Marsh said.

"What?" Edna was surprised he had spoken to her. He was so strange, she would have been less surprised if he had just put his hand on her neck and begun to strangle her near one of the exit signs.

"Skip it," he said, disappearing into the cafeteria lines.

Edna wanted to bite her lip off for being so slow. Her first reaction to everything seemed to be one of fear. And here it was, just some kid talking to her, and it wouldn't have been any skin off her back if she just made a civil answer and started a conversation. It wasn't that she could ever possibly be interested in someone like Marsh. A high-school group-therapy class isn't exactly the best place to shop for a date to the Junior Prom. But he did seem so worldly. She'd never heard of a boy who did so many fantastic things with his father. Most of all, she decided what she would really love to do is pet his raccoon. She loved all kinds of animals. Even most insects, except roaches. A month ago she had found a baby mouse in the cellar of her house and made a beautiful nest for it complete with four varieties of cheese. Every year she tried to save at least five or six mice, but they always croaked. She had decided there was really no way to save a baby mouse because once they've been seen by a human being a mechanism seems to go off inside of them that tells them to hurry up and die because their life is over.

She was biting into an apple when Marsh squeezed in at her table with a tray containing the Curtis Lee High lunch special of the day. The dieticians had some fancy name for it, but all it consisted of was a container of milk, an apple, a bowl of dishwater and a plate that looked like it was the final resting place for a stuffed, roast rodent.

"Your name's Edna, right?" Marsh said.

Edna nodded, and looked up at him just for a split second, then she began to furiously butter a piece of bread.

Marsh began blabbing a mile a minute, slurping up the dishwater soup and prodding his roast rodent with a fork. *My God, he looks zany,* Edna decided after sneaking a few more glances at him. His hair was three colors of dull blond, and sprung out from the side of his head like corkscrews. His face was interesting, she had to admit, but only in a slightly twisted sense. And his eyes looked like unhappy, blue laser beams. He looked a little bit like the kind of person that would run around with a sign around his neck saying "Support Mental Health or I'll Kill You." And, on the whole, it was sort of unbelievable that he could possibly lead the life he said he did during the group-therapy sessions. They drank their milk at the same time and Edna shared a Devil Dogs with him.

She didn't want to give him a piece, but he was making drooling sounds and she didn't see any way to avoid it.

"My father and I think love is really a super way to say hello," he gurgled. "See, the way we see it, love is like patting each other on the back. And we find, my father and I, that we can eliminate months of baloney by getting down to brass tacks with a girl the first time we take her out. Last week we took a couple of swingers from Jersey City to a gargle factory and blew their minds."

Edna sucked in a big lungful of air and then finally found her voice. "I think it's great the way you can say the things you do in front of all those kids."

Marsh smiled. "Well, when you've had as much mileage in romance as I've had, it's easy. I mean, we've really got it down pat. My father and I rate girls on a scale from A to Z, and if you see me acting a little nervous right this minute, it's because a C is heading this way."

Edna looked up and saw he was talking about Mary Lou Bibbs who swayed like a palm tree when she walked, supporting an impressive pair of coconuts.

"I take it back," Marsh said, "she's an H. Couldn't see her zits until she got up close."

"Too bad you and your father can't just find two girls and have a steady relationship rather than all the running around you have to do," Edna said. "And in your father's case, it's too bad his steady wasn't your mother."

"Oh, he's still married to my mother," Marsh said. "But she's full as an egg half the time."

"I'm sorry, but I don't know what 'full as an egg' means."

Marsh laughed. "It means she's a drunk."

"I'm sorry."

"Don't be sorry," Marsh said. "I mean, the day comes when eventually we all have to face up to it that love doesn't exist anymore the way it used to in the great classics like *Summer of '42*."

"That was a movie. And I don't think it's old enough to be considered a classic."

Marsh looked at her coolly. "Look, your problem is that you haven't accepted movies for the art form they are. You're behind the times. But all I'm saying is that love today is nothing more than *Chitty Chitty Bang Bang*. Say, why is your face red?"

Edna was furious that her facial capillaries were betraying her feelings. "My face isn't red! It's just that I don't happen to think that love has to be what you say it is. Some people get embarrassed talking about the things you do, you know."

"Oh, that's great," Marsh said.

"What's so great about it?"

"Well, keep up talking like that and I'm going to think you're a virgin," Marsh clarified.

"It's none of your business if I'm Helen the Harlot," Edna said.

"Well, if I knew you were going to be so defensive about it I wouldn't have even mentioned anything as sophisticated as I did. I wouldn't have come on so strong if I knew you were a teenage nun."

"I'm not a nun," Edna said.

"How old are you?"

"Fifteen," Edna said quietly.

"Wow," Marsh said, "fifteen and still a virgin. That's mind-boggling!"

Edna glared at him. "Well, I think carrying around a baby raccoon in your raincoat is mind-boggling!"

"Edna, honey," Marsh said, reaching over and giving her arm a little pinch. Edna was so shocked by the touch of his hand, she almost screamed. "I think this group-therapy stuff is going to be good for you," he continued. "Edna, why is your head jerking?"

"My head isn't jerking."

"Yes it is."

"I don't think it's very polite for you to point out that a person's head is jerking."

"I don't care whether it's polite or not, I just want to know why is your head jerking?"

Edna squirmed. "My head happens to be jerking because, subconsciously, I always feel my mother is hiding behind a corner spying on me. Especially when I'm thinking something I shouldn't be thinking. Or doing something I shouldn't be doing."

"Far out!"

"When I was ten she finally let me go down to the corner on Hylan Boulevard to wait for the school bus, and she thought I never saw her trailing me, and the way she used to peek from behind oak trees. She shadowed me for years. And now my head still jerks to see if she's hiding behind a corner or a post."

"It looks very freaky," Marsh said, trying to understand what she'd just said.

"Well, I apologize to you. I'm sorry I'm not perfect, I'm not as cosmopolitan as you are, and I can't just sit

/ 34

down with a member of the opposite sex and rattle off at the mouth the way you do." Edna saw Gert Ronkiwitz, last year's football queen, heading by the table and licking an ice-cream cone loaded with jimmies. She drew Marsh's attention to her by a tilt of the head. "I suppose you think she's a B."

"Nope. An E," Marsh said, expertly. "But my father would really like that stuff, only it would have to be a little older. He likes them vintage, thirty years and up with a lot of flash. I like them young myself."

"Well, that's all very nice, but I'm not interested."

"Oh yes you are."

"No, I'm not. What I am interested in is that raccoon you have in your pocket."

Marsh gave her a big wink. "Yeah, I'll bet you'd just love to see Raccoon, wouldn't you. But I'll tell you, I only let very special people pet him—like girls I make the scene with. In fact, my father's in California so I've been doing a lot of solo dating lately. What do you say you and I go out on the town some day. It'll make your stock go up and I'll let you play with my raccoon all you want."

Edna took a good look at him, and then balanced her books on the end of her lunch tray. She picked everything up and felt the capillaries in her face filling with blood, only this time it wasn't because she was embarrassed, it was because she was angry. "Thanks, but no thanks," Edna said. "You see, I happen to rate boys alphabetically according to how much of a human being they are, and you're an X! Besides, you talk about your father too much."

Chapter 7 /

Edna figured there was something on Jacqueline's
mind the minute Edna saw her come into the *Crow's
Nest* office. Jacqueline looked like she'd been through
an ordeal, so Edna just said a few words about how
nice the weather was and then decided she'd better
just continue trying to get a few gimmicks into a new
story about the General Organization student candi-
dates. She had eight pictures of these different kids
from the two political parties and all of them looked
like they'd just popped out of some beauty contest.
That was one thing that always burned Edna up. Only
the good-looking kids seemed to be the most popular
ones. They were the ones that got everything out of
school. And it had been the same way in grammar
school. Only once in a while some kid that was on the
ugly side could make the big time, but even then it
was usually some funny-looking girl that was ugly in
an acceptedly comical way. Like, she'd have to have
a big nose and be fat and throw a lot of parties, or at
least be able to play "Malagueña" on the piano.

"You know what Butch did?" Jacqueline finally
said.

"What?"

Jacqueline pulled Butch's Varsity jacket closer around her. "I want to tell you, I was worried at first. When he gave me the jacket I got this feeling he was only trying to be nice to me so he could take advantage of me. I mean, he knows my family has money. He knows I've got a little money, and he used to ask too much about my house, and what kind of cars my folks have, and when can he come and see the house, and all that stuff. And then, a couple of days ago, he told me his carburetor was on the blink."

"I'm sorry," Edna said, expecting that Jacqueline was going to say the whole thing was off.

"No, you don't understand. You see, he didn't ask me for money directly, but he just was really worried about the carburetor and my instinct was not to give him any money, because I did that with a few other guys and all it did was to get me in trouble. I didn't know whether I was coming or going, so I went back to the witch for another palm reading and she said there was some kind of evil—something terrible was going to happen to me, and so she was no help at all. If it was up to her, I wouldn't have even given him the money."

"You gave him money?" Edna asked.

"Yes."

"But you haven't known him that long."

"Look, he gave me his jacket, and I think there is such a thing as love at first sight, I really do. And I think the witch was right the first time when she said a boy was going to come into my life. But I figured she had to be a little off-base about the fire-and-brimstone routine."

Edna felt like telling Jacqueline that she thought she'd made a mistake. She decided it was better just to keep her mouth shut. She watched Jacqueline sit down at the desk next to her, and they both looked out the window to the athletic field where the football team was jogging.

"See, my problem is that I've never been able to share," Jacqueline said sadly. "In fact, when I gave Butch the money I felt terrible."

Edna looked away from the window, directly at Jacqueline. "Then why did you give it to him?"

"Well, I felt terrible not because I gave him the money. What really made me feel rotten was that it took me so long to be able to share something with someone without feeling like it was the biggest thing on earth."

What Jacqueline said depressed Edna because she understood only too well what it felt like not being able to share something with somebody, not being able to tell somebody how you felt inside. And the more Jacqueline talked about the witch, the more it sounded like that witch was really on the ball. That witch was right about that one girl's brother being dead, she was right about Jacqueline meeting a boy, and just maybe she was going to be right about something awful happening to Jacqueline. And that something awful was sure as hell going to involve Butch Ontock.

Edna was still depressed when she got home that night. Her mother had gone out to a Tupperware party and there was only she and her father eating dinner alone, facing each other.

"Is something wrong?" her father asked.

There were shadows, she felt very strange, even faint. Edna didn't remember getting up from the table, but somehow she kneeled down beside her father's chair and rested her head on his knee. She hugged him and the tears started pouring from her eyes. She heard her father put his fork down on the plate and felt his arms slip around her and lift her so she sat snuggled against him like when she was eight years old and her second-grade homework had been too hard.

"Don't be so impatient," her father said in a gentle voice. "With me you're relaxed because I'm your father and you know I love you. But one of these days a boy will come along and take one look at you and see all the beautiful things I see, and let me tell you, you'll never get rid of him. He's going to love you the rest of his life."

Chapter 8 /

On Thursday, Edna and the rest of Mr. Meizner's specially selected students reported to Room 101 for the active sessions of their group-therapy-experience class—now simply known as GTE. GTE was supposed to be a code so the rest of the kids in the school wouldn't know exactly what the class was. But it was already common knowledge that GTE was for the teenage insane. It was the same kind of pretense with all the other classes that were called "Applied." Everybody knew that if they were in a class called Applied Chemistry or Applied Geometry that "Applied" simply meant that they were more stupid than the kids who were taking the real thing. But that kind of thing didn't really bother most of the kids at Curtis Lee High because almost all of them were more interested in playing poker during their study periods.

Room 101 had been a sewing room, and Edna was surprised to see Mr. Meizner had taken out all the machines and converted the room into a sort of cross between a Zen Buddhist prayer temple and a wrestling arena. The only furniture to speak of was Mr. Meizner's desk which had a phonograph on it and a swivel chair behind it. The rest of the decor was a pack of strawlike mats which covered the floor. There was one blackboard and somebody had written in big letters on it "Don't be a high-school dropout. Stay and learn how to read and riot."

"Put on your blindfolds," Mr. Meizner crowed, waving a handful of black pieces of cloth. "Pick out a straw mat, stand by it and put on your blindfold. Today we're going to say hello to another face."

Edna didn't know what on earth he was talking about, but she was much too jittery to do anything but comply. She put her books down on the floor, grabbed one of the blindfolds and went to a straw mat. The last sight she saw was that of the seven other kids lined up and looking like they were going to be executed by a very plump psychologist.

"No fair peeking," Mr. Meizner instructed. "Just turn around in place until I come to get you. I want you all disoriented."

Edna heard some of the kids laughing, but her own aorta seemed like it was going to tie itself into a pretzel.

"One by one, I'm going to take you by the hand and lead you to your own special spot," Mr. Meizner droned on. "When I squeeze your hand, you just sit down and cross your legs Indian style. Don't do anything until I tell you."

"What if I have to burp?" somebody yelled out in a falsetto voice.

"Shut up!" Mr. Meizner bellowed. In a few minutes he had led the last student to his place. "You are all in position now. But let me tell you what you're going to do. Each of you is squatting, facing another person.

41 /

And when I give the signal, you're going to reach out your right hand and gently touch the face of the boy or girl who's directly in front of you."

"Cheap feels at Happy House," the falsetto voice squeaked out again. And this time everyone burst into laughter.

"You are to touch only the face of the person in front of you," Mr. Meizner clarified with even more volume.

Edna felt extremely uncomfortable. Now her entire heart felt like it was tap dancing on her kidneys. She hadn't the faintest idea who she was paired with, whose fingers would be reaching out to touch her. With her luck, she figured it would be someone so obtuse they'd stick their thumb in her mouth or something. Besides, there was no one in the room she wanted to do anything like this with. It wouldn't be bad if it was Jacqueline Potts, but Edna knew she definitely didn't want it to be Mario Lugati, the mama's boy who, at the last GTE session, had confessed to the group that the biggest thrill in his life was the time when his mother took him for a ride on the Crazy Mouse. The two bed wetters were Doris and Elaine Bach. They were sisters who had very little in common except matching rubber mattress covers, and a father who worked for Wells Fargo. The boyish girl turned out to be called Jo by her friends, and more than anything on earth, Jo wanted to be a Comptometer operator. The girlish boy turned out to be called Snooks, and at the second meeting of GTE he confessed that he loved trying his mother's Avon products. The one thing Edna knew for certain was that the face she didn't want to touch most of all was the face that belonged to Louis "Marsh" Mellow. There was something about him that scared her.

Mr. Meizner sat in his swivel chair and cleared his voice. He was dead serious. "Now boys and girls, the one thing all of you have in common is that you're all socially miserable. You've all been in to see me at one time or other either on your own, or your parents dragged you in. But your common denominator is that you've got trouble expressing your emotions. The only emotion any of you seem to be able to feel is that you're depressed. And that means something is interfering with all the other emotions in life that you should have. I'm making you wear blindfolds because that way you're going to be more in touch with your feelings and not confused by what you see. Most of our prejudices come from the fact that we see too much with our minds and not enough with our gut. It will also help cover up a lot of the embarrassment that you'd feel if you didn't have the blindfolds."

"Hey, Mr. Meizner," Edna heard Snooks' voice call out. "Did you hear the one about the couple called Kelly who went around belly to belly?" Everyone laughed again until Mr. Meizner let out a sound like an ape. Then there was silence again and Mr. Meizner returned to a more civilized tone.

"All right boys and girls, let's just get on with it. Reach out and say hello to another face with your fingers."

Edna heard herself gulp.

"Come, come, come! Get those happy fingers out there! Move that right hand forward until you touch someone," Mr. Meizner continued.

Edna forced her arm to move, but now she could feel adrenalin cascading into her bloodstream. She felt ridiculous! The idea of saying hello to someone's face with her fingers was absurd. Then she felt someone touching her brow and her head jerked. But a second later her own fingers made contact with something and she froze. At first she thought it was some kind of a hairy golf ball, but then she realized her fingers were clasped around a tiny head with little teeth. She let out a scream and yanked her blindfold off. There in front of her was Marsh with a big grin holding his raccoon in his left hand. Edna had grabbed the raccoon's head.

"Keep your blindfolds in place!" Mr. Meizner demanded. He rushed toward Edna. "It's only Mr. Mellow's raccoon which I will stick in the closet for the rest of this period." He stood over Marsh yelling, "If you dare bring him in here again, I will notify the ASPCA."

Marsh looked a little frightened and handed over the raccoon. "Look, Mr. Meizner," Marsh said, "I'll tell you one thing, if you hurt Raccoon I'm going to send you up the river."

"Quiet!" Mr. Meizner insisted, putting the raccoon in the closet and slamming the door. "Do not break your concentration, boys and girls. Just keep saying hello to a face."

"Mr. Meizner, do I have to?" Edna asked softly.

"Yes, you have to!" Mr. Meizner shot back. "Put your blindfold back on immediately!"

Finally, Edna reached out her hand again, this

time knowing whose face she was going to have to say hello to. She was saying hello to a face that she'd much rather say good-bye to. Marsh had started in again on her brow, kneading it like he was squeezing a grapefruit, as Edna's fingers made contact with Marsh's chin. It was very strange, Edna thought after a minute of exploration, that touching Marsh's chin was only half as revolting as the mere thought of touching it. There were a couple of little hairs growing out of it, but she knew you wouldn't call it a beard yet, it was more like slight bursts of alfalfa.

Marsh found a very strange thing happening to him as he began to creep down Edna's face. The more he touched her face, particularly her lips, the more unusual he felt. In fact, suddenly nothing was very funny to him anymore. He didn't feel he had to let out some smart-aleck falsetto remark. He didn't feel he had to honk Edna's nose like a horn which was what he had intended to do. And he was rather oblivious to Mr. Meizner's voice which was chanting, "Don't be afraid, don't be afraid. Touch each other's eyebrows and ears and hair. Realize that you are touching another human being who is very much like yourself; who has feelings like you do. Remember, even monkeys pick nits off each other."

Another couple of minutes went by and Edna felt her fingers were doing things in rhythm with Marsh's fingers. She found the two of them were feeling each other's chins at the same time, and then they'd feel their lips at the same time, and then their fingers would run up the sides of their faces at the same time.

They ran their fingers gently along the bottom of the blindfolds, softly sliding the tips of their fingers under the edge of the blindfold as though trying to feel each other's eyelids. Mr. Meizner then put a record on the phonograph and the strains of a string orchestra playing "On the Sunny Side of the Street" began to play.

"Let your fingers dance on each other's faces," Mr. Meizner called out.

Crazy thoughts were galloping through Marsh's mind. He couldn't stop them. His thoughts didn't seem to make any sense to him. It seemed like his mind was turning into a short-circuited computer. Book titles, headlines, jokes, everything seemed to come pouring silently through his head. For some reason he remembered a book he once saw on a library shelf called *How to Conduct Your Own Divorce and Save Lawyers' Fees.* Then he had this vision of a dozen waltzing Oscar Mayer wieners. And after that, he pictured himself smacking his mother around with a rubber duck. That led to him remembering a giant billboard he'd seen out in California with a huge girl saying "Come for the filter, you'll stay for the taste." And the memory of a bus bench came back to him with an ad for Murphy's Mortuaries. Somebody had written below it "You kill 'em, we'll chill 'em." Then he remembered some guy in one of the bars telling him that heaven was a tin box in the sky. And he remembered being with his father one time and having a pastrami sandwich at the Regina Deli. And then the thoughts went so fast they didn't seem to have any connection. Hit a shark on the head in the right spot and it'll go cross-eyed. Ordinarily Marsh knew he would blurt out such thoughts as jokes, or do something funny or idiotic, work them into a gag. But now, as he was feeling Edna Shinglebox's face, he couldn't do anything but sit still and marvel at the shape of her nose. What an interesting nose, he thought.

Edna found her mind was spinning. She couldn't think of anything except a whirlpool. It seemed she was just whirling around. Then for some silly reason she began to remember an ad she had read once in an underground newspaper. It was a personal plea that some man had published. "I'm forty-two years old, nice-looking, male, a bachelor father. My boy is fifteen years old, we enjoy tennis, golf, dancing, camping, movies, music centers and Winnebagos. Need very much to meet an honest, nongaining woman who would like to love and be loved and be mother to my son. Let's have more beautiful children together. My wife died of cancer. I offer integrity and devotion and happiness. I and my kid need you very much. Those interested, please write Box A317."

Suddenly Edna felt Marsh grab her hand. He moved it quickly away from his face, but it was too late. The first thing she felt was embarrassment. She wished it hadn't happened, but it was too late. She had felt something wet slide from Marsh's left eye, and then she heard a whisper. She thought it was Marsh, but she couldn't be sure. Again there came the whisper, and this time she heard every word.

"They've got my father in a nuthouse. Can you hear me?"

Edna didn't know what to do for a moment. Finally she heard herself whispering back, hoping that her voice couldn't be heard by anyone else.

"Yes," she said, "I heard you."

Chapter 9 /

On the way to the cafeteria, Edna knew Marsh was following her. She was more confused than ever because she had felt something she couldn't quite put into words when her finger had felt a tear on his face. She tried to stop thinking about it by repeating a ditty she had memorized once. "Remember *'Sisi sa si Sasa si susi'* means 'Sisi, I wonder if Sasa is up in Sicily.' " But then there was another voice inside her that took over. This voice said, "I've never been able to share," and at that moment Edna remembered Jacqueline Potts confessing to her, and Edna knew the reason most of the things Jacqueline told her were haunting was because Edna, herself, was very much like Jacqueline, but times one hundred. Edna had caught herself a dozen times in situations where she was horrified at sharing anything. She remembered once breaking into a cold sweat when it came down to splitting a pizza with a couple of girlfriends. The way it had worked out, there were two pieces left on the pizza platter and all three of them wanted more, but Edna never had enough guts to say so. What was worse, she'd make believe she was full and then hate the other girls because they ate the slices. She knew that she was probably wasting her whole life being scared and selfish. She knew it was part of the whole reason boys and girls didn't warm up to her. They could see in her eyes and hear in her voice that she was uptight. And no matter how she pretended nothing bothered her, she was really Miss Stingy Bachelorette of the Century, and she knew who made her like that too, but she decided she wasn't going to blame anyone anymore. There had to be a certain age when a girl had to take responsibility for what she thought and did, and Edna felt her time had come. By fifteen, any kid has to start taking the blame for what they are.

The cafeteria special for the day looked like three smelts on two Pop-Tarts, but she ordered it anyway. She hadn't been at the table a minute before Marsh was sitting opposite her eating a bologna sandwich and slurping down pickles. She was surprised that he seemed less repulsive looking than she had thought he was before her fingers had said hello to his face. His hair was still screwy and blond, but the way it stuck out now seemed to give him a type of energy like his fingers were rammed into some 220 electric socket. She even found his neck muscles weirdly fascinating. And his laser eyes were much more interesting now that she knew he was capable of crying— well, maybe it wasn't crying, maybe he just had something in his eye. But beneath the table she rubbed the finger that had touched his tear. Why was she making excuses for him? Of course it was a tear. When something wet rolls out of your eye, it's a tear. And nobody had set off a tear-gas bomb, and nobody was cutting up an onion. The only thing she really cared about, she decided, was that Marsh wouldn't be embarrassed. She felt like telling him that she cried all the time.

"I have to talk with you," Marsh pleaded.

"What?" Edna said, trying to smash one of the Pop-Tarts with her fork.

"They've got him in a nuthouse, but he's not nuts."

"Who?" Edna asked, just to make sure she was clear on the matter—at least as clear as she could be, although she still thought she must have been hearing things.

"My father," Marsh whispered.

Edna looked at him suspiciously. "How can they have your father locked up in a nuthouse, when all you tell everybody else is how you and your father go around picking up girls? You never said anything about him being in a nuthouse."

"I had to lie," Marsh said.

Edna thought that over a moment. "*Who's* got him in a nuthouse?"

Marsh shrugged. "Look, I can't tell you here. They're watching me too you know. Sometimes they have child spies. I mean, you think they don't, but they do." He slipped a letter under the table and smacked it against her knee. "Here, read this when you're sure nobody's watching you."

"What is it?"

"A letter."

"I don't want any letter."

"Take it!"

"I don't want to."

He threw the letter on her lap. "I've got to talk to you tonight. I'll pick you up sometime between eight and ten-thirty." He broke off a piece of his sandwich and stuck it into his jacket pocket. Edna could see a pair of little beady eyes looking out at her.

"You can't pick me up," Edna said.

"Why not?"

"Because I don't want you to. Besides, you don't know where I live."

"Yes I do. I stole your Delaney card out of Meizner's attendance book."

"Between eight and ten-thirty is such a wide range. Why don't you just pick eight o'clock?" Edna inquired.

"Because it all depends on what time my mother passes out. She doesn't let me drive the car while she's conscious."

A million excuses ran through Edna's head why she couldn't see Marsh that night, but it was too late. He just picked up his stuff and was gone, leaving her with the letter in her lap. She sat still for a minute with nothing but the sound of her chewing. He'd been so furtive, she didn't know if he was playing some kind of joke on her or if he was serious. What did he mean "they" had his father in a nuthouse? Who's watching him? She'd been in school for years and never once saw a child spy. But there was something about the way he talked and the way he looked that made her feel he wasn't joking, that there was something sinister about whatever he was talking about. She'd heard the expression "A matter of life and death," and his voice sounded like it was just that. Then she felt annoyed. It had to be a joke. And her head started jerking reflexively. She decided to use the jerks to scan the kids around her to make sure no one was looking at her, and then she reached down and slipped her hand inside the opened airmail envelope. She pretended to be eating, but her eyes were glued beneath the table. The letter was handwritten with very neatly formed letters: *Dear Marsh*, the letter said. *I'm sorry I haven't written in a while, but they've got me locked up in solitary confinement. It's taken me this long to bribe a guard who promised to mail this to you. I had to give up a piece of chocolate cake. Whatever you do, don't show this letter to anyone. I've had a lot of time to think about things, and I'm positive the FBI, the CIA, and several politicians are involved. This includes the President of the United States, the Governor of New York, and the Mayor. They're all criminals. And there are a lot of other governors and mayors involved. Particularly the Governor of California. He's got to be in on this. It's the only way they could have kept me here this long. Marsh, they are afraid of me for the things I was saying about them. I can tell you now that they had to put me away because I was blowing the whistle on them. You know that as well as I do. The union bosses want me knocked off, but I don't care about me. It's you I'm worried about, Marsh. Are they still poisoning your mother? Does she still slug down the juniper juice? They've got ways of making people into alcoholics and junkies. Don't let them get you, Marsh, play it their way. I fought them, but I couldn't win. Our country's going down the drain. Just hold on to your own thoughts. Don't tell them to anyone. Don't let them know what you think. Marsh, I want you to know I can see the top of a eucalyptus tree from my padded cell. It's a giant eucalyptus tree, just like the one next to the firework stand in South Carolina where I bought you that three-stage firework rocket that was supposed to explode into the shape of an American flag. Remember how impressed we were when we stopped at that firework stand, and I pointed out the terrific eucalyptus tree? Do you remember that? It's very important that you remember it, because I can see the sky and the very top of that eucalyptus tree. I think you can read between the lines, Marsh. I can't tell you any more than that. I love you very much, my son. I will write you again if I can. I think of you often. Don't let them step on your eyeball—you know what I mean. Love from Dad. P.S. Don't forget the eucalyptus tree.*

Edna put the letter back in the envelope and stuck it into her chemistry book. She let it sit a minute, and then took a peek at the envelope. There was the same handwriting staring up at her, and it was addressed to *Mr. Marsh Mellow, 619 Richmond Avenue, Staten Island, New York 10302.* The return address, in very small letters, read *Peter Mellow, Esq., Los Angeles Neurological Hospital for the Insane and Crazy, Los Angeles, California 90023.* The postage stamp looked strange to Edna. It looked like it had been glued back on and the stripes didn't quite match up. In fact, there was something very strange about the whole thing, and yet, she really didn't think it was a joke. No matter what kind of a liar Marsh could be, there was no way for him to really put her on like he'd been doing. It wasn't a put-on, it was genuine. As freaky as this kid was, Edna knew he was desperate. Several times she felt as though he was ready to break down in front of her. And then she felt a chill run up her spine because she didn't think the letter was written by a crazy man either. There was something terrible going on and she couldn't put her finger on what it was. Edna's first thought was to send the letter back to Marsh and refuse to talk to him. She had felt the old "negative click" in her head. She was not going to get involved with this whether it was true, or it was a stunt, or whatever it was, she'd just pretend it didn't exist. She wanted no part of it. If he kept after her in the halls, she could fix him. She'd tell a teacher, and she could tell her mother and father, and if that didn't work they could call the Principal and they could demand that this lunatic be kept away from her. She could get out of Mr. Meizner's GTE sessions. She didn't think she belonged in them anyway. A lot of people cry a few times a day and don't know why they're crying. Even Marsh was dripping tears, at least once, and that was a real tear. There are laws and police and people who protect citizens from things they don't want to know about. She could make the police go right to his house and warn him. And while they were there they could tell his mother, and they could tell his father who was probably sitting in the living room right now, for all she knew, that Marsh Mellow was not to go near Edna Shinglebox. After all, she was only a high-school junior, she had enough problems of her own. You had to be a little off your rocker to walk around with a raccoon in your pocket. Raccoons are health hazards. People get rabies from raccoons. Edna found her mind racing ahead and dreaming of a million charges she could make against this weirdo, and she found herself chewing on the last of the smelts with a vengeance. Somebody would stop him. She could get her parents to call a Congressman, or the Police Commissioner. She was getting absurd now, and she knew it. But the thing that worried her most of all was she didn't think the letter she read was really from some guy with a screw loose. Somewhere in the back of her mind she could very easily imagine the system taking an innocent man that knew too much and locking him up in a nuthouse. And then she felt this onrush of anxiety that she used to feel once in a while when she thought someone was hiding somewhere with a rifle and ready to shoot at her. And she used to think of zany ways to protect herself like, if she was rich she could walk around in a transparent bulletproof box. But she knew the rifle pointing at her was only her mother's eyes, and it had nothing to do with reality. Besides, this whole thing didn't even have to be political. That was the craziest part of all. It wasn't so crazy that someone could know the great secrets of life and have to be hidden from the rest of the world.

Chapter 10 /

Mrs. Shinglebox was thrilled that Edna had a date. She'd told her daughter that there were certain nights when Fate was at work and Fortune smiles, and this was going to be one of them. Edna protested. She said she definitely didn't have a date. But Mrs. Shinglebox said, "When a boy is going to come by to pick you up, even if it is between eight and ten-thirty, that's still considered a date." Even Edna's father was in a good mood, because he'd received an order to make up one of the largest floral funeral horseshoes of his career. And on top of that, the Friday Night Movie was going to be *Scream of Fear*. Mrs. Shinglebox was so excited she even got out her Guatemalan shawl and made her husband wear his nicest tie, which happened to be one that had a lot of hula dancers on it. Edna was fidgeting in her room, putting the finishing touches on her makeup. She'd worked on her hair for an hour, and her mother had helped to put on her makeup. Mrs. Shinglebox assured Edna she looked better than Barbara Steele who was one of the most famous actresses in low-budget English and Italian horror films. Edna thought she looked pretty good herself, but she would have preferred to be thought of as

Natalie Wood in *Splendor in the Grass*, before Natalie had had her nervous breakdown.

Mrs. Shinglebox worked on her daughter right up until the last minute.

"That's enough, Mom," Edna said.

"It's never enough," Mrs. Shinglebox insisted, extending Edna's eyebrows until they almost touched her ears. "When a boy takes you out, you've got to remember he's the fish and you're the bait."

"Mom, I'm not a worm."

Mrs. Shinglebox frowned. "Honey, just don't act like a zombie. That's why nobody takes you out. They think you're going to be a mummy. You've got to be more like a Playboy Bunny. In my day it was okay just to sit still and look like a well-groomed corpse."

"Mom!"

"Okay, I know you don't like anything to do with deceased persons. I just mean, nowadays you've got to let a little hanky-panky go on."

"I don't know what hanky-panky is," Edna said.

Mrs. Shinglebox blushed. "Edna, I don't mean going all the way, but we mothers talk you know. A lot of mothers come into the florist shop and we compare notes, and they tell me their daughters have to do research to be popular."

"What kind of research?"

"Well, some of them get out books and find out where all the erogenous zones are."

"I want a relationship, Mother," Edna complained, "not a rape."

Mrs. Shinglebox gasped. "Did I say rape? Did I? Did that word come out of my mouth? I'm just saying you've got to do something so that boys will remember you the next day. You don't want them to go to Phys. Ed. and do once around the track and forget your phone number, do you? And remember, if you need pills, just let me or your father know. It won't come out of your allowance."

Edna felt like screaming. "Mom, I'm not going to need anything. He hasn't even kissed me yet. The only thing he's done is stuck a raccoon's head in my hand."

"How weird." Mrs. Shinglebox adjusted her Guatemalan shawl to make certain all the tassels were hanging perfectly straight. "I just want you to be safe, and know that your father and I are with-it. God knows we don't want a Rosemary's Baby on our hands, do we?"

The doorbell rang and Mrs. Shinglebox almost fell running to answer the door. She yanked the front door open, and there stood Marsh. She took two steps backwards from the explosion of color. Marsh was wearing a red-and-white headband, a blue, patched-denim jacket, skintight Levi's, and a pair of high boots made of purple, orange and red squares. Taped on the shoulder of his jacket were three small blue-and-white feathers. The introductions took only a minute. Edna's simple red dress went quite unnoticed in the presence of Marsh's costume.

"Well, that's enough small talk," Marsh said. "We've got wheels, and we've got to move."

Mrs. Shinglebox practically ran after them to the door. Marsh bent over for a second to tuck his Levi's into his boots, and Mrs. Shinglebox had just enough time to whisper into Edna's ear.

"Very freaky," Mrs. Shinglebox said, "but very cute."

A minute later they were in a beat-up, green-and-white Mazda and pulling away from the house.

"I'm sorry I'm late, but Schizo Suzy didn't pass out until ten, and then I had to do some fast driving to make sure no one was following me."

"Where'd she pass out?" Edna asked, all the while feeling that something was missing, but she just couldn't put her finger on it.

Marsh made a sharp turn onto Hylan Boulevard.

"At the piano. She thinks she can play the third movement of the 'Moonlight Sonata,' but she never gets past the first eight bars—no pun intended."

"Are you old enough to drive?" Edna asked.

"No."

"Oh."

"But I'm a great driver."

"Where are we going?" Edna asked.

"You'll see. A great joint, up near Wagner College. We can talk there."

Edna remembered what was missing. "Where's Raccoon?"

Marsh stared straight ahead at the road. "Home in my room, sleeping. He's another reason I don't leave until Schizo Suzy passes out. She'd feed him rat poison or something. She's knocked off every pet I've had for the last five years. Even a neat chameleon my father bought me in Florida at a pecan emporium."

"You've been to Florida?"

"Sure, I've been a lot of places."

"You're lucky."

"Nah, me and my father used to take a lot of trips. It wasn't anything unusual. The best one we ever took was to California, and the second-best was to Florida. But we didn't do Europe or anything like that, you know. Once we went through Georgia and stopped at a freak farm that had a cow with two heads and a six-legged pig, and you can feed them and touch them and get your picture taken with them. My father knows about all those weird kinds of things which is one of the reasons they locked him up."

Edna felt herself slide back into the seat like she was in a rocket ship that just took off. The car was climbing swiftly up a hillside.

"There's the place," Marsh said, pointing ahead.

Edna braced herself by grabbing on to the dashboard, and caught sight of a large mansion set high, overlooking South Beach and the Verrazano-Narrows Bridge. She was very impressed because it looked like a very fancy place, and when two boys in uniforms came out to park the car, she knew it had to be something special.

"It's so fancy," Edna said.

"No," Marsh assured her, leading her towards the huge, ornate entrance.

A doorman was already swinging the massive front door open for them.

"Thank you, my good man," Marsh said as they marched by.

Edna glanced behind her for a moment and caught a sight of the parking lot. There seemed to be a lot of cars there.

The entrance foyer had a lot of college kids waiting in a line and paying money to a rather glamorous woman behind a cash register. It was three dollars per person for three drinks.

"What kind of a place is this?" Edna asked, imagining that at any minute there might be a police raid and she'd be taken home to mother in a Black Maria.

"You'll see," Marsh said, as he flashed a card and paid out six dollars to the cashier.

Marsh led her further into the dimly lit foyer, and Edna began to notice there was something very strange. First of all, the foyer was very small, and it was designed like a little, elegant, Victorian study. It looked like some 1890 library that someone like Sherlock Holmes would have had. And there was rather malevolent organ music vibrating the floor and leaping from speakers somewhere. What was most peculiar, was that there was no door leading out of the foyer, except for the door they had entered with a few of the other college kids. It was as though everyone was now trapped, and the only escape was back out the entrance which was getting more and more blocked by other people that were arriving after them. Edna felt very claustrophobic, as though she were being sealed in a tomb, and she wanted to yell, but Marsh grabbed her and rushed with her to beat everybody else to a mean-looking gold elephant that was perched on one of the bookshelves. It was only about four inches high and six inches long, but it looked like it was made of pure gold.

"Speak to it," Marsh instructed her.

"Why?"

"Just tell it to open the door."

Edna's head jerked, thinking she may have to run for her life at any moment.

"Talk to the elephant," Marsh repeated. "Say hello, Magic Elephant."

Edna decided it was best to suspend all reason and just do as she was told. She spoke the words quickly and frantically. Instantly, an entire section of the bookshelf wall swung open, and everybody laughed and filed through. It was a secret door, like in the old spook movies. "Boy, would my mother love this," Edna said, as Marsh led her down a passageway. Suddenly another wall shot straight up into the ceiling and there was a cabaret filled with a college crowd that was chug-a-lugging beer and dancing to a small band. Everything had been controlled by secret microphones and electric eyes, Edna realized, but she decided not to let her rational mind pick all the gimmicks apart. There was a long, exquisitely carved, wooden bar with sumptuous stools, and the wall behind it was filled with backlighted transparencies which made everything seem hypnotic. There were people at tables doing card tricks, and little, side alcoves with a lot of people having fun and performing magic tricks.

"What'll you have?" Marsh asked.

"A Coke," Edna said, her head still whirling, dizzy from the dozens of colored-glass lampshades that hung from the ceilings.

Marsh squeezed her arm. "I'm talking about booze, Edna, what kind of booze do you want?"

Edna's eyes widened. "They serve kids?"

Marsh looked impatient. "This is a private club. That's why I had to flash the card to get in. It was my father's favorite bar before they took him away. Mainly college kids, but he used to get into all these philosophic discussions up here. Besides, the police get paid off not to bother the joint."

"I never had anything alcoholic," Edna said.

"Leave it to me," Marsh smiled, pushing his way through the crowd to the bar. "Two Harvey Wallbangers," he called out to a bartender who was twisting his handlebar mustache and sporting a straw hat.

"I feel like I just got out of a time machine or something," Edna said, but she knew Marsh couldn't hear her over the din. Finally he had the drinks and came back, handing one of the Harvey Wallbangers to Edna. "What's in it?" she asked.

"Swamp gas and pasta fazool," Marsh said, taking her hand and pulling her into another room, located just off the main bar. It was a smaller chamber with only five or six tables and a grand piano that was roped off by a chain. There were imitation cobwebs all over the place, even on the piano stool, and especially hanging in the corners. Next to the piano was a wrought-iron birdcage with a few dollar bills on the bottom of it, and an elaborately printed sign that said "Gertrude, The Ghost Piano Player."

"I can see why this was your father's favorite bar," Edna said. "It's wild!"

Marsh sat Edna at a table near the birdcage. "Look, I didn't mean that this was his favorite bar, all I meant was that this was *one* of his favorite bars. He also liked Joe's Bar in Huguenot, and the Stumple Inn on Richmond Avenue, and he thought Dirty Irma's in St. George was pretty neat too. He said bars were the best place to get away from the FBI. And every payday, since I was four years old, he'd take me with him on rounds of his favorite saloons." Marsh moved close to the piano and Edna could see his face reflected a thousand times in the mirrors behind it. "What do you want Gertrude to play?" he asked.

"How can she play anything if she's a ghost?" Edna said, puzzled.

"Gert's a ghost, but she plays just the same. Just tell me what you want to hear, but it's got to be something corny. Gertrude only knows corny songs," Marsh specified as he took out a dollar, crumpled it up and threw it into the birdcage.

Edna couldn't think of a song, until finally she remembered an old one that had been revived and she blurted out the title: "Laughing on the Outside (Crying on the Inside)." That song had stuck in Edna's mind for two reasons. One was because she liked it, and the second reason was because when she was in the seventh grade, and it had just had its revival, she knew there were two boys who told her that they had a game where they'd sit in a room with a bayonet and drink beer, and if that song ever played on the radio while they were sitting there, they'd get up and run for the bayonet, and then whoever got it first would have to stab the other one to death. They were really weird kids and Edna never forgot them.

"Hey Gertrude!" Marsh yelled out. "Do you know 'Laughing on the Outside (Crying on the Inside)'?"

Instantly, the piano started playing the song, the

keys going up and down, and Edna burst into laughter. It was really quite a gimmick. Whoever the real piano player was, was probably behind the mirrors, and then there was probably a hidden microphone somewhere near the front of the piano. Edna wondered who was really at the remote keyboard, and it gave her a funny feeling to know that somebody was staring at her that she couldn't see. Or maybe the person wasn't staring. Maybe that was just her being paranoid. Whatever, it was a terrific arrangement of "Laughing on the Outside (Crying on the Inside)" and it sounded even better after the third sip of her Harvey Wallbanger. In fact, the only person in the world she knew who could play that well was Mary Ann Scarmadella who sat next to her all through grammar school, and who specialized in playing the "Warsaw Concerto." Edna began to sing the lyrics on her fourth sip of the Harvey Wallbanger. "The crowd sees me out dancing, carefree and romancing. . . . they don't know what I go through! I'm laughing on the outside, crying on the inside 'cause I'm still in love with you."

Edna laughed when she found herself singing. "That'd make a good theme song for Meizner's class, wouldn't it?"

Before the song could finish, Marsh dragged Edna back to the main bar. He seemed to shove her onto one stool in particular, which Edna thought was a little strange. She'd been heading for the one on the left, and then he did a quick switch and she ended up on the one on the right. It was like he was trying to control her behavior or something, and in a way it seemed sort of nice that somebody beside her mother and father cared that she was in a particular place.

"That stool you're on is the most comfortable one in the whole bar," Marsh explained.

"Oh, thanks," Edna said, noticing her stool did seem more ornate and plush, like she had the place of honor at the bar. She still clutched her Harvey Wallbanger and was going to say something else, but Marsh gave her a signal not to speak. He had his finger up to his lip for a full minute while he checked all around them. Then he leaned very close to her. His voice was somber.

"I need you to help him escape."

Edna found herself checking to see if they were being watched. Then she fumbled in her pocketbook and slipped back the letter he had given her.

"Did you read it?" he asked.

Edna nodded, affirmatively.

"Good. We can talk here," Marsh assured her. "Nobody's followed us. And I recognize a lot of these flunkies. Most of them are college kids who never knew half as much as my father did. He used to really give it to them about existentialism. And did he have the jokes! He used to say things like 'Old postmen never die, they just lose their zip.' And another favorite of his that used to always get a laugh out of anybody he met was, he'd say, 'Is it fair for us to look through the yellow pages when we don't know whether the Chinese look in the white pages?' He also knew a lot of stuff like that Hitler's favorite movie was *King Kong*."

Edna was surprised when Marsh reached out and

took her hand. Her first instinct was to yank it back, but instead she just let it hang limp while he clutched it. She wanted to close her fingers around his so that he would know he could at least trust her. She tried hard to make her hand respond, but it just wouldn't. The whole thing was so eccentric. She really had no reason to trust him, so why should she show him that he could trust her? He could be a raving lunatic along with his father. She didn't even know what existentialism was. Everybody in the joint could be nuts for all she knew. She wanted to help, deep down. She wanted to help this weird boy with the corkscrew blond hair. She decided maybe the best way would be to try being a little honest about how she felt.

"Your father sounds paranoid from his letter," Edna said. She no sooner had let the words out, than she wanted to bite her tongue off. Why did she always do and say the wrong things? She could have waited, warmed up a little bit, and then hit him with the paranoid accusation. She could hear Meizner's words bouncing inside the walls of her head: "You're all depressed about your lives. Something is interfering with all the feelings of life you should have." Meizner might look like a pregnant manatee, but he certainly had her number on that, she told herself. And if she was miserable, just think how miserable Marsh must be. Particularly if his father really was in a nuthouse.

"It's funny you say that," Marsh said. "That was my nickname for him, *Paranoid Pete*. The problem is that he isn't paranoid. It's only that his mind is so far ahead of the rest of civilization, everybody thinks he's paranoid, except the ones that locked him up. They socked it to him because he was telling the truth and they knew it."

Edna felt peculiar. She couldn't put her finger on why, but something was happening to her. It had to do with perspective, she decided, and thought it must be the Wallbanger.

"See, your problem is you don't have any feelings for my father," Marsh said. "I mean, you're not emotionally involved like I am."

"How can I be? I don't even know your father," Edna said shrilly.

"Do you know Abraham Lincoln?"

"I know who he is. I don't know him personally."

"But don't you have any emotional involvement with Abraham Lincoln? When you hear that name, Abraham Lincoln, doesn't that produce some emotion in you?"

"Of course it does."

"Well you never knew him."

Edna took a big sip of her Harvey Wallbanger. "Look, I've had that problem with people who've been dead for a couple of hundred years."

Marsh sat up straight. "Look, what I'm saying is that you can love people, you can have an emotional involvement with them even if you haven't met them. Even if you don't know everything about them. Some people think Abe was on speed half the time. I mean, I don't believe that theory. Of course I don't believe he walked miles to borrow books either. I mean, that would be nuts, in my book. You've got to feel for a human being to know what they did. My father loved Louis Pasteur, Winston Churchill, and Marilyn

Monroe. He loved all the big ones. He always felt that if he'd ever met Marilyn, they could have had deep philosophical discussions and she would never have died from an overdose of barbiturates. He told me there was a time when he was hoping to correspond with her and get together with her, and maybe she would have ended up as my stepmother, I don't know."

The bartender seemed to be standing too close, and Edna was aware that Marsh was suspicious of him.

"Another round," Marsh said.

"No!" Edna spoke up.

"Yes!" Marsh overruled.

When the bartender had left, Marsh reprimanded Edna. "Look, anytime I say something, don't butt in. Somebody could be a spy, and sometimes I have to do things that seem a little peculiar. Edna, I'm telling you, if you knew my Pop you would have loved him, no kidding."

"Oh, I'm sure of it," Edna said, bordering on being sarcastic.

"I mean it. He was the kind of guy who'd do things like wake me up at midnight and cook waffles."

"Oh, that's terrific," Edna said, putting her empty glass on the bar and watching the bartender replace it with a fresh drink.

"You think that's dumb, don't you?" Marsh said.

"No, I don't. I really don't," Edna insisted. "I think it's terrific that a father would wake you up at midnight and make waffles. Even pancakes for that matter."

Marsh smiled at her and she liked that. She noticed

he had very nice teeth, and even his tongue had a healthy color.

Marsh continued talking. "It's not the big things about a guy that make him great, it's the off-the-wall kind of things that tell you his character, that's what I always say. If I felt bad because I had flunked arithmetic, my father would come home and he'd tell me that the math tree had square roots, get it?"

"Oh, that's funny." Edna took a sip of the fresh drink. She wasn't sure whether it had less alcohol in it or whether her gums were suffering from sugarshock.

Marsh leaned closer to Edna, practically rubbing against her. When he turned his head his hair swung by and tickled her ear. "My father was my pal. He taught me right from wrong. That's what we used to talk about all those paydays when we'd make the rounds and he'd drink beer and eat pickled eggs. I'd ask him how to spell inconspicuous, and he'd tell me to go look it up. See, he knew how to teach me a sense of independence. And he taught me that S D R A W K C A B is backwards spelled backwards. He was a riot."

"He sure was," Edna slurred.

"And he gave me loot whenever I needed it. He was always there to protect me and Schizo Suzy, as much as he thought she was a loser. Every bar we ever went into, he protected me by punching somebody in the face. Paranoid Pete had guts, let me tell you! He was tall, skinny and bald, but really good-looking. A real idol. That's where I get most of my charisma from."

Edna smiled to cover up that she didn't know what on earth he was talking about. In fact, she was angry that so many times in her life she didn't know what on earth anybody was talking about. She wished she could think of herself as not knowing what people were talking about in some different way, like she didn't know what in *heaven* anybody was talking about, but it was always, she didn't know what on *earth* anyone was talking about. Then she became aware of a feeling that she was growing smaller. She thought maybe that the effect of the Harvey Wallbanger was to make a person feel like they were getting tinier. It was like she was Alice in Wonderland, and either that bar was getting higher, or she was getting smaller. It seemed Marsh had to look down at her.

"See, Pete felt if a father didn't smack his brat around once in a while that that father didn't really love his kid. But let me tell you, Pete really loved me. He used to throw me against the wall like clockwork and he'd always tell me it was for my own good. One time he even kicked Schizo Suzy; and let me tell you, she was a lot better off for it. After that he used to kick her around regularly. It was kind of therapeutic. She'd be sweet for a week. Good ole Pete was king of the hill; dominated the television; hated sitcoms because they were so phony, and he used to yell at the television set things like: eat, drink and be merry, for tomorrow you may be radioactive. I used to think he didn't understand me because he had such a political mind. But then he'd tell me that when he was a kid, he didn't think his father understood him. See, that was the way I knew he understood me."

Edna silently nodded, but by this time she was certain she was growing smaller. Now it was definite that she had to look up in order to see Marsh. She tried to interrupt, but Marsh just rattled right on.

"See, my father wanted to help out around the house but he couldn't," Marsh said, clinking the ice in his glass and then closing one eye to look through his drink. "He used to pick me up and hold me whenever I was freaked out, especially after he'd take me for roller-coaster rides when I was in kindergarten. You know, I mean we kids don't usually think about this, but without our fathers, I mean, we wouldn't have our mothers. That's how important a father is. And, my mom's only a temporary dipsomaniac. She's kind of nice when she's not nipping, but even if she was sober she wasn't as much fun as Pete. My father used to sit at the head of the table and he'd slice the turkey—that was, of course, before he became a vegetarian—but he wasn't the kind of two-faced load of bull who'd tell you to cut your hair while he grew a goatee. Everybody respected my father wherever we went, even Dirty Irma's. People shaped up when he went into a saloon. Okay, biologically he could tie one on better than my mother; hold a lot more. But I'll tell you, he was real cool because I knew that once he was a boy himself, and all Schizo Suzy ever was was a girl. See, that's the kind of thing you wouldn't understand."

Edna took her limp hand out of Marsh's grasp. She knew something was terribly wrong when her hand dropped and touched the floor. Suddenly Marsh burst into laughter and Edna realized that the stool she'd been sitting on was some kind of trick pneumatic contraption that lowered very slowly after the bartender had pressed a button somewhere. It was like a car lift in a gas station, except instead of going up, this one went down. Ever since she'd been sitting on the stool it had been moving down bit by bit until now she was almost on the floor.

Marsh howled and howled until he almost fell off his stool, and there were a lot of other people and kids standing around that were laughing, even the bartender had a fit of the giggles. Marsh took Edna's hand and helped her up and then the bartender pressed the button so the stool shot back up to its normal height, but Edna had no intention of sitting on it again. In fact, she knew she'd have to think twice about anything Marsh asked her to do. Maybe he thought it was a great big laugh; she decided there was something about him she couldn't trust anymore.

Chapter 11 /

Edna scolded herself for having finished three Harvey Wallbangers. She could hardly see the road in front of them, but Marsh didn't seem to have any trouble driving. He zipped that Mazda around corners, and burned rubber when stoplights turned green. Her brain felt so weird, and she knew she must be quite loaded to have agreed to go to Marsh's house. The last boy's house she had ever been to was when she was nine years old and a kid on the block had a birthday party, during which he had broken down crying because he realized at six-thirty that he had missed a rerun of "Batman."

"I don't think we should really be going to your place," Edna said. "I mean, I don't think we really have to, do we?"

"Oh, yeah," Marsh said, pushing his face closer to the windshield. "See, if we don't do that, you're not going to believe me, you're just going to go around thinking I'm crazy."

"Well, I mean, I already think there is something screwy, so I don't know whether going to your house is going to make me stop thinking you've got a little curvature of the brain."

"See, that's why you need proof."

"No, I think I've had enough proof already. I've had three-hundred proof or something," Edna said, and then she let out a little laugh because she'd thought it was a very funny joke.

"The kind of proof you need is that my father knew too much. See, his mind was so complicated, I've got to show you things so you'll understand. I can't do it justice."

"Well, why don't you just get all the stuff and bring it to school tomorrow."

"There isn't any time. They're preparing him for a lobotomy."

"What?" Edna asked, sticking her head out the window to let the air smack against her face. Her cheeks felt like they were petrifying.

"They're going to cut a hole into his skull and go in and slice out a piece of his mind. They take out just enough to turn you into a vegetable."

"I think you'd better drive me home," Edna said.

"Look, I just put you on that trick stool to give you a good yuk. See, this stuff I've got to show you is too depressing, and I figured you'd better be in a good mood first. Besides, I had to test you to see if you were ready for the evidence."

"Well, let me tell you, I don't think I'm quite up to it," Edna moaned, sticking her head out the window again. It felt good having the cold air blast her in the face. As they drove around a sharp bend she saw a huge sign in the shape of a hand. She realized they were passing the witch's house. There were floodlights that lit up both sides of the giant hand, and writ-

ten across the sign, in large letters, were: PALM-
IST—READER AND ADVISOR. As they whizzed
by, Edna noticed a red light inside one of the downstairs rooms, and she couldn't help wondering what
the palmist must look like. The thought even crossed
her mind that maybe even Jacqueline was in there
with the witch right at this very minute for some kind
of refresher course. A minute later, Marsh braked the
car and pulled into a driveway. Edna had the distinct
sensation she was back to normal, but she wasn't sure
whether the gusts of oxygen had done it or the sight
of Marsh's house.

"You live near the palmist," Edna said.

"Oh, yeah. She's an old hag. She used to chase the
kids with a razor strap, and put ads in the local newspapers asking people to end psychedelic employment
by sending her a dollar."

"Do you think she's a real witch?" Edna pursued.
"That's what a lot of the kids think."

"Nah, she's a big phony. Some kid I know went to
her to find out if he was going to pass the Geometry
Regents and she told him not to worry about it because he wasn't going to be able to take it. And sure
enough, the Regents came and he couldn't take it
because he had fallen off a chopper."

"I thought you said she was a phony."

"She is. I mean, that kid went to see her on a chopper. And all you had to do was to see him drive up and
you knew he wasn't going to last on that thing very
long. See, that's what they do. They look for little
things about you that you think don't say anything;
but they do. It's like wearing an advertising sign right

around your neck when you walk in. And these gypsies can pick it up before you can say ring-a-levio."

They got out of the car and Edna stopped a moment to really drink in the sight of Marsh's house. The overall impression from the driveway was that this house made a slum look good. It was an old, two-story, wood frame house with half a porch. The other half had fallen off. It looked like seven ghosts were jumping around in the backyard, but Marsh explained that Schizo Suzy always leaves sheets on the clothesline so burglars are going to think somebody's home even if she went out to buy diet beer. The color of the house was barf green, and the shutters were done in a chic termite-tinted orange. Two windowpanes were broken and some very attractive black-plastic garbage bags had been stretched to seal the holes.

Marsh opened the front door and led Edna inside. The first thing she was conscious of was the slight odor of a dead mouse. If there was one thing she had become an expert in, it was in what a dead mouse smells like. Next she noticed a dining room that looked like it was a Walton's Mountain reject. She also noticed that all the floors tilted different ways like some kind of earthquake was running through the house, except that it got frozen somewhere along the way. To the left, there was a large living room that buckled several times with furniture that looked like there had been a very smart decorator from the Salvation Army. Either that or some upholstery hints had been given by Helen Keller. Lying on the floor over near the piano was Schizo Suzy, snoring, in a nightgown that made her look like she was an extra from *The Snake Pit.* Marsh took Edna's hand and just led her right up to the body.

"I want you to meet my mom," Marsh said.

"No, don't wake her up."

"Don't worry, she's not going to wake up." Schizo Suzy let out an extra-loud snore. "A bomb couldn't wake her up," Marsh said as he got a pillow from the couch and slid it under his mother's head.

"Are you just going to leave her here?" Edna asked.

"I'm sure as hell not going to drag her upstairs. Besides, she and Pete used to play 'Chopsticks' together all the time, and sometimes they had a special arrangement worked out for 'Blue Moon,' and when they didn't do that, sometimes they'd just wrestle romantically in this area. So I think she passes out here basically for sentimental reasons. Come on, we've got to get upstairs."

Edna's head began to twitch, and it wasn't long before the twitches turned into outright jerks. "Do we have to?" Edna asked.

"Of course we have to."

"Why don't you just bring the stuff down here and then we could examine all the proof down here. I mean, what are we going to do upstairs?"

"What do you think we're going to do? Sit on whoopy cushions?" Marsh asked. "My father's life is at stake, can't you get that through your head?"

Edna looked at Marsh and could see he was getting angry. She went with him, meekly, up the stairs, but her mind was galloping again. She remembered reading an article in the *National Enquirer* about some boy who used to bring girls up to his room, hack them to death and then cement them in his shower stall.

Marsh put the light on in his room and Edna almost passed out. About fifty giant faces were staring at her. She felt like she was really Alice in Wonderland now, small and facing a mountainous deck of cards.

"Hi, Raccoon," Marsh said. "I'm back." He went over to a cage in the corner, grabbed a bag of Keebler Pecan Sandies and tossed a couple of the cookies to Raccoon. Then he lifted the animal out and started to hug and pet it. By now, Edna had recognized most of the faces on the posters that covered the walls of Marsh's room. There was Robert Kennedy, Winston Churchill, Jean Harlow, Einstein, Shakespeare, Jimmy Hendrix, Eisenhower, Cervantes, Clark Gable, Janis Joplin, John F. Kennedy, Jack Benny, Babe Ruth, Leonardo da Vinci, George Bernard Shaw, Jesus Christ, Trigger, Sigmund Freud, Marilyn Monroe, Louis Armstrong, Black Beauty, Moses, Cass Elliot and Edna St. Vincent Millay, among others. Over the unmade bed was a montage of what seemed to Edna to be another hundred people or so, photos snipped from newspapers and little mottoes and things from magazines and history books. Marsh had written the names of each person under their location in the montage, many she hadn't heard of. Every country seemed represented. There were famous faces from England, South America, Africa, Europe, Russia, Norway, Sweden, Japan, China, Italy, Denmark. It seemed like every famous person in the world was there, including Betty Grable and

Mahatma Gandhi. Marsh noticed Edna's eyes ready to pop out of her head.

"Neat, huh?" he inquired.

"Oh, yeah," Edna agreed. "Who put them all up?"

"Me."

"No kidding."

"Yeah, it took three years. I'm still adding every day." Marsh dumped Raccoon on Edna's lap and started digging through the bottom drawer of his dresser. She had to admit, after the first few minutes, that she loved holding the little animal. Especially now that she wasn't wearing a blindfold. He had the cutest little brown face with large eyes set in black circles, like he'd been out too late the night before. And he would take a bit of the cookie and then stare up at her while he chewed. His little paws were very much like fingers, and when he reached out to examine Edna's chin, she felt he was saying hello to her face. Maybe he picked up a few points from Meizner's class. Then the raccoon took another bite of the cookie he was holding and climbed up on Edna's shoulder. He was munching away, right next to her face, and reaching out one set of fingers to examine her ear.

"See, this is what you've got to read, and we couldn't do it anywhere else. Up here we're safe," Marsh said, taking Raccoon off her shoulder and giving her a very thick letter. "This is the main evidence of why they want to knock him off. Pete set it down while we were in L.A. for three days, staying at the Hollywood YMCA. I was out trying to get a job as an usher at Grauman's Chinese Theatre so we'd have

enough money and never have to come back to Schizo
Suzy. You know, that's the place where they've got
everybody's feet in cement? Then, when I got back to
the Y that afternoon, they'd already taken him away.
But I found this letter."

"Marsh, look, I don't know whether I should read
it. I mean, it's getting late," Edna said. "I really think
I should go home."

"Now look, please, just read this. It won't take
long, honest."

"What I'm saying is, if this is really important,
maybe you should just bring it to a private eye or
something. You know, hire somebody professional or
bring it to some public service. I mean, there are
departments that take care of this kind of thing—
maybe the Chamber of Commerce. I mean, I don't
know. If you don't trust the police, there must be
somebody."

"No!" Marsh said definitively as he moved next to
her on the bed and put his arm around her shoulder.
"Edna, just read it. Just read half of it, that's all I'm
asking you."

Edna felt very strange with Marsh's arm around
her. And when he put the raccoon on the floor it
started to yank at her left shoe. She looked from
Marsh's eyes to the raccoon's eyes, and she had to
admit there seemed to be some kind of family resem-
blance. They both looked like sad koala bears in a
Qantas Airways ad. She decided all Raccoon was desperate for was another cookie, but she didn't know
what it was that gave Marsh his look. Against her
better judgment, she unfolded the several pages of

the letter. The familiar handwriting was easy to read:
Dear Marsh, They have me surrounded, and will soon bust in here to take me away. I don't want you to think that I left because I wanted to. They may machine-gun me to death and make it look like a suicide, but I'm going to pin this letter behind the drapes and pray you find it so you know I didn't run out on you. Whatever you do, don't report me to the Missing Persons Bureau because they'll be in on this to cover up. I'm sorry, kid, if what I'm telling you scares you, but I want you to know the least I'm being is kidnapped. Whatever you do, don't show this letter to anyone.

Edna stopped reading and handed the letter back to Marsh.

"I want you to read it," he said.

"Yeah, maybe you do, but your father says you shouldn't show it to anybody, and that includes me."

"No it doesn't."

"What do you mean it doesn't?"

"My father never met you. If he'd met you, he'd know it was all right for you to read this. Besides, he didn't really know how tough things were going to get."

The raccoon began pinching Edna's ankles. "Well, I can't read it with Raccoon salivating for another cookie. Why don't you just take care of feeding him and giving him hugs, I mean, he looks like he's love-starved. I mean, I have to go home, I have stuff that I have to do tomorrow, and then some other time, maybe I'll read a little bit more."

"No. You've got to read it now," Marsh said.

"Look, my mother has hypertension."

"Oh, please stay, Edna," Marsh said, looking more and more like some kind of animal you'd feed by putting a quarter in a machine and getting a handful of corn or something at the Catskill Game Farm. "Don't leave me alone," Marsh said. "Some day you might need somebody and I promise I'll be there. I promise."

Edna looked into Marsh's blue eyes again, and then reluctantly took the letter back.

You won't be able to stop them, Marsh, the letter went on, *but remember, evil spelled backwards is "live." There are evil people everywhere. We're in the middle of a curse. I know you're going to be able to understand that, because you're a kid, and kids understand everything. You sound nasty sometimes, but I know you don't mean to. Something terrible happened to me and I don't want it to happen to you, which is one of the reasons I'm writing this letter. They can decapitate me like they did to that boy we read about in the newspaper that had that done to him when he was in the car crash. But I won't care as long as this letter gets to you.*

"What does decapitate mean?" Edna asked.

"Cut his head off."

"I thought so," Edna said, keeping her eyes glued on the letter.

You're my only son and the only thing I've found worth living for in this whole, rotten world. If you read in the papers that they put me away because I'm nuts, that'll be a crock. And this letter's going to be pretty long, only because that's how much I love you, and I want you to know exactly why the evil ones in this country had to shut me up, although I think you've got a sneaking suspicion already. They're all those people who are trying to step on our eyeballs. All those kind. There are horrible things I have to tell you at the end of this letter, but I'll save the most horrible for the very end. But first of all, there's a lot of little junk up front that I've got to remind you about, and that's all those evil people that are the small-fry ones. Watch out for those people that brag all the time, and say clever little things like "Tolkien spokien here." And watch out for people who lie about their age and say smarty things like "One good turn-on deserves another." You see, that's one kind of evil person. You've got to be careful of all those. Careful of people who try to put you down, like conniving wives and confirmed bachelors and tightwads and chatterboxes and bores and snobs and show-offs. And then you've got chiselers and gossips and henpecked husbands and a whole lot of other rotten phonies like juvenile delinquents and meanies and old fogies and pessimists and liars and those awful teachers who give busywork. Now you know, I never let any of those people get away with anything and I don't want you to let them get away with anything either. And don't worry, it's safe to stand up to them. They don't do anything like kill you off for that, they just give you bad marks and say mean things behind your back.

Edna squirmed a little at the expression "kill you

off" and then let out a yell.

"What's the matter!" Marsh said, leaping to the alert.

"That animal is climbing up my leg," Edna said.

"All right, stop it, Raccoon!" Marsh yelled, pulling the animal off and giving him a big hug. "No matter how much you like Edna's legs, leave them alone." The animal simply continued nibbling on a cookie and looking cute and innocent and rolling his big black eyes. Edna groaned, and held the letter back up towards the light. She decided she'd read a little bit more of the letter, but if anything got too unpleasant she'd just skip over that part.

Also, watch out for banquets, Marsh. They're all rip-offs, phonies, jerks sitting at a dais. Phony speeches. Politics is horrible, Marsh, and death isn't so hot either. Don't you believe all those people who tell you death is the greatest kick of all, which is why they save it for last. And TV is so phony, isn't it? Advertising is so phony. See, what I wanted to do was try to make all that stuff disappear from the earth, but I couldn't because there were too many rotten people and corporations behind it. Even breakfast cereals are getting out of hand now. And you know the way I feel about military children's toys, and the National Rifle Association.

Just then Edna was reminded of something about the first letter Marsh had asked her to read. There was something about the style of the writing that bothered her. It wasn't smooth. She'd known a lot of kids where the kid sounded like the father, but this seemed to be sort of the reverse situation. In this case the father seemed to write just like his son talked. It was a little crazier, but there seemed to be something very similar.

"Did your father really buy you a three-stage American flag firework rocket?" Edna decided to quiz because the thought just happened into her head.

"Oh yeah, you bet he did. It's terrific. See, when you light it up, the first stage is supposed to bring everything up to about five hundred feet in the air and then the second stage explodes and there's these long banners of red and white that are supposed to run across the sky, horizontal to the earth, and then there's another stage or two and all these stars are supposed to appear in one corner at the top so that it looks like a great big United States flag."

"Where is it?" Edna asked.

Marsh looked at her as though he knew she didn't believe him. "It's under my bed," he said.

Edna took in a deep breath. "Oh, I'd love to see it," she said, noticing a strange expression on Marsh's face. She was positive she had caught him in a lie now.

"All right," he said. He got down on his hands and knees and reached under the bed until he pulled out a long cardboard box which looked like the kind of thing Edna's father would send a dozen gladiolas in from his florist shop. But this box was a dull brown and looked like it had been made in Japan or something. Marsh opened the box, and sure enough, there was the rocket, about three feet long with a stand, and even a set of instructions attached to the body of the rocket by a rubber band.

"Nice," Edna said, going back to the letter while

Marsh rearranged the rocket, closed the box and shoved it back under the bed.

Marsh, you already know what I think of doctors, the letter continued, *especially that cruel one up on sixty-seventh street east, between Madison and Park Avenue that wouldn't take your grandmother when she had cancer, but no money. Always remember what Longfellow said: "Joy, temperance and repose, slam the door on the doctor's nose." And cigarettes! They're as bad as the Surgeon General says they are. I only smoke because I don't know any better. And a friend with a weed is not a friend indeed. Marsh, life is a hereditary disease. And one thing I want you never to do is to pay taxes, because it only goes to welfare to pay for heroin. And all that talk I did against abortion, suicide and moguls who foul up the earth with their factories, and millionaires who hire lawyers so they don't have to pay taxes, but the rest of us do? Remember all that? Well, that's all true. They're wrong, and our government is wrong, and the politicians are wrong because they're always trying to throw bones to the poor and save the real meat for the rich ones. Marsh, if it was up to me, I'd have a couple of television programs called:* Mace the Nation, *and* Beat the Press. *I'd rather have you vote for Buddha or Godzilla. I just saw another car pull up outside, Marsh, so I guess they'll be breaking down the door any minute. Please remember, even though I was your father and much older than you, that I hated flag-wavers, parades, guns, missiles, A-bombs, and thought welfare got out of hand.*

/ 88

So did food stamps. And the unions and their crim-
inal bosses. I never could understand how people
could let criminal bosses run all those unions.
Everybody's ripping off everybody else, and the
only thing that would make them be nice is if the
whole country went down the drain, and then peo-
ple were selling apples on the street again after
they finished killing off as many as they wanted to
kill off. Also, Marsh, I hate to tell you, but there's no
God, and I'm afraid Jesus was just a carpenter, and
Lord only knows about Mount Olympus. Death is
more than Nature's way of telling you to slow
down. Death is horrible. And what makes me feel so
sick is that you've inherited it from me. Every-
body's always inventing something to believe in,
but tough luck, Marsh, they're all wrong. I don't
care if they use Yoga, tarot cards, Transcendental
Meditation, Zen, I mean, all that garbage. All
they're doing is kidding themselves because when
you're dead, you're really croaked. Everything we
do is unimportant.

Edna stopped reading and put the letter back on the
bed. "That's it. I don't want any more."

"You've got to finish it."

"Look, I said I'm not finishing it. I've done it. That's
enough. I gave it enough attention, I understand, I've
got the gist, I don't want to read any more."

"What'd you do? Get to the part about death?"
Marsh asked.

"It doesn't matter what part I got to. Look, it's
getting late and my eyeballs hurt."

"You've got to finish," Marsh pleaded.

"Some other time."

"Edna, please." He put his arm around her again and she felt like she'd been wrapped in an electric coil. He looked so charged up it was like he had *both* his hands and feet shoved into an electric socket. It was the first time she ever felt like a human electromagnet, and her head gave a couple of jerks as though she thought her mother was hiding under the bed with the American flag firework rocket. Maybe it was just all the huge faces staring down at her, but she felt like she was going to explode with guilt, and she didn't even know what her crime was.

Marsh put the pages of the letter back into her hand, and against her will she started reading some more:

Marsh, the mean politicians in this country want me out of the way because I'm hitting them where it hurts, and that's in their money belt. See, public schools have gone too far away from liberal arts, I mean that's part of the problem. I want you to know how sorry I am you've got to study all that junk you don't need now and you're never going to need. I mean, all that stuff is old stuff they have at school. Who do they think they are, they give you this little sprinkle of current events and they think it's a big deal. Curtis Lee High is so hung-up on the old days it's enough to make you engage in reverse peristalsis which, as you know, means throwing up.

Edna reread a couple of the lines of the letter and the thought crossed her mind that for a drunk, Marsh's father was really emotionally involved in the school system.

Marsh, his father had continued writing, *I don't want you going to Curtis Lee High School on a regular basis. I don't want you jumping at their bell. I think it's a good idea if you cut lots and lots of classes, particularly those who have phony teachers who aren't up-to-date and never admit they're wrong. Remember what I always said to you at Dirty Irma's: School is going to disappear pretty soon, and there is going to be a whole new way of getting smart. Remember, Einstein failed everything. And who the hell does our president think he is fooling the way he runs around the country doing public appearances to help the other jerks in his political party get in. Our president is so corrupt he'd go to New Hampshire and say Marcel Proust was a yenta. Our president is just like all the rotten politicians in this country who want nothing except to get rich, go to parties, have poor people think they're terrific, hang around with celebrities, stash away a whole pack of loot to pay off their houses, and store up certificates of deposit, and think of any new ways they can to take your money away and shove it in their own pockets. The whole gimmick is that everybody on earth is out to make money and have as much fun as possible before they die and get stuck in a casket and are cremated or frozen like Walt Disney.*

Edna slapped the pages of the letter down on the bed and stood up. "I'm sorry, Marsh. That's it. I've got to go home. I really appreciate it, it's been very interesting. I've never read a more fascinating letter, and I really wish you a whole lot of luck, and I feel very badly about the whole thing."

Marsh looked surprised. "There's more."

"Well, that's nice, I'm glad there's more, I'm sure it's very interesting, I'd love to read it, but I'm tired." Edna walked quickly to the door of the room and turned back to see Marsh. All the faces of the posters seemed to be looming over his shoulder, staring at her and making her feel guilty. Marsh looked very sad.

"If you don't finish the letter," Marsh said, "I'll know you don't care about the human race!"

"Well, you can think whatever you want, but if you ask me, that's thinking a little too broadly. All I want to know is are you going to drive me home or do I have to walk?"

"I want you to finish the letter."

"I'm not reading any more."

"What do you want me to do? Get down on my hands and knees and beg and crawl and say Jesus, for God and the Country, and the Flag and whatever else —for Raccoon! Please finish reading the letter; that's all I ask. I've got nobody else. You're the only one I can trust."

"I said I want to go home!" Edna screamed.

"Please, Edna."

"No!" Edna quickly lowered her voice, afraid that she'd already awakened Schizo Suzy. For all she knew, Schizo Suzy could be running up the stairs with an ice pick in her hands. Maybe Schizo Suzy and her son were some kind of bizarre murder team that lured high-school girls to their house and then cut them up into little pieces and sent them out in parcels of something like she read in an English news report.

"I'll finish reading the letter in the car," Edna said. She would have agreed to stand on one finger to get out of there, even swallow glass, anything. But that room and that house were giving her the spooks. Even the raccoon was eerily squealing when Marsh put him back into his cage. Edna went over to the cage and threw a couple of cookies in to shut him up. The raccoon looked just as grim as she did.

Edna was still grim, sitting in the Mazda with Marsh driving slowly by every streetlight so she could finish reading the letter. Edna spotted the giant sign of the palmist and looked back once as it disappeared into the night. Edna couldn't help but feeling that she caught the sight of a figure in one of the downstairs windows.

Sugar is evil, Marsh, the letter went on. *They put sugar in everything so you can get hooked, my son. Our whole country is high on sugar, not to mention pot, hash and coke. Marsh, the world is a big bowl of loneliness, frustration, desperation, insecurity, deceit, disappointment, hopelessness and disillusionment. And it's tough that women think pay toilets are antifeminist devices. That's another part of the mental sabotage. If a woman tells you she's the same as a man, I want you to punch her. There are differences between men and women. They should have the same rights, but let me tell you, they're really not very good at unloading refrigerators. I mean that. I've seen them trying to unload refrigerators and they don't do a very good job at it. Maybe they could learn to do a good job at it, and then I'd change my mind, but as of yet, they don't seem to do so good. Son, I'm sorry I'm a drunk. I'm sorry I was such a wise guy and went around saying that absinthe makes the heart grow fonder. Booze is a bummer, kid, and in my book, George Orwell was an optimist. See, life is like a dog race. You've heard of the greyhound races? Well, politicians and moguls are the greyhounds, see? And we're the rabbits, strapped to an iron bar that whirls around the racetrack so fast that our mouths are ripped open from the wind while the greyhounds are chasing us. The greyhounds don't eat us in public. They wait until the race is over, and then we're taken to a private room and then we're thrown to the dogs. And what's even worse, is that all the races are fixed, because they give us doped meatballs; that's the kind of poor dogs we are. There's a pack of guys around that are just like the Marquis de Sade, and let me tell you, he really knew how to hurt a guy. Marsh, I hear them coming down the hall now. I'll yell and kick while they're dragging me out and socking me over the head with blunt instruments. But they'll only tell everybody at the Y that I'm a crazy person. Marsh, I've got to tell you quickly now, thank you for having been my son. Thank you for having been my only friend in life. Remember, two things I always told you: One, don't be placid with acid, and two, life is like the situation where a ferocious tiger has chased us to the edge of a cliff, and we climb down a rope and are hanging in the air above a ledge that has another ferocious tiger waiting to eat us. Now I know all those Zen people think we're supposed to just reach out in front of us and be able to grab a bunch of grapes and eat them and be happy in that situation, but I can't do it. With a tiger above and a tiger below, I'm not going to be able to eat grapes and say, "Oh my, aren't they delicious." They're trying to break down the door now. Please, oh please, Marsh, don't let them step on your eyeball. Remember, Lake Erie died for our sins. Good-bye, son. Love, from Dad. P.S., I hope you find this pinned, as I said, to the drapes. Adieu. If it's my fault our leaders are such bums, and your school is a dumb-dumb factory, I apologize. Maybe I should have done more than talk. I will never forget you, my wonderful son. Love again, from Dad. P.P.S. You can give my clothes back home to Goodwill Industries.*

Edna's eyes hurt from having read the letter under such transient conditions. Without saying anything, she folded the pages of the letter back up and put it on the seat between her and Marsh. Marsh kept glancing from the road to her face to see what her reaction was. She just remained silent and she was very relieved at that moment to see her house just ahead. It was plain and simple; a split-level ranch, just like every other house on the block; it was very middle-class, but somehow middle-class didn't seem like such a bad word anymore. Even the artificial wishing well on the front lawn didn't look so bad. In fact Edna was never as glad to see an artificial wishing well before in her life.

"Now do you believe me?" Marsh asked, looking as though his whole life depended upon what she would say. "He wants us to help him."

"Oh, sure," Edna said, not even positive of exactly what he was talking about. She felt like she'd just spent a night on the town with a hobbit. Edna opened the door of the car and started to get out.

"Wait," Marsh said, that strain of desperation returning to his voice. "There's one more thing you've got to read. It came in the mail this morning." He shoved another paper towards her and she felt like running towards the house screaming like a crazy lady.

"It's just a note," Marsh emphasized. Edna let out a big groan and kept one foot out the door of the car as she held the note beyond the shadow of the car roof. The streetlight wasn't far away, and since the note looked mercifully short, she decided she might as well make it a night completely devoted to bizarre correspondence.

Dear Marsh, I thought of you again today because I saw the top of the eucalyptus tree and the church steeple behind it out the window of my padded cell. Like I told you, it is just like the giant eucalyptus tree next to the firework stand in North Carolina where I bought you that special $14.98 American Flag Firework Rocket. I hope you still have it. They are going to operate on me soon. Oh, God, son, please help me. Now that they're going to really operate on me I'm scared. Forgive me, son, but please help me. Love, Dad.

Edna handed the note back to Marsh and got out of the car. She felt numb again and just started walking towards her front door.

"Edna," Marsh called after her, "don't you see?

There *was* no giant eucalyptus tree next to the firework stand. That whole part is a clue."

"Sure it is," Edna said as she opened the door. She stood for a moment looking at the boy in the car. She gave a slight wave as she closed the door to block out the sight. Then she leaned against the door.

"Edna? Is that you, dear?" she heard her mother's voice call from upstairs.

"Yes, Mama," Edna said, and then burst into tears.

Chapter 12 /

All the way home Marsh could think of nothing except how terrific Edna Shinglebox was. He never told anybody as much as he had told her; never showed anybody the letters. All of that was something he thought he'd just have to keep inside of him and never let out. And it was so strange—he knew the minute he had first seen her in the lunchroom that this strange girl was going to be the one to help him. She had looked so pretty that night. Everyone at the Magic Elephant had noticed her, and it wasn't just because he'd stuck her on the trick stool. He knew they were going to be great friends. And now it seemed like he was going to have some kind of family again. There was his father, Raccoon, and the terrific Miss Edna Shinglebox.

When he got back home he noticed Schizo Suzy's head had rolled off the pillow. He stuck it back on so she'd be more comfortable. She might have less of a hangover that way, he figured. There was a little draft under the piano, so he took a quilt from the sofa and covered her, then went upstairs to his room.

He gave Raccoon a big hug, hurled his clothes around the room and then shoved a cassette into his secondhand Sony tape recorder. There was nothing he liked better than just lying in bed with the earphones strapped on. It seemed to shut out that whole horrible house, and it did a pretty good job of shutting out the world too. But tonight he could hardly hear the music because his thoughts were pounding too loudly. He used to like to try to control his dreams; program his mind for what would happen while he was asleep. He thought it would be nice if he dreamed about his Florida trip. He'd wanted to tell Edna about that one; how he and Paranoid Pete had run away because Schizo Suzy was getting on everybody's nerves about being afraid of everything. She had phobias about phobias. The first thing she started with was being afraid that the boiler was going to blow up while she was sleeping. And then she used to think a burglar would come in and knife them while they were sleeping, or try to suffocate them with a piece of foam rubber. After that, she was afraid that a dog down the street was going to run out and tear her into pieces. For days she went running around the house saying "Where can I go for a walk now? Where can I go for a walk now?" And it didn't matter that she could have gone for a walk anywhere except down near where the dog lived. Finally it got so bad Pete just took Marsh by the hand one day and said, "You know, Suzy, Marsh and I are going to go take a little stroll."

Marsh had been really surprised to find that the little stroll ended up right in Florida. That was the way Paranoid Pete did things. It was really a lot of fun. He'd make believe he was going down to the corner to buy a pack of cigarettes and then he'd end up in New Orleans for the Mardi Gras. He never made a big fuss about it; no bragging, no threats, nothing. If somebody did something he didn't like, he'd just say, "Well, I'll see you around." And then he'd go to Canada. That was the terrific thing about him. And if he didn't run off somewhere, then he'd just slug somebody. The California trip started the same way. Schizo Suzy had been getting really ugly around that time. Marsh himself had to admit that as a wife she was the pits. She was really low in intelligence quotient, at least compared with Paranoid Pete. Pete had smarts. Schizo Suzy used to have to ask directions, even how to get back from the post office. That's how spaced-out she was. She had what was known as "poor spatial relations." Marsh knew a lot of that psychology stuff because Pete loved those kinds of books.

Pete used to always love telling Schizo Suzy that she had the worst spatial relations in the world. The best part about telling that to Schizo Suzy was that she never knew what spatial relations was. And then he used to also use some Spanish curse words with her, but say them in a nice way so she thought they were complimentary. Then finally the day came when Schizo Suzy called Pete for directions back from only a block away. Now, all that kind of thing wasn't really Schizo Suzy's fault, Marsh felt. It just happened to be the way she was raised. Her parents always told her she was this precious little thing, and everybody should take care of her. That's how she ended up getting retarded because that's not the way the world is. Schizo Suzy just couldn't wise up that she was supposed to take care of herself. And she used to always try to correct Pete even though she, herself, had some kind of screw loose. She'd say things like "Hey, Pete, how come there's so many colors in a sunset?" And Pete would let out a loud groan and say "Suzy! We both saw the same TV special yesterday that explained the whole thing, so why do you make believe you don't know the answer?" Marsh tried to analyze the whole thing and he decided it was just Schizo Suzy's desperate way of making conversation. Still, it was annoying, and she was so inept at making conversation she really came out sounding stupid. Sometimes she'd make believe she heard birds chirping all over the place and accuse Pete of having hooked up an artificial bird-chirping machine as a joke. She was a real flop in the domestic department! She hated washing clothes, she never did dishes, she didn't know how to cook for beans. Her idea of housecleaning was to run around with a Windex bottle for two minutes in the morning. She was really useless.

She used to do things like "calculated lying around the house." She used to lie awake nights, thinking of what she could do to manipulate people into waiting on her. She was really terrific at pretending she didn't know how to do something. And the one time she even tried to make a pork roast, she looked at this recipe, and then she doubled everything and the thing came out tasting like a salted brick. Thank God, Marsh thought, that Edna Shinglebox was nothing like that.

Marsh continued dreaming with the earphones still blasting away. He wanted to remember the best time in his life, and he decided that it was when Schizo Suzy said she thought Pete was a stinker.

"You're a stinker, Pete," Schizo Suzy said.

"Oh yeah?" Pete asked. Pete didn't wait for an answer. He just took Marsh by the hand, and Marsh knew they were going someplace. He thought it might just be to Dirty Irma's, or the Magic Elephant. But this time it turned out to be three thousand miles to California—Los Angeles, to be exact. What a trip that had been. That was Marsh's idea of paradise: Paranoid Pete and him in Hollywood.

He remembered everything about that trip. The terrific headlines that used to be in the newspaper machines they had on all the corners: I LOVE WOMEN FOR WHAT THEY CAN DO FOR ME; A LACK OF LOVE CAN KILL YOU; AN EASY, DIGNIFIED METHOD FOR MEETING SINGLES. The day they got off the Greyhound bus in downtown L.A., he and Paranoid Pete rented a Dollar-a-Day Rent-a-Pinto and went cruising down Holly-wood Boulevard looking at all the belly-dancing emporiums near Vine Street. That was the great thing about Hollywood. From the moment they got there they could tell it was a weird place. There'd be things like a kid standing on a street corner yelling out "Remember that today and yesterday are the good old days someone will talk about tomorrow." Everybody seemed to be spaced-out on drugs or religion. There was a terrific hypnosis institute near Hollywood and Vine. And Marsh always read the billboards. There was a terrific cigarette ad for Tramps all over the place that exploited a shot of Charlie Chaplin, and they had Yul Brynner on another sign saying how he drinks a special kind of Scotch. And there were a lot of weirdo stores. They even had a store that thought it was so special because it had huge signs saying that they sold living plants and trees. What a triumphant drive it was down Hollywood Boulevard! Past the Great American Food and Beverage Company which looked like a plain old hamburger place, all hyped-up. There was a bar called Filthy McNasty's where Pete stopped and threw down a couple of boilermakers. Some woman was standing in front of a restaurant called The Lost-On-Larrabee Burger Palace, and she was yelling "Cancer cures smoking! Cancer cures smoking!" That's what kind of a nifty place Hollywood was. Marsh was really getting off thinking about what a riot that place was. Day after day of running around with Pete to freaky places and seeing such freaky people. One time they had breakfast at a Mexican restaurant called Por Favor. And they shoplifted their lunch at the Yum-Yum Supermarket. Instead of eating in the Pinto, they sat in the backseat of a 1936 Rolls-Royce which was left unattended on Selma Avenue.

"Yoo-hoo!" Pete had yelled out at one point. Pete used to do that when he was having a good time. He'd just yell out, "Yoo-hoo!" Sometimes you didn't even know what he was talking about, but "yoo-hoo" and you knew everything was okay. Once Pete let Marsh take the wheel of the Pinto and Marsh crashed right into a Granada but they got away. It was just a little sideswipe. And another time, a taxicab hit them in the back, but nobody got hurt. A little whiplash. But it was a lot of fun. Actually there was another thing they got used to. Everybody found it normal to crash into the back of cars in Los Angeles. Every street corner you were at you'd hear CRASH, and there'd be another car smacked into somebody. It was like a natural phenomenon, so everybody'd get out and look at their bumps and then get back in and drive off. There were dopeheads all over the place. Hollywood had everything. Marsh started to laugh out loud as he lay in bed. He could still see the expression on Pete's face when the owner of the Gourmet Nibbler grocery store caught him stealing three jars of chocolate-covered grasshoppers and told him to put them back. That was the same day the money started running out.

Marsh lay in his room and began to feel frightened. He knew his mind was moving forward to the main thing he didn't want to remember. He knew he could remember only so far, and then he'd have to stop himself. Rather than let the most horrible memory of his life come any closer, he tried to turn his mind off, but he couldn't. He remembered that last morning when Paranoid Pete and he had gone out to have homemade burritos for breakfast, and then they just stumbled around, and Pete was tying a real load on that morning. Marsh felt he could have told Pete not to drink so much. He could have made his father take him to an early movie or something.

For lunch they stumbled in and had pizza at Pizza Galore, which had a sign in its window saying "Our English, she no good, but our pizza, she speak real better." Then they went next door and looked in a book place that sold things like *Winged Hordes of the*

Yellow Vultures and *The Ant Man.* Some of the subtitles on the books were even more wacko: "His size alone doesn't frighten me, but there is some sinister secret behind the coming of GARGANTUS!"; "Who is the hunter? Who is the victim on the night the streets ran red with gore?"; "Vampirella and the duel of her life against the Blood Gulper"; "Hulk on the Rampage, the terrifying story of a blob." Then after the bookstore, Paranoid Pete wanted a few more drinks. That's when he should have told his father "No!" Marsh had counted ten boilermakers, and he had three Singapore slings, and then he switched and he had two water glasses of stingers, and on top of that he had half a bottle of Thunderbird wine. Marsh knew he should have stopped him but it seemed like such a hoot. Then Pete started to sing out loud and dragged Marsh into Madame Tussaud's Wax Museum which advertised: ONE HUNDRED SEVENTY FIGURES OF STARS AND FAMOUS PEOPLE. It seemed really freaky to be walking up and down the aisles past all these waxed imitations of people, because they all looked like corpses. There was even a wax duplication of the man that founded Grauman's Chinese Theatre and his arm had fallen off and was lying on the floor next to the exhibit. There was just something about the whole morning, about the way everything had begun, that Marsh knew something rotten was going to happen. Why didn't he listen to his conscience? What happened was his fault, not Pete's. Pete was drunk. It was Marsh that should have known better!

When they got out of the museum they bought a

pound of Barton's Continental Chocolates, and Pete started to drive, throwing the chocolates down his throat like they were peanuts. He only drove a block and then he wanted to go to another bar for a boiler-maker. Marsh refused to go with him. He figured if Pete went in alone, he wouldn't stay as long if Marsh wasn't there. Marsh could feel the old guilt about to explode inside of him. Marsh just stayed outside the bar, walking up and down the street reading the stars' names in the cement memorials set in the side-walk. He should have been inside with his father. That's where he belonged—next to Pete! Lou Costel-lo's memorial imitation gold star was next to some guy called Joseph Schildkraut and the two of them were smack in front of an occult jewelry store.

The memories kept pouring in on Marsh as the mu-sic clanged in his ears. It's as though the reality of a tape deck was screaming for him to stop, not to re-member any more: "Turn off the guilt machine! Turn off the horrible guilt machine!" Marsh felt himself beginning to shake as his mind spun closer to the worst of the nightmare. "It's *your* fault!" a voice in his mind cried out. "It was all your fault!" For a minute he thought he would have no control and the full terror of it would sweep across him, but he started counting backwards from a hundred; started pulling a lot of mental tricks that would prevent him from remembering that part tonight. He kept telling himself over and over that he wasn't going to think any more; he wasn't going to remember any more. Finally, he resorted to his surefire trick, remembering the graffiti in Hollywood like "Benjamin Franklin got a charge out of life" and "Convertibles are topless." Thank God all the fences and bathrooms and buildings had jokes written across them like "Nuns kick the habit" and "Impeach God, Evil Works"; "In case of atomic attack, the federal ruling against prayer in schools will be temporarily suspended"; "Come home, Judas, all is forgiven"; "God is an usher at the Astrodome, and what's more, She's Chinese"; "God isn't dead, He's just trying to find a parking place"; "Jesus Saves! But He couldn't do it on my allowance." And two of his favorites that were always surefire were: "Tomorrow will be canceled because of lack of interest" and "Count Dracula, your Bloody Mary is ready."

Chapter 13 /

Edna didn't go to school for three days. She told her mother she had an upset stomach. But all her mother wanted to know was why Edna wouldn't answer the phone all the times Marsh had called. Every day her mother called her seven times from the florist shop where she was working with Mr. Shinglebox, and she had to work out a special, one-ring signal so that Edna would know it was her and answer the phone. Mrs. Shinglebox even stayed home with her on Thursday, she'd become so concerned about her.

"It's not an upset stomach you've got," Mrs. Shinglebox insisted, "when you don't take twenty-seven phone calls from a boy. You've got to have something like indigestion of the heart, if you ask me."

"Look, I hardly even know him," Edna said. "Don't go giving me that heart business. I don't know him, and I'm not going to know him, and that's all there is to it. It didn't work out. He was interesting, nice shoes, I liked the three feathers on the side of his jacket, but, let's just say it was not a match made in heaven. Besides, he wasn't the least bit romantically interested in me from the beginning any more than I was interested in him."

Mrs. Shinglebox made Edna sit down at the breakfast table and finish eating all of her eggs. "Edna, darling," she started in, "have you ever considered getting romantic assistance from a computer? Maybe your father and I haven't been keeping up with the times as much as we should have been. Maybe I'm too old-fashioned."

"Mother," Edna said, "this boy that came to pick me up the other night, if he was a car, I'd have to tell you that it's got a loud knock in its engine. Do you know what I mean? All the pistons aren't hitting quite right."

"Maybe it's a temporary condition," Mrs. Shinglebox said. "You know, maybe he needs just a little oil, or you've been putting in the wrong kind of gasoline."

"Mom, it's more than a petroleum difficulty."

"Well what is it then?"

"I can't tell you, but in general, I think he's a loony. He's always talking in terms like 'LBJ and the CIA did away with JFK.' I mean, everything's got initials in it or about politics. I mean, there's just something very freaky going on and I can't tell you all the facts about it. It would just blow your mind."

"Honey, your father used to blow my mind when I married him. He was active for some kind of cause that used to say that they should keep New York clean by dumping all the trash in New Jersey. All boys are crazy. You think I didn't know that boy was crazy when he came to pick you up? But, my God, I said, what a nice-looking crazy person my daughter has taking her out." Mrs. Shinglebox poured herself a fresh cup of coffee, then took out a notebook and sat down opposite Edna. "Now look, honey, this woman came into the florist shop yesterday and ordered four dozen mums in an arrangement with a zebra-head vase for a base. It took us a long time to make it up and she waited for it, so while she was waiting, we started chatting and it turned out she's some kind of an interviewer for a computer-dating service. She told me that this might be something good for you."

"Mother, I don't need a machine."

"Honey, I know you don't need a machine, but I asked her for some of the sample questions that they kind of ask and program into the thing, and I thought I could try them out on you, and then maybe we'd know why you're sort of like a teenage, frigid person."

"I'm not frigid!"

"I didn't say you *were* frigid. I just said you were *kind* of frigid. Now, just shut up because I could be boxing corsages now with your father, but instead, I'm home with you because I'm worried. Now, all I'm asking is that you listen to me."

"Do I have to?"

"Yes, you have to. I'm your mother and you owe me that courtesy," Mrs. Shinglebox insisted, squirming herself into a comfortable position and taking on a professional tone to her voice. "See, now this first question they always want to know about is, Are you cheerful? And then you get multiple choice, you see, Are you cheerful all the time? Are you cheerful half the time? or Are you cheerful none of the time?"

"I'm not doing this, Mom."

"Yes you are! Now what's the answer!"

"What were the choices?"

"Are you cheerful all the time, half of the time or none of the time."

"Half of the time."

"Good, that's normal," Mrs. Shinglebox said with joy. "Now, question two: In the last year, what was the average number of times you were kissed by a boy? None. One to five times. Ten to thirty times. Thirty to eighty times."

"None."

"Are you trying to tell me you weren't kissed the other night?"

"You got it." Edna was surprised to hear herself be so blunt.

"Well, at least you got a hug or two. Maybe we could just insert hug for kissing, and then it would have the same kind of meaning and we could stick that in the machine."

"He didn't even put his arm around me, Ma. Well, yes, he put his arm around me, but he only did that so I wouldn't run out of the room."

"What room?"

"Mom, stop giving me the third degree, it wasn't a romantic date. It was something very ordinary. All he wanted was for me to help his father escape from a nuthouse."

Mrs. Shinglebox's eyes tripled their size. "Edna, stop making things up. I'm trying to be serious with you. A lot of families get fleeced trying to come up with questions like these. Psychology costs a lot of money these days, you know that. And my God, if you have to go under intensive analysis, we're talking about a fortune! You could go to Princeton for the money we'd have to spend to send you to the kind of shrink who'd really find out why you're so weird."

"Mother, I am being serious."

"Edna, don't you try to kid your poor old mother. That boy didn't show up here looking like a rock star for nothing. One look at him and I could see he's got you under his skin." Mrs. Shinglebox let out a wicked little laugh and danced back to the coffeepot singing "He's got you under his skin; he's got you deep in the heart of him."

"Mother!" Edna protested.

"All right," Mrs. Shinglebox said, filling her cup and zipping back into her place. "Question Three." She squirmed to get into position and adjusted her voice. "Where, in your opinion, is the most appropriate place to express your love for a boy? In school? In a park? At a movie? In a car?"

"On a horse," Edna said.

Mrs. Shinglebox wanted to pull her daughter's hair out along with her own. "Edna, I'm trying to help you. I gave that woman a special price on the mums and she said she'd give you a good deal to hook you up with her machine."

"I don't want to be hooked up to her machine."

"Darling, darling," Mrs. Shinglebox said, brushing a few strands of Edna's hair out of her eggs, "the whole trick in life has to do with four crucial steps, this lady was telling me. First you've got to know what your hang-up is, and then you've got to get all this information together about how come you're so strange. I mean, you've got to think of all these solutions and you make lists of the whole thing. Things you can do about it. And last of all, you have to make a decision and act. Act! Not talk! You talk too much; that's your problem."

"Look, you're the one that does all the talking."

"I am not!"

"Yes you are!"

"I am not I said!"

"Mom, I told you, I'm not seeing that crazy boy anymore. He's from hunger."

"Edna, I don't care if he's on cloud ninety-four. He's the first boy that's asked you out in your life. How can you say you're not going to see him anymore? He calls this house night and day. What, you're making believe you're sick so you don't have to go to school and see him? Honey, he's in that nutty class with you. You can't hide out forever. Eventually, you're going to have to go in there and confront the boy. Did it ever occur to you that maybe you've got just as many problems as he does? Oh, excuse me, that came out wrong. I mean, he's got just as many problems as *you* have?"

"Yes, Mom, that did dawn on me. And let me tell you, my main problem is you."

"Me?" Mrs. Shinglebox cried out incredulously. She almost spurted a mouthful of coffee across the table. *"Me!"*

"Yes, you," Edna said firmly. "It's not your fault, but you're the one that got me going like this. Why do you think my head swivels so much? All through grammar school people called me Swivel Head."

"Oh, I see. That's what that ignoramous, fat school psychologist told you. Is that what he's done all this time! Put the blame on me, huh? My God, is he behind the times!"

"Mom, look. I don't want to be a suburban housewife. I don't care if I ever get married. Don't you understand that?"

"Edna, the way you're going, you're going to be lucky if you end up as a suburban nun."

"Mom, I thought the whole thing over and, look, a lot of the things about how I am come from you. I mean, I'm not complaining, I'm not blaming you. I mean, I'm old enough to handle it all myself. I'm sorry I'm not doing so well with it, and I wouldn't mention it except that you're trying to hook me up with some kind of machine, and if I don't talk up you're going to get the wires all plugged into me, and I'm not going to let it happen. Mom, I'm not going to do too well at this middle-class waltz you've been drumming into me."

"Oh, you're doing a great job not blaming me, I'll tell you that," Mrs. Shinglebox wailed. She grabbed an appliance, pulled it to the center of the table and held her hands over it. "Edna, look, if I've hurt you in any way, may God take my two hands and shove them into this toaster and kill me."

"Oh, for crying out loud!"

"I never thought I'd hear a daughter of mine say 'Oh, for crying out loud.' Never! My God, I don't even know what you mean by 'a middle-class waltz.'"

"Mom, all you want to do is see me married, with two kids and living in a split-level ranch just like this one."

"Oh, it'd be such a curse for you Edna, wouldn't it! Just such a curse!"

"Mom, you're enough to make me want to take a cannibal to lunch!" Edna said clearly.

Mrs. Shinglebox gasped. She tried to say something but her mouth simply hung open. Finally she decided to sit down quietly and cry. Then Edna started to cry. In a second the two of them were bawling their heads off, but Edna continued eating her eggs and her mother continued sipping her coffee. They bawled and bawled for a very long time. Then Mrs. Shinglebox dried her eyes and got up from the table. Edna couldn't stop crying so she just sat still, mushing her eggs into different patterns on her plate. Her mother left the kitchen and five minutes later she was back with her hat and coat on. Edna was still crying and refused to look at her.

"Are you all right?" Edna asked, although she was the one still in tears.

"I'm going down to the florist shop," Mrs. Shinglebox said in a very composed tone. Edna couldn't quite tell what she was up to. "I'm going to tell your father the good news," Mrs. Shinglebox said.

"What good news?"

Mrs. Shinglebox gave her daughter a Mona Lisa smile, and then started to exit dramatically.

"What good news, I asked."

"That you started to *express* yourself," Mrs. Shinglebox said, disappearing.

Edna was so glad to hear the front door slam that she wanted to yell with joy, but the tears were still coming down her face. She was crying as she scraped the remains of her breakfast into the garbage pail under the sink. And she was still crying by the time she went upstairs to her bedroom. It was only when she happened to look into the mirror on her wall that she noticed how ridiculous she looked with tears rolling down her face. In fact, she felt at that moment that it was a good time to take a good look at herself. She didn't even know why she was crying anymore. Actually, she thought the girl in the mirror looked different, and it was very strange because when her eyes looked at the eyes in the mirror, the tears instantly stopped. And something even stranger about it was that Edna had a feeling she was never going to be able to cry as easily as she had before. It was like she had had all she could take and then there wasn't any more that could hurt her. Maybe if somebody died, or if a truck ran over her arm, maybe then she'd cry. But it had to be something more important than what she usually cried about. At the very least, she wasn't going to cry without a damn good reason. She hunted through her makeup paraphernalia and finally found a clean tissue to dry her eyes. Then she looked back at herself in the mirror. "Who are you?" she asked herself. "Aren't you tired of being some kind of emotional clunk? Aren't you ever going to tell how you feel in this life? Aren't you ever going to have the guts to say the things you think? As crazy as all those letters Marsh's father had written, at least the guy had guts. Mad as a hatter, but some of those things took nerve. And you, Edna, what do you do? You sit in front of a mirror, and you're worried because you're fat. And you're not too fat. Maybe you're a little fat, and maybe you overeat a little bit. Edna, you don't have to have a pint of Breyers butter almond ice cream every night before you go to bed. You don't have to have twenty-three cookies. Edna, what you've got to do is lose weight, because, Edna Shinglebox, you're ashamed of yourself." She continued staring at herself in the mirror. It all seemed very freaky, and yet it seemed to make some kind of sense. "Take better care of your nails, Edna. You need better body tone. Join the tennis and swimming club. And don't be so ashamed of what you look like because Rosalie Potkins, who sits in front of you in English, is two hundred pounds heavier than you and she plays on the war-ball team. If you're so worried about what you look like, go on a diet. Just because your mother and father eat corn crunchies during *The Fall of the House of Usher* doesn't mean you have to. Okay—you're not a movie star. But you look decent, in fact you look good." Edna even felt she looked better, the more angry she was getting at her image in the mirror. "Edna," she told herself, "you look more interesting when you're angry about something. When you're sad, that's when you look dull. And dull people only do what other people tell them to do."

Edna leaned closer to the mirror and let her thoughts spin on. She was going to give herself a good talking to even if it killed her. "It's tough luck that Joey Kapinolli got poisoned on the mushroom project. He isn't known as Dumb Joey for nothing. And so what if you get your hair caught in escalators. Nobody's got any right blurting that out and embarrassing you, especially in front of a school psychologist that looks like he's married to Sara Lee. And you should have been straight with Jacqueline Potts and told her exactly what you thought about Butch Ontock. No wonder Jacqueline didn't really consider you as a friend. All Miss Edna Shinglebox ever did was keep her mouth shut and nod and be boring and try to agree with everybody. No more," Edna said to herself, wanting to shake her finger at the girl in the mirror. "Oh, yes, you're lonely all right, and you need friends, but you've got to do something to earn them. Edna Shinglebox, you're a yes-woman, that's what you are! All you do is say 'yes.' Kids who say nothing but yes all the time don't have any backbone. Edna Shinglebox, you're a jellyfish."

The phone rang and Edna let it continue ringing. It rang five times, ten times, twelve times. It was still ringing as Edna finished putting on her makeup and fixing her hair. She let the phone ring and ring while her thoughts began to fly like machine-gun bullets. She knew there was only one person in the world who would call someone and let the phone ring forty-nine times. "Who do you think you are, Mr. Marsh Mellow," Edna said to herself. "I think you're a liar, and I think you're cruel. And I'm going to tell you that in person. It's not going to be on the phone." She continued talking to herself as though she were rehearsing a speech. "Don't you think I hear the remarks you make under your breath in GTE? I don't think it's very nice the way you make fun of Doris and Elaine Bach. You may think referring to them as the pee-pee twins is very funny, but I don't. And with the kinds of problems you have, you shouldn't dare even open your mouth. If Snooks wants to wear his mother's platform shoes to school and sing 'I'm Looking Over a Four Leaf Clover,' let me tell you that's normal compared to you. I'll tell you what you are, Marsh Mellow. You have as much compassion as a squash."

Edna's mind was racing on. Everything was getting clearer and clearer for her now. It was as though things were suddenly beginning to fall into place now that she was believing in her own thoughts. It seemed like there was a voice inside of her that was growing stronger and stronger, and that voice belonged to whoever the real Edna Shinglebox was going to be. And that voice was saying, "Marsh Mellow, you are the world's biggest liar. You think I don't know that's your handwriting in those letters? You think I don't notice the handwriting in your notebook is the same as in those letters? You think I didn't notice the way you phonied up the postage stamp on the envelope and with that return address to a nuthouse called the Los Angeles Neurological Hospital for the Insane and Crazy? You must think I'm an idiot! I don't fall for your gibberish about your father who hasn't written, and is locked in solitary confinement waiting for a lobotomy. Those kinds of crazy ideas are fiction! Those letters read just like you talk, Mr. Marsh Mellow. And let me tell you one thing, Edna Shinglebox may look dumb, but she's not dumb anymore. The big plot . . . the eucalyptus tree . . . they're going to operate on your father's brain, my foot! You're the one that's freaked out, buster, and when I see you, you're going to get yours, that much I can promise you!"

Chapter 14 /

Marsh was euphoric to see Edna walk through the door of the GTE classroom. He'd called her house in the morning as soon as some kid from her section told him that she'd been marked absent, but there had been no answer. The thought of going another day without seeing her had been driving him up the wall.

"Why wouldn't you talk to me?" Marsh asked, rushing right up to her.

Edna pushed by him and put her books down. She wouldn't even look at him. "I didn't talk to you because I didn't feel like it," she said, walking towards the rest of the kids who were swarming around Mr. Meizner like he was a honey dispenser. Marsh was so taken aback by the tone of her voice that he almost tripped on one of the straw mats on the floor. He hung his coat up in the closet, making sure that Raccoon was able to look out of the left pocket. He gave Raccoon's chest a little scratch and was thankful that at least somebody still liked him; at least there was one faithful pal in the world, even if this pal happened to be a little less than eight inches long and hairy. Raccoon gave a big smile at Marsh, and then the animal continued eating a half of a Clark bar that Marsh had bought him for brunch.

"Move it!" Mr. Meizner yelled at Marsh as he continued explaining to the class what was planned for the session. "And make sure that raccoon stays in your pocket," Mr. Meizner added. Marsh grunted and watched Mr. Meizner waving his hands up and down while he was rattling on about some kind of celebration-of-life experiment they were going to do that day. And Mr. Meizner looked like he'd put on at least another twenty pounds overnight. Marsh also noticed that Mr. Meizner had to leave the top catch of his trousers open because his stomach had gotten so big it was defying enclosure.

"Everybody get in a circle around Edna," Mr. Meizner ordered.

"Mr. Meizner, I'm not feeling so hot today," Edna moaned. "Why do you always have to start with me?"

"We don't always start with you," Mr. Meizner said. "But you've been absent and you've missed out on a lot of sensitivity exercises. Just lie down on the mattress and everybody will stand around you," Mr. Meizner continued, instilling as much guilt as possible.

Marsh thought Edna wasn't going to do what Mr. Meizner asked, but she did. She moaned and groaned and lowered herself onto the floor and then stretched out, making sure her skirt was pulled down. Marsh caught Edna looking at him out of the corner of her eye, but then she looked quickly away. Jacqueline, Doris Bach, Elaine Bach and Mario Lugati were already in position, and Mr. Meizner had to let out a special bellow to get Jo and Snooks to stop giggling.

"When I give the signal, you're all going to bend down and take hold of Edna," Mr. Meizner stated. "Mario and Snooks, get her shoulders; Doris and Elaine, grab her around the waist; Jacqueline and Jo, you each get a leg; Marsh, you're the strongest one, so you're going to be in charge of her head. Keep your eye on her upper torso and make sure that you don't drop her and crack her head on the mat."

"I've got a headache," Edna grumbled.

Mr. Meizner grumbled right back to her. "All you do, Edna, is relax. That's all you're supposed to do." Then he blew a whistle. "Okay, everybody, grab!"

Marsh could see a flash of fright in Edna's eyes as everyone stooped over and clutched the various designated parts of her anatomy. Mr. Meizner cleared his voice and prepared for action.

"On the count of three, everybody lift Edna into the air. One . . . two . . . three!"

"Oh, my God," Marsh heard Edna whimper as she went up into the air. Now she was in a horizontal position, but about three feet off the ground. Marsh couldn't help thinking the vision began to look like a Mexican funeral where nobody could afford a casket and you just carried the person up to a mountaintop and shoved them in a hole with rocks on top so that wolves wouldn't dig up the body. He saw that once in a movie.

"Now we rock her," Mr. Meizner said in a singsong fashion. "Rock her, rock her, rock her. Rock her like she's in a beautiful hammock of humanity. Rock her wider, and wider . . . and now, everyone begin to hum; hum louder and louder."

Marsh started to laugh as Snooks lost his grip on Edna's leg, and it flew wild, losing a shoe. If anybody was off their rocker, it was Meizner. Mr. Meizner screamed. "Grab her leg! Grab it! Come on now, everyone, march with Edna. March her around the room. March proudly! March joyously!"

Marsh couldn't stop laughing, although he tried as best he could to muffle himself by pressing his mouth against his shoulder, but he was well aware that the upside-down eyes of Edna Shinglebox were glued on him, and she knew very well that he was having a good time at her expense. In fact, the eyes of Edna Shinglebox looked so fierce, Marsh tried glancing across the room to look at Raccoon whose head was peeking out of his jacket pocket, munching a mile a minute on the last of the candy bar. Even Raccoon seemed to be enjoying the shenanigans. Marsh loved Raccoon, because when anything like this went on, the animal would get a look in his eyes as though he were watching a pack of people that had flipped their wigs.

"Now, Edna, just close your eyes and think of this room as your personal space," Mr. Meizner guided. "Concentrate on how much everyone is supporting you—how much they like you. Everyone is willing to carry you, to float you through the air. You are sharing this experience with everyone, Edna, and everyone is sharing their experience with you. Edna, I want you to feel like you are in the center of a beautiful balloon; your own, personal, blue balloon and you are bobbing in the wind of good wishes."

Suddenly Mr. Meizner blew his whistle. "Everybody halt!"

"What?" Jo complained in a gruff voice.

"Make sure you've got a good grip on her now," Mr. Meizner insisted. "Because now we're going to toss Edna up into the air."

"Oh, come on!" Edna protested.

"Shut up and trust," Mr. Meizner said, riveting his attention on her attendants. "Edna is now that fabulous, inflated, blue balloon; she's filled with helium, and we're going to float her higher and higher. Come on now, everyone, toss her up."

Marsh couldn't believe what was happening as everyone began to throw Edna into the air. She went up and down more like a pizza crust than a balloon and he could hear her making cries of protest, the most frequently repeated phrases being "Don't drop me" and "Ouch." While everyone was busy tossing Edna and laughing their heads off, Mr. Meizner rushed to the phonograph and put on a record.

"Sing, everyone," Mr. Meizner ordered. "Sing, as we celebrate life for Edna! Trust us, Edna. We're your friends. Trust us, and listen to us sing. Raise your voices, everyone!" Edna went higher and higher, and everyone began to sing louder and louder. "Happy birthday to you, happy birthday to you, happy birthday dear Edna Shinglebox, happy birthday to you."

"One more time!" Mr. Meizner ordered. "And then we'll do a couple choruses of 'The World Owes Me a Living.' You must think of only beautiful things,

Edna, only beautiful and truthful things. You are a worthy bubble. Keep telling yourself you are a bubble of enormous value; people love you; people care about you; these boys and girls are your friends, and you're happy that they love you. And cherish your bubble, they're celebrating you as a person. Happy birthday, dear Edna Shinglebox! Feel the promise of hope and affection and respect that makes pain and loneliness disappear. Throw Edna and her bubble higher and higher! What a heavenly, blue balloon she is. A heavenly blue balloon!"

Marsh was very disappointed that the class only had time to celebrate Edna, Mario Lugati and Jacqueline Potts. He was hoping that everybody would have been able to pick him up because he wanted to know what it felt like to be in a bubble and have everybody love your bubble. But, the bell rang. Marsh was exhausted and still trying to get his breath, and was so busy getting his things together, he didn't even notice that somehow Edna Shinglebox must have grabbed her books and run out the door as fast as she could go. Marsh grabbed his jacket with the raccoon still peeking out of it and checked the halls and stairway, but Edna was gone. She must really hate him, he thought. After all, if somebody is your friend, they don't usually take off in a wild sprint to get away from you.

He finally caught up to Edna in the lunchroom after he had fought the ice-cream lines and had lifted a piece of white bread for Raccoon. As he approached the table where Edna was eating, he could tell by the way she was pretending to savor the daily special that she was not going to be a bundle of laughs. Marsh plopped his book down on a chair, and sat across from her. Edna still wouldn't look at him. Actually, he knew he was running the risk of her going into a bit of shock when he told her about his father, but he didn't think she was going to be completely thrown by it. It made him feel that maybe he hadn't picked the right girl to help. Maybe that was the mistake. He knew he had a tendency to fictionalize what people were like; too many people he met were so different when he got to know them, but this time, maybe he was really off base. He didn't even know whether it was worthwhile trying to check it out a little further. He took Raccoon out of his pocket and began to feed him the piece of bread. Suddenly, Edna lifted her head and stared straight at him.

"I think you have nerve," Edna said.

"Why?" Marsh said.

"Because that animal could have rabies, that's why. I think you've got some nerve bringing him into the school cafeteria, and I think you even have more of a nerve bringing him over here and sitting down right opposite me, because I've got enough problems in this world without having to worry about rabies."

Marsh checked to see where Mr. Fettman was patrolling and spotted him far down the other end of the lunchroom where kids were throwing pennies dipped in peanut butter at him. Marsh decided to put the raccoon on the table. "Raccoon doesn't have rabies, Edna. You see, when animals get rabies they foam at the mouth and then they freak out and they try to bite you. And you can just take one look at this guy and you can see he's in great shape."

Edna almost growled. "I not only think you've got nerve, but I think you're cruel. I don't think you have any right dragging that animal around with you. You've got him in your stuffy little pocket; there's not another kid in this school that's allowed to run around with an animal in his pocket. I've heard of kids with a frog or maybe a snake, but they do it for a day, not day in, day out. Raccoons are wild animals and they belong in the woods."

"Why should they stay in the woods?" Marsh said. "Don't you think anybody has a tame raccoon? It's not so weird. I know somebody that's got a tame skunk." He could feel he was getting angry at the way Edna was talking. She was obviously going to pick on him and if there was one thing he really hated in life it was being corrected.

"Well, I see you've got a screw loose, and you don't have any regard for that animal," Edna said.

"Oh yeah, I know what you'd like—just let him loose up near Bald Hill or something, and he'd be knocked off crossing the street in less than a week." Marsh remembered the sight of Raccoon's mother, splattered all over Todt Hill Road. "Besides, you're not being nasty to me just on account of the raccoon. You've got a bug up you because of some other reason. And you know very well what that reason is. If you don't want to help me and my father, then don't. Just say that. But don't pin the rap on Raccoon or look for any other way out. I'm sorry I asked you. I'm sorry I showed you the letters. I'm sorry I trusted you at all. I should have known what a royal crumb bun you really are."

Edna looked hurt. "I'm not a royal crumb bun."

"Well, you don't want to help him, do you?" Marsh asked. "You don't care what happens to my father. You're just like one of the killers, aren't you?" Marsh felt terrible when he saw Edna deliberately take another big mouthful of what looked like sliced pig's pancreas and nonchalantly open up her history book and start reading as though he wasn't even there. He could see in her eyes though, that she was ready to explode, no matter how she pretended nothing was getting to her.

"Edna," Marsh said, "for once in your life, please, even if you never cared about anything else before, please help me." He no sooner had the words out than Edna's head shot up again and her eyes practically tore into him. She took a big swallow, and then her voice came blasting out.

"Look, I think those letters you showed me are phony, that's what I think. I think everything about you is phony, and I don't want anything more to do with you. I've given this a lot of thought, and I've decided that I don't have very much character because I just sat back and let you make a fool out of me. And all I'm saying is that I'm tired of the gag; the jig's up! So, if you don't mind, just leave me alone. And if you've got this thing about having to be cruel to raccoons, I'd appreciate it if you didn't flaunt it in front of me. I don't happen to like people who torture animals or who transplant them to places they don't belong. You may think it makes you Mr. Hot Shot, but I think it's barbaric."

Marsh felt as though someone had grabbed him by the throat, and he couldn't speak for a long time. He just looked disbelieving at her. Finally he lowered his head and said softly, "I'm not lying." He jumped back reflexively when Edna suddenly shot her right hand over the table, grabbed his loose-leaf notebook and threw it open. She pointed to the scribbling on the pages.

"Are you trying to tell me this isn't the same handwriting as in those letters?" Edna attacked. "You must really think I'm stupid that I never noticed. Even a dodo bird would see that the writing in your books is the same as in those letters. I'm not an idiot! And neither is the whole world, which is probably why nobody else will listen to that story of yours. You thought I was some kind of Neanderthal teenage dumb girl that would put up with that; go for it hook, line and sinker. Well, forget it. The days of Edna Shinglebox being a dummy are over."

Marsh felt sick to his stomach and he could feel his hands starting to shake. He was glad when Edna pulled back and took her eyes off him. If he had felt before like someone had grabbed him by the throat, he felt now as if those hands were strangling him. Slowly, he picked Raccoon off the table and began petting him, trying to look as casual as possible. He was thankful to have something to do with his hands to help disguise their trembling. He looked up towards the windows of the cafeteria and could see a few trees that had been planted along the street. Then he focused on the ceiling and stared at one of the lights that was covered with a large, frosted-glass casing. He had all he could do to make his tongue move, but he finally said it. "I'm not a liar." He could hardly get the words out, and he wasn't certain that she'd even heard him. He stood up and put Raccoon back into his jacket pocket, then he gathered his books together.

"You took me for a dope," Edna said. "Maybe you thought I was going to be your freak-of-the-week or something. Well, the week's up. I've got feelings and I'm going to fight for them from here on in, and I don't like being taken for a fool."

"I'm . . . I'm not lying," Marsh repeated softly.

"Who are you kidding?" Edna said, her voice sounding like it was getting very fragile and about to crack. "You're the biggest load of baloney in this butcher shop. The Los Angeles Neurological Hospital for the Insane and Crazy! What a load. The lobotomy, the eucalyptus tree, you're a liar. The only real thing about that whole ton of bunk is that three-stage American Flag firework rocket. And as far as I'm concerned, they ought to take you and your father, strap you both to it and light the fuse."

Marsh looked at Edna's angry face. Her voice had broken on the last words and she wouldn't look at him anymore. She just kept eating, and seemed interested in filling her stomach. Marsh took a step to leave, and then he took a step back and was going to say something but the words wouldn't come out. He started to go again, and before he reached the end of the table he turned and came back and leaned over towards

Edna. "You shut up!" Marsh screamed at the top of his lungs so loudly that Edna almost fell over backwards in her chair. He screamed it with such force that everyone in the lunchroom stopped talking and whirled to look to see what was happening. Even Mr. Fettman started rushing from the other end of the cafeteria. "I am not a liar! I am not a liar!" Marsh screamed over and over. He knew he was out of control and that he was yelling things at a girl, who at the moment looked frightened to death. The next thing Marsh was aware of was that Mr. Fettman had him by the arm and was pulling him away from the table. Hundreds of kids in the cafeteria began to stamp their feet and bang on the tables like they always did when someone dropped a platter of dishes or a fight broke out. Edna kept her eyes glued to her plate as Mr. Fettman led Marsh to the nearest exit. He screamed at her again and again, "I am not a liar!" A moment later, he was gone.

When Mr. Fettman came back he asked Edna what had happened, and if she wanted to make a report.

"No," Edna said, quietly, continuing to eat her lunch. "It was just a little misunderstanding and he was only expressing himself." She ate the rest of her lunch very slowly. She had all she could do to raise her forkful of food to her mouth and chew it, and she had to fight in order not to get sick to her stomach. She called upon a little trick she'd been practicing lately whenever things seemed to get out of hand. She'd always tell herself to stop and just think of a tropical beach with palm trees and beautiful water. But at the moment she found it very hard to think of such a pretty picture. She thought for a long while and was well aware that some kids around her were still turning to look at her. When she was finished, she cleaned up her place at the table, stacked her books and walked to the cafeteria exit. A nasty-looking kid with a badge stopped her.

"Do you have a pass?" he asked, like a state trooper. Edna hated that. Give some kids a marshal badge and suddenly they were power crazy.

"No," Edna said.

"Well, you need a pass."

Edna looked him right in the eye. "Look, if you don't let me get out of here and go to the girls' room, I'm going to throw up."

The marshal took a close look at Edna and cleared out of the way real quick.

Edna did want to go to the girls' room, but she had other business first. She went directly to Room 110, knocked on the door and went in. Mr. Meizner was alone, sitting at his desk eating something out of a plastic bag.

"What do you want?" Mr. Meizner asked.

"Can I talk to you for a minute?"

"I'm in ketosis."

"I beg your pardon?" Edna asked.

Mr. Meizner looked proud. "I'm on a diet of proteins and fats, and the only thing crunchy I'm allowed to eat is fried pork rinds."

Edna didn't know what he was talking about, but figured it was safe to come in. She shut the door behind her and walked over to his desk. "I want to ask you about someone; somebody in GTE."

"Who?"

"Marsh."

"What about him?" Mr. Meizner asked, placing another handful of fried pork rinds into his mouth and bringing his teeth down on them with a loud crash.

Edna didn't quite know how to get into it, but then she decided the only way might be to just get to the point. "I want to know about his father," she said.

Mr. Meizner stopped chewing for a moment, then swallowed. Edna stared at the immense contractions in his throat as the mouthful of fried pork rinds tumbled down his esophagus. The only time she'd seen any action like that was when she'd watched an eleven-foot python at the local zoo eat a dead guinea pig. She was also quite aware that Mr. Meizner was looking at her as though she were crazy. It seemed that Mr. Meizner wasn't going to say a word, and she shifted her weight from one foot to the other.

"Is there anything about Marsh's father I should know?" Edna clarified.

"What makes you think you think you should know anything about anybody's father?"

"Look, I'm just asking," Edna said.

"If you want to know something about anyone's father, maybe you should just ask the person who has the father."

"Well, it wasn't that I asked him, it's just that Marsh decided to tell me about his father. I just wanted to know whether you knew anything about him."

"Well, what did you ask Marsh?"

"I don't remember," Edna said, sensing she'd better lie.

Mr. Meizner looked morose and put all his attention into opening a small jar of caviar and mixing it into a container of sour cream. The sight of black fish eggs on a white background being spooned into his mouth was grotesque and Edna took a step backwards.

"You're lying," Mr. Meizner said.

Edna was so startled by the accusation she shifted weight again, and the straw mat beneath her feet squeaked. "Well, look, maybe I shouldn't have come in here," Edna said with a forced smile. "I'm sorry I bothered you, and I didn't mean not to tell the truth. It's just that I'm confused about something; I thought you could have helped me." She started for the door.

"Wait a minute," Mr. Meizner said, grabbing a fried pork rind and dipping it into the fish-eggs-and-sour-cream mixture. "I could tell you something about Marsh's father, but I'm not going to. Do you know why?"

"No, Mr. Meizner."

"Because it's none of your business, that's why."

"I can appreciate that point of view," Edna said. "Like I said, thanks anyway. It's all my fault; I shouldn't have come in here, and, let's just forget about it, okay?"

Mr. Meizner fixed her with his stare. "Edna, I'm going to tell you a little story, and maybe you'll learn something out of this. See, once I had a boy in a class like ours that did nothing except whirl around in circles and scream at the top of his lungs 'Would Jesus

Christ carry a draft card?' You see, everybody used to wonder why he did that, and I knew. But I wouldn't tell anybody else. What kind of a psychologist would I be if my children didn't trust me? If a kid came to me and wanted to know about your parents, you wouldn't want me to say that your father's a dull little petal pusher, and your mother's as overprotected a mummy as King Tut, would you?"

"No sir."

"So there."

"Oh, I see now," Edna said, finding herself doing a slightly oriental bow, again trying to move towards the door.

"No, you don't," Mr. Meizner corrected her. "You see, the really interesting part about you coming in here is, why are you so nosy? Did anyone ever tell you that what you're doing is nosy, Edna?"

"No, they didn't."

"Well it is, Edna. It's nosy, nosy, nosy."

Edna felt for a moment that she should defend herself, but the expression on Mr. Meizner's face killed that. She decided it would be better to get out of there.

"I'm sorry, Mr. Meizner."

"Well, you should be, Edna. You see, if you'd spend a little time just thinking about why you're nosy, you'd learn a lot more than making believe you're Police Woman or somebody."

"Be seeing you," Edna said, taking another step towards the door.

"Edna, you're feeling things," Mr. Meizner said, crunching on his pork rinds again. "If you'd think about that you'd find out more than if I was to feed you the gossip you're trying to squeeze out of me. Solve your own hang-ups first, Edna. Keep that beak of yours out of other people's business."

Edna opened the door and was going to slam the door and run down the hallway, but she decided she hadn't said everything she wanted to.

"Do you know something, Mr. Meizner?" Edna said.

"What?" Mr. Meizner asked, reaching deep into his cellophane bag.

"I think you're a crank," Edna said.

"So would you be if you were in ketosis," Mr. Meizner said as Edna slammed the door.

Chapter 15 /

Edna really got a going-over at home that night. Her mother didn't let up for a minute, and what was worse, was that everything her mother said was so complimentary on the surface that it was only the *way* she said it that was so awful. It was so subtle at first, her father didn't even catch on.

"You would have been so proud of Edna," Mrs. Shinglebox said to her husband.

"You told me at the shop," her husband reminded her as he continued sipping his tea at the dinner table. "You were so busy blabbing, you didn't even finish the spider-mum arrangement and I'm supposed to get that delivered tomorrow morning. How am I going to do it? It takes twenty-five minutes to do a good spider-mum arrangement."

"Oh, forget your spider mums," Mrs. Shinglebox said. "Just be happy that we've got such a wonderful daughter."

"Mother, please," Edna said. "I apologize for the way I was this morning. I didn't mean to say all the things I said."

"Oh, don't apologize," Mrs. Shinglebox insisted. "You were one-hundred-percent correct. Jack, isn't it wonderful that we have the only daughter on earth who's one-hundred-percent correct!"

"Nobody's one-hundred-percent correct," her father said, flatly.

Mrs. Shinglebox gritted her teeth. "Oh, our Edna is. She knows more than computers; God forbid technology should give her a hand. So what if I wasted all those flowers on that interviewer in order to get those questions. I asked Edna one of the questions about where she thought the best place to make whoopy was, and she said on a horse."

"Mom, would you please drop it."

"Isn't that humorous, Jack?"

"Yeah, it is pretty funny," Mr. Shinglebox agreed. "It is."

"Well, I'm glad you do think it's funny. Such a blessing to have a daughter who can gag it up on her way to being an old maid. She's so smart, our daughter, no suburban housewife in her future. Did I tell you that, Jack? Edna's so with it, there's going to be no kids—what it is, it's going to be a royal boot in the behind for Mother Goose. Jack, if we ever plan to get grandchildren, I think we're going to need pacemakers to play with them."

"Mom, you're being ridiculous," Edna protested.

"Oh, all mothers are ridiculous," Mrs. Shinglebox wailed. "So wonderful to have a kid tell you where you really stand." Mrs. Shinglebox's voice began to drift towards complete hysteria. "You're going down the tubes, Edna. That's where you're going."

Mr. Shinglebox looked up. "What's that mean? How can you go down the tubes at fifteen?"

"That's right, Jack. Go ahead, take her side," Mrs. Shinglebox cried. "You always do."

"I'm not taking anybody's side."

"Yes you are."

"No he isn't," Edna inserted. Then for five minutes nobody said a word, they just chewed, and the sound of chewing made Edna remember Mr. Meizner. A couple of things he'd said were still spinning in her brain, and her mother's big scene at the dinner table only helped her make up her mind.

"*I Was a Teenage Werewolf* is on channel seven tonight," Mrs. Shinglebox finally said, breaking the silence. "Maybe you'd like to watch it with us, Edna. You could pick up a few more hints."

"No thanks," Edna said. "I've got to do some research at the library."

"What kind of research?" her mother asked suspiciously.

Edna tried to invent something as fast as she could. "I've got to check on the synthesis of trimethylchlorine from dihydroxybenzene after hydrogenation by catalytic combustion."

"Oh," Mrs. Shinglebox said.

During dessert, Edna decided to lay an even better foundation for her need to go to the library by telling how hard she found the chemistry course, particularly now that they were going into biochemistry. She also decided that she really didn't like lying to her parents, but lately it seemed like the world was slowly teaching her that there's a real need for creative prevarication. Later, in her room, she picked out clothes that looked like she was really going to go to the library. She wanted to look nice just in case she met anybody she knew. At first she'd gotten over-dressed, and she knew her mother would notice, so she had to simplify her outfit. Then she decided it'd be good if she didn't seem overanxious, so she made sure she was very calm before coming downstairs again. Finally, she picked a couple of books that would make everything convincing. One was a real library book that she took out two and a half years ago and was something like six hundred days overdue. It was called *Dreams and Their Meaning*, and she found that book so interesting she could never bring herself to return it. The other book she took with her was a large notebook that she once used as a diary when she was recording her dreams. She recorded one dream every day for something like sixty weeks, and then it began to be too much of a bother and it was only lately that she'd started jotting a few dreams down. Somehow she felt Marsh had something to do with the reason she was turning back to her dreams in order to find out what was really going on inside of her, and how she felt.

Edna walked nonchalantly by the living room and waved in to her parents who were watching the seven o'clock news. There was a human-interest item on it about a certain Max Guttman who was a school-teacher in the Bronx. Apparently, he had expired while his students were attending class around his deathbed. Edna wanted to hear the details on that one, but kept moving and made it out the front door without a grand inquisition from her mother. At the corner of Hylan and Guyon Avenue she got the number 103 bus and decided to look at a few of her old dreams in the diary during the trip. One thing she noticed from her dreams was that apparently there was a part of her that really didn't have such hot feelings about her mother. Edna knew she liked her mother well enough, but still there was this other side that used to show up in her dreams. During one period of when she was recording her dreams there was a recurrent nightmare where there was an older woman who used to chase after her trying to shove gigantic glasses of orange juice down her throat. There must have been fifty dreams about compulsory eating. But the dreams Edna was most fascinated by were the ones that were off the wall. Like the one when she dreamed she was in a geometry class and some boy behind her tapped her on the shoulder and said, "I like squeezing you, but I don't love you."

As the bus bumped its way down Hylan Avenue, Edna tried to skim through most of the diary. There were so many kinky things she had dreamed. There was a dream about a fat woman hostess at a Holiday Inn who wore a double-heart pin with an arrow through it, and wore a long, dramatic black dress. Then there was a dream about larvae jumping up and down on an English muffin that she was trying to eat. And in another dream there was an earthquake in which she tried to run out of a tall building, but stopped for a shot of vodka in the lobby. Not long after that there'd been a dream about a man with no arms, and a woman wrestler called Sock-It-To-Them-Mary who was teaching her how to make frozen hot chocolate in a blender. There was also a dream about her mother dying, and a very recent dream in which she was trying to explain to her father that God marks on a curve. There were two dreams in which there was a child on a television game show where the kid's mother jumped out of the audience and took over and won the $25,000 prize instead of the kid. And the mother in that dream was terrible. She jumped up and down and hugged the MC like she was crazy. And there was even a dream about Marsh that she'd written down a few days before. She had a lot of dreams about Marsh lately, but there was only one that she bothered to write down because she felt it meant something important, even though she couldn't figure out what. In this dream she figured that she was going to be executed by soldiers. Somehow she managed to steal a ferryboat and as the boat was sailing towards Manhattan she saw Marsh swimming in the bay and she pulled him aboard. She wanted to help him, but all he did was stare at her and hold a small, drowned animal in his hands. Then Edna became afraid the ferryboat would never dock, but finally it headed for a beautiful beach and Edna was really happy until she saw that the beach was covered with fish that had bullets in their heads.

Edna transferred to the number four bus which went up Richmond Avenue. As soon as she saw the palmist's sign, she pulled the buzzer to get off because she knew Marsh's house wasn't much farther. Besides, she knew Marsh's house was distinctive enough to find even if she was blind and had to go around feeling each house with her hands. All she'd have to do is feel for the oldest, dumpiest house with half a porch. As it turned out, the bus stopped practically right in front of the house.

Edna got off and took a deep breath of the night air as the bus pulled away. As usual, there were sheets strung on a line in the backyard, and tonight they looked even more like ghosts than the first time she'd seen them.

There were lights on in the house, but she also noticed that the Mazda was not in the driveway. She figured that meant that either Schizo Suzy had gone out to buy diet beer, or that Marsh had cleared out and was down at the Magic Elephant or someplace. If that was true, it would probably mean that Schizo Suzy was passed out under the piano, and that Edna wouldn't be able to find out what she had to know.

As she walked closer to the house, the awful green color made Edna dizzy. She went up on the porch and rang the buzzer. She waited a minute and then knocked because she figured, like everything else in the house, the doorbell was probably out of order. After a few minutes there was still no answer so Edna banged very hard on the front door and stepped back to check the front windows. Now there were three broken windowpanes with black plastic garbage bags covering the holes. Edna waited another couple of minutes. She figured maybe Schizo Suzy was crawling out from under the piano or something. Then she went to the door and raised her knuckles to give a really loud rap, when a face appeared in the window of the door. Edna almost cried out at the sight. It was Schizo Suzy, but perpendicular she looked more like Fist-Sandwich Frieda.

"What do you want?" Schizo Suzy asked gruffly. Edna could tell, just from the few words, that Marsh's mother was quite loaded, and that she was well-endowed with what was known as a whiskey baritone.

"Is Marsh home?" Edna asked meekly.

"No."

Schizo Suzy's face disappeared from the window and Edna thought perhaps she had just stepped back to open the door. After a couple of minutes Edna realized that Schizo Suzy had just gone away altogether and Edna had to bang on the door again. This time the face appeared quicker.

"What?" the low voice growled. Schizo Suzy brushed her long, gray hair away from her face so that it fanned out like some kind of heroine in a Greek drama who had just burned her children offstage.

"Do you know where he went?" For some reason, Edna found herself talking loudly like she was speaking to a deaf person.

"No."

"Mrs. Mellow, could you open the door a minute?"

"What for?"

"I need to ask you something."

"What?"

"I can't tell you through the door."

Schizo Suzy's face disappeared for another minute, and then there was a click and the door opened. Schizo Suzy was wearing the same nightgown Edna had seen her in when she had been sleeping one off under the piano. But tonight there was a big spot down the front of it as though she had recently spilled a Cup-a-Soup on herself.

"I'm Edna."

"So what."

"I'm a friend of Marsh's."

Schizo Suzy swayed slightly and rolled her eyes. "He stole the car tonight. He thought I was sleeping, but I heard him go out the driveway. He's a punk."

"Mrs. Mellow, I need to ask you something." Edna took a deep breath because several thoughts ran through her mind at the same time. Somehow she thought she was bungling the whole thing and if she hadn't bungled it yet, she would any second. Maybe she shouldn't be talking to Marsh's mother. Maybe she should just wait, or maybe she should say nothing at all. Maybe, what she really hoped was that Marsh would be home and that she could just ask him. And then again, maybe she was just kidding herself about the whole thing. She wasn't at all sure that she even cared what happened to Marsh, to his father, to this house, to the whole world, to anything. And besides, she knew he was a liar. So what if he freaked out when she called him that; if she was going to be honest she'd have to say it all over again. He's a liar. She knew he'd been feeding her a line. But there was something about the way he was doing it that she felt he *thought* he was telling the truth. That was the twist about it. So maybe she was only being nosy. She never really asked him if he had a phone. She never really showed any great selfless interest in him. It seemed like all she did was lie around her home and in school and be worried about her relationship with him. It was like she'd been doing nothing except wondering if there was anything in the whole thing for her.

"I need to know about your husband," Edna said quickly. "Marsh's father." Edna noticed a flash of fire in Schizo Suzy's eyes. Edna followed up instantly. "Do you know where he is?"

Schizo Suzy looked like she was going to grab a bazooka and rush out the door and get off a fireball at Edna. In fact, Edna got ready to run, but then a smile crept across Schizo Suzy's face and the woman looked less frightening.

"I know where he is."

Edna felt her usual large dose of adrenalin surge into her bloodstream and she could feel Schizo Suzy wasn't being completely honest. It seemed like she was playing with Edna, as though Edna was some kind of mouse and she was some kind of weird cat.

"May I know where?" Edna asked, trying not to sound like she was a buttinski.

"He's upstairs," Schizo Suzy said.

"Upstairs?" Edna repeated the word, quite surprised.

Schizo Suzy wasn't saying anything else and she started to close the door.

Edna blurted out, "He's not in Los Angeles?"

"No."

"He's really upstairs?"

"Yeah, that's what I said, he's upstairs. He's up in Marsh's room. What's the matter, have you got wax in your ears?"

"It's just that I didn't think he'd be here."

"What? You don't believe me?"

"I believe you, Mrs. Mellow."

"Maybe you'd like to meet him," Schizo Suzy inquired.

"No, I don't think so."

"Oh, I know Marsh would love you to come in and say hello. You could have a nice little chat. Not too many people are interested in talking to Marsh's father. A lot of them give him the cold shoulder."

"Is he sleeping?" Edna asked.

"You might say that."

The thought that Mr. Mellow was up in Marsh's room seemed very peculiar. It also brought back the image of all those faces plastered all over the walls. The idea of Marsh's father being in that room seemed improbable. There were probably other bedrooms in the house; why wouldn't he be in one of those? Why would he be in Marsh's room?

Schizo Suzy's smile grew wider and made her look even stranger. "We'll go up and say hello. Pete'd love to meet you," she assured Edna.

"I'm not a good friend of Marsh's," Edna said nervously. "I just know him a little."

"Well, that's even nicer."

Edna stood motionless for several moments trying to really size up Marsh's mother and decided the old lady was too drunk to be very strong, and that if she had to, she could knock Schizo Suzy over and get out of there. The main thing she'd have to do is not turn her back on her in case Schizo Suzy did have a sharp instrument hidden somewhere. Edna smiled back at Mrs. Mellow and then moved slowly into the house, being careful to face her at all times. Edna waited, and let Schizo Suzy lead the way upstairs. Edna let her keep far in front and disappear into the dark hallway at the top of the stairs. Edna wouldn't go to the top of the landing until Mrs. Mellow had put on the hall light and the light in Marsh's room. It was only when Mrs. Mellow was far into the room that Edna walked to the doorway. Mrs. Mellow turned to her and was smiling even more bizarrely. Edna looked slowly around the room.

"There's nobody here," Edna said softly.

Mrs. Mellow looked exaggeratedly puzzled by Edna's remark; almost sarcastically puzzled. "But he's under the bed," she explained as though it were the most logical place in the world.

Edna was ready to bolt down the stairs but Schizo Suzy made the first move. She got down on her hands and knees and reached under the bed. She swung her arms and threw out some old shoes and a pair of sneakers; after that she flung the long cardboard box Edna had seen once before. The box slid the full length of the room and hit against the wall, and Edna hoped that the American flag rocket that she knew was inside of it wouldn't be damaged. She also took that moment to check Raccoon's cage and saw it was empty, so she knew wherever Marsh was, he was out with Raccoon in his pocket. And for some reason, and against everything she'd said about the proper place for raccoons, she was glad that at least Marsh had company, wherever he was. The force with which Mrs. Mellow threw things out from under the bed made Edna realize she had underestimated the drunken woman's strength. She decided now that this woman had plenty of strength to strangle someone if she wanted to.

"Here he is," Schizo Suzy said, rolling an urn out from under the bed. "Pete, I want you to meet . . . what's your name?"

"Edna."

"Yeah, Pete! Edna's a friend of Marsh. Ain't that nice, Pete?"

Edna stared at the small urn Schizo Suzy was now holding out to her. It was about a foot tall and made of a shiny, bronze metal. Edna knew what it was because she'd seen one before when an aunt of hers had been cremated. And she'd seen a whole mausoleum filled with them in a photo about Valentino's fan club that met once a year to celebrate his death. Edna took a step forward because she saw some writing on the funeral urn. The inscription was: Peter Charles Mellow. And according to the dates, it would seem that Peter Charles Mellow had been dead for over a year.

"May I ask how he died?" Edna said softly.

"Of course, dear," Mrs. Mellow said, rolling the urn back under the bed. "He got drunk and stumbled out onto a street where he got hit by a bus. On Hollywood Boulevard, of course; nothing but the best for Pete, you know." Schizo Suzy then burst into laughter.

Edna didn't know what to say. Somehow the words "thank you" came out but she didn't mean to say that. She backed slowly out of the room and then began to move down the stairs. She was suddenly aware of someone moving behind her very swiftly. There was a shadow racing across the wall in front of the stairwell, and instinctively, Edna began to jump down the stairs two at a time. She didn't even have to turn around to know that Schizo Suzy was after her. She heard the woman yelling; it was as if Schizo Suzy had suddenly become another person, her voice going higher and higher. She was yelling like a hysterical ventriloquist's dummy erupting filthy and obscene language. Edna heard words like "sneak" and "pig" and "slut" and a few others she'd never dreamed anyone on earth would call her. A moment later Edna was out the front door and slammed it behind her before Schizo Suzy had made it to the bottom of the stairs. Edna leaped off the porch, and then, in an instant, she was running down the street as fast as she could. She looked over her shoulder to make sure that no one was behind her, and she was thankful that all she could see was the ugly, dilapidated green house with the line of ghosts flying in the wind in the backyard. Edna turned again and again even though she was a good distance from the house by now. Finally she was out of breath and slowed down to a fast walk. Her head kept jerking to look behind her and the thought crossed her mind that maybe Schizo Suzy had run out a back door and was running along the woods behind the other houses and would suddenly come roaring out of another driveway. The first thing Edna thought of was that she should knock on somebody's door; stop at a stranger's house and ask them if she could use the phone. She'd call her mother and ask her to come pick her up, and she could stay inside the house until the car came. She started to run again and then stopped. Actually, she felt ashamed of the way she was thinking. It was really ridiculous to be as old as she was and still be such a baby. Wasn't she ever going to grow up? Big deal! She went over to the house and some drunk lady chased her and called her a few dirty names, and the first thing she thought of was calling her mother. Wasn't she ever going to grow up and take care of her own business? It was embarrassing to always think of her mother whenever she got in trouble. The time had come that she should take care of herself. If she was going to lie and go out on her own and do things on her own, then she shouldn't suddenly decide to switch everything around and become Mama's little girl just because things got a little sticky. It had gotten so it wasn't even unfair. At her age it was getting so that it was a boring thing to do. Edna walked farther down Richmond Avenue, and somehow her feet came to a halt in front of a sign shaped like a huge hand. The illuminated hand looked like it belonged to a giant who was buried deep into the earth.

Chapter 16 /

Edna stood reading the sign. For the first time she noticed the name: *Miss Aimée.* The number four bus only ran once an hour, so Edna knew there wouldn't be another bus for at least forty minutes. That was the main trouble of going anywhere on Richmond Avenue. She could remember Jacqueline giving Miss Aimée such a good review about what a super witch she was. Big deal. The tall, dark man in Jacqueline's life turned out to be Butch Ontock and as far as Edna was concerned, that wasn't exactly successful witchcraft. But the part she'd thought about a number of times was how the palmist had told Mary Louise Carter about her brother being dead. And that seemed to be in the right department with what Edna was interested in at this moment. Meizner wasn't a barrel of laughs; her mother hadn't been much help; so why not go to a witch? A couple of young kids, around ten years old, came running towards Edna and asking in shrill voices, "Who you looking for? Who you looking for?"

Edna glanced at the sign again. "Miss Aimée," she said.

With that, the kids began to scream and hold their

noses. They went away, jumping up and down yelling "Pew, pew, pew, pew!" Edna didn't know what to think of that except there must be something stinky about Miss Aimée. Either that or these kids were just let out of a nuthouse somewhere. Edna could still hear them yelling as she went up the steps to the front door. The door opened even before Edna had a chance to ring the bell. Miss Aimée was standing there, looking anxious for business. She was about sixty years old with short, bleached-blond hair and wore a long skirt that looked like it had unicorns embroidered on it. The thing Edna really noticed about her right off the bat was that, for an old lady, she was wearing a very low-cut purple blouse. In fact, it was so low, Edna could see the channel running down the middle of Miss Aimée's chest, and the only place she'd seen anyone wearing clothes like that was on some of the television variety shows and in ads for triple-X flicks.

"What do you want, little girl," Miss Aimée asked.

"I saw your sign."

"Yeah, a lot of people see my sign."

"Well, I was just wondering if you were open."

"Of course I'm open. I wouldn't have the sign all lit up if I wasn't open. What do you want—your palm read? I do phrenology too, you know."

"What's phrenology?"

"That's where I feel the bumps on your head. Who sent you?"

"Nobody," Edna said, knowing she was off on a lie again. In a sense it was a half-lie, because Jacqueline didn't really send her, she'd only hinted it would be a good idea if Edna stopped by. Edna felt it was more important to have Miss Aimée not even know she knew Jacqueline, that she didn't know anything about Edna. Then she'd find out just how much of a real witch Miss Aimée was.

"Ten bucks," Miss Aimée said. "You'd better have ten bucks."

Edna cleared her voice. "I heard it was only five."

"I thought nobody sent you," Miss Aimée spit out at her, at the same time as she hustled Edna into the house.

If the odor in the Mellow house had been slightly like that of a dead mouse, there was no way that Edna could think of to describe the stench in Miss Aimée's abode. It practically knocked her off her feet. The front doorway led directly into the living room, and the only light was from candles. Edna could see there were at least three mangy German shepherds pacing back and forth in the rear of the room along a narrow pathway between huge stacks of junk. There was only one small, clear area right near the front door that had a couple of chairs around a desk. On the desk was a bowl that looked like it was made out of imitation carnival glass, and inside the bowl was a good supply of burning incense. Edna knew the incense was an attempt to kill the odor in the house as well as set the atmosphere for sublime, spiritual experiences.

"Five bucks is the regular," Miss Aimée said. "Ten bucks is the special," Miss Aimée clarified.

"I can only afford the regular," Edna said. Then she wanted to kick herself because she remembered that all she had with her was two ten-dollar bills and some change for the bus.

"That's in advance," Miss Aimée said, sliding into a chair at the table like she was going to prepare Edna's income tax or something. She beckoned for Edna to sit opposite her, and when Edna stepped forward the dogs froze and began to growl.

"Shut up!" Miss Aimée yelled at the dogs, and they returned to their pacing, looking more like panthers in the shadows, stepping over pieces of furniture and piles of books and newspapers. Edna slid one of her ten-dollar bills out of her pocketbook and Miss Aimée grabbed it like a Las Vegas cashier. She shoved it into a cigar box and counted out a handful of ones like she was dealing a poker hand.

"I thought you said it was only five dollars," Edna asked when she realized she'd only gotten four dollars back.

"What, do you think there's no tax?"

"I'm sorry. You didn't say anything about taxes."

"Well there's taxes. That's a fact of life. Now what's your problem?"

Edna didn't quite know how to begin. She felt like she was in the presence of a very smart gypsy and she noticed the wall behind the gypsy seemed to have been a rather creative integration of all the religions of the world. She had symbols of Catholicism, Judaism, Indian sculpture, hanging rugs that looked like they were from Peru, and some horrible thing that looked like it was dug up out of an Egyptian tomb. Edna decided to play it smart. "I want you to tell me," Edna said.

Miss Aimée gave her a fish eye and reached out towards her. "Give me your hand. I want you to know, I don't usually do all this for six bucks. The kind of thing you're asking for is the special, and I told you that's ten dollars. But you look like a nice little girl, so I'm willing to go along with it for now." Edna offered her hand and Miss Aimée snatched it and started peering into Edna's palm. It tickled the way Miss Aimée ran her finger up and down the crevices and she was angry that her hand was shaking a little, because she knew Miss Aimée would know that she was nervous.

"Very interesting," Miss Aimée said.

"What?"

"Don't rush me, I'm still looking."

"I'm sorry."

"You see this line here?" Miss Aimée said, pointing to a deep line that ran from her index finger toward her thumb. "See, this is a weird line. Most people don't have this one. This other one's your Lifeline, and that one says you're going to live a long, long time. And these bunches of little lines, near the fat part of your palm mean that you've had a miserable childhood, and that you're demure."

"What do you mean, demure?"

"You know, you're skittish, timid, a little out of it. You go to school, don't you?"

"Yes," Edna said.

"Well don't you notice you're a little out of it?"

"Yes," Edna said solemnly.

"So see, I know what I'm talking about."

"Yes," Edna agreed. At that moment Edna's eyes

saw something that made her almost get up and run out the door. Miss Aimée was bending over, engrossed in Edna's palm, but Edna noticed something crawling up the center of Miss Aimée's purple blouse. It was a dark, oval-shaped thing, about an inch long, and it took Edna a full minute to ascertain that it was a cockroach. Miss Aimée bent a little farther towards the light, and there was no doubt at what it was ... a big, healthy cockroach crawling right out of Miss Aimée's cleavage.

"Why is your hand jerking?" Miss Aimée asked.

"I'm sorry," Edna said. She didn't know what to do. She didn't think it was right for her to say "Excuse me, but there's a cockroach crawling up your chest." She didn't know what protocol was in a situation like this. Besides, maybe the cockroach was some kind of pet of Miss Aimée's. All Edna knew was that it made her skin crawl, which in itself was really a horrible verb to think of.

"See now," Miss Aimée continued, "all this messy pack of lines clear up when you get a little further into your teens. How old are you now?"

"Fifteen."

"Right. That's when they clear up," Miss Aimée said adamantly. "You see, they're going to clear up any day now. All your problems are going to be solved. What's going to happen to you, is you're going to meet a boy soon and fall in love."

Edna tried to block the sight of the cockroach out of her mind so she could concentrate on what Miss Aimée was telling her. It would be stupid to let an insect interfere with her getting her money's worth.

"Have you met any boy lately?" Miss Aimée asked.

"Yes," Edna said.

"See, I told you. And the reason you came here is because you want to know if it's going to work out. Right?"

"You might say that."

"Well, what I'm telling you is that you're a very lucky girl. This boy is a prince, honey. He's a prince. Just grab him and don't let him get away. You're going to be very, very happy, and you're going to have five children; two of them are going to be identical twins."

Edna rummaged through her pocketbook to find a piece of Trident gum. She broke it in half and stuck it in her mouth. "Miss Aimée," Edna said, "I didn't come here to find out if the boy was going to fall in love with me."

"Well, what'd you come here for?" Miss Aimée said, quite annoyed. Edna decided to speak as fast as she could, because the cockroach was beginning to crawl around Miss Aimée's upper bosom and it was giving Edna the creeps.

"Look, I met a boy and I don't love him and he doesn't love me, but he makes me read letters. And these letters are from his father who's in an insane asylum in Los Angeles. And, supposedly, there's this whole political structure that stuck him there and wants to give him a lobotomy. But I know that his father isn't in a nuthouse, what he is, he's really dead. Because his mother just showed me an urn that's got his father's ashes in it. See, he was a drunk and he got hit by a bus, and they cremated him in California—I think. So, what my problem is, is that I want to be a friend to this boy, because I've never been a friend to anybody. All I've been in my life is selfish and interested in myself and so worried about myself. I've been a spoiled brat. Sometimes I make my mother so mad she says she wishes I were a pig so at least by the end of the year I could be butchered and they'd have sausage in the freezer. See, my problem is, I don't love the boy, but I just want to know how to help him accept the fact that his father's dead so he doesn't have to go around writing these phony letters and being a social outcast."

Miss Aimée's eyes looked like grapefruits. She dropped Edna's hand and sat back in her chair. For a full minute she refused to speak, then she began to groan and itch her head. The motion of her arm made the cockroach run the rest of the way up her neck, and now it was peeking out from under her double chin. "Oh, honey," Miss Aimée said. "You need the special!" Miss Aimée put forth her own palm.

Edna looked at Miss Aimée's hand and then fumbled in her purse. "All right, here's four bucks, but that's it. I can't pay tax."

Miss Aimée grabbed the bills and shoved them into her cigar box. "What the government doesn't know doesn't hurt it." She grabbed Edna's hand again, and Edna was very careful so that Miss Aimée's chin didn't come close enough to be right over her hand. She didn't want the cockroach jumping off Miss Aimée's chin and landing in her palm. And it was exactly at that moment that Edna made the mistake of looking at the floor. There were at least five of the cockroaches scurrying around, just to the left of her foot. It seemed like they were all running for Edna's shoe, and when they got close, Edna just tapped her foot and they all reversed and ran back a few inches. Edna had to keep tapping her foot, and she found herself shaking her legs, hoping none of the bugs had started climbing up her. She had a terrible thought that hundreds of cockroaches were crawling up her chair at that moment, and God only knew what was going on in her hair.

"Listen to me," Miss Aimée said, looking up from Edna's hand and staring at her. It seemed as though for the first time Miss Aimée was taking her business seriously because she was going to be direct; that she knew Edna hadn't come there for some sort of mundane problem. She wasn't there to hear about any prince that was going to come and sweep her away on a wild horse. Besides, Edna had a rather low opinion of some of the young ladies in fairy stories. Even when she was six years old, she decided that Cinderella had married for money.

"There may be a way I can help you," Miss Aimée said.

"How?"

"You just keep your mouth shut," Miss Aimée said. "I'm talking, and I've got to get into a little trance here, so just let me talk out loud, and you just shut up. At these prices, I'm only going to tell you once, and it isn't going to be very exact, but you're going to have to figure it out for yourself. It's the best I can do. Never in my life have I ever been willing to do this much work for ten dollars, but you look like a nice little girl, and you look like a desperate little thing. I only had one other case like this, and that involved a librarian. Some old bag who couldn't face the fact that her mother had kicked the bucket. Are you following me? And this old bag of a librarian, she comes in here and she paid me a thousand bucks for me to fix her up, and you're getting this for ten dollars, so you just remember that."

"Yes," Edna said.

"Look, I told you just to shut up," Miss Aimée reminded her. "Let me tell you, the first time I looked at that librarian's hand, I knew she was a weirdo. I get a lot of librarians in here. But this one took the cake. See, the problem is when a kid—no matter what age they are—has their parent kick the bucket, they've got to be able to break down and cry and to know that the person is dead. And not everybody does that in the same amount of time. See, it's very common that somebody will have somebody die on them, and they keep seeing them around the house sitting in chairs and lying on beds, and things like that— wherever they used to see the dead person . . . when the dead person was alive, of course. And it's no good if someone like me comes along and just says 'Hey, they're dead, now just face up to it. They're dead, that's reality and that's the way it's going to be.' It's like they've got a curse on them, and if you tell them what the curse is, it doesn't mean anything. I couldn't just tell the librarian that her mother was dead. The trick is, you've got to get the person to tell someone else that their beloved is dead. See, it took five visits before I got the librarian to say it to me. Finally, she was sitting right over there, right on the other side of that incense bowl, and she broke down crying, and finally she was able to say the words. She said, 'My mother's dead.' And that's the first step in getting over the curse. But, it gets more complicated than that. Because just telling someone isn't enough. They've got to do some kind of symbolic act. They've got to come up with some kind of ritual. The person's got to lay the whole death trip on to some kind of object, or some kind of action. And that's where this gets really complicated. I don't know the boy you're talking about, and I don't know how you're going to use it, but I know that what I'm going to tell you has the answer that you're looking for. Now, what I did with the librarian was, I worked with her guilt. See, that's usually the main reason why someone can't admit another person's dead. And this librarian felt a whole lot of guilt because she had written a book while her mother was dying. And the reason she felt guilt, was because she spent a lot of the time writing, when she thought maybe she should have been taking care of her mother, because it took six months for her mother to die. The whole thing was so horrible, because when her mother died, she died in a terrible way, of screaming and asking for her daughter to inject poison in her veins or to throw her out the hospital window, or to do anything. But finally, this woman coughed up her insides and she choked to death right in front of her daughter, which was this librarian. And then it was a few months later when the book the librarian wrote got published, and it was a big bomb, and it didn't sell well—was no best-seller or anything like that. But she felt an enormous amount of guilt over the book. And even though she knew her mother was dead, there was still something else she had to do before she could go on living a normal life and accept her mother's death."

"What?" Edna asked. It was as if her heart had stopped beating and wouldn't beat again until she heard Miss Aimée's answer.

Miss Aimée leaned still closer and the cockroach ran all the way up the side of Miss Aimée's face, then detoured back down her left cheek and under her lip. Finally it disappeared again behind her right ear. "I told her to take a copy of this clinker book she wrote, and go out to the cemetery and bury it in her mother's grave. I didn't mean she should dig six feet down to the coffin, or anything like that, you know, but just like a half foot or so and then put dirt on top of it. And when she did that, then she was able to go on living, and she didn't sit around feeling guilty about her mother's death anymore. Do you understand me?"

"I think so," Edna said.

"Yeah, well you better, because that's all you're going to get for ten bucks. That's the most I ever gave anyone for ten dollars—you know that, little girl?"

"I appreciate it," Edna said, getting up carefully from her chair and checking to see if there were any things crawling on her. She moved towards the door and was glad to see there were no roaches on the doorknob. Miss Aimée got up and walked with her.

"Now, honey," Miss Aimée said, "I want you to know that I was very moved by meeting you. A lot of terrific things are going to happen to you and that boy."

"No, you don't understand. We're just friends."

"Yeah, you're just friends today, but wait till tomorrow."

"No, I mean it."

"Look, honey, some day you and that boy are going to get married and live happily ever after, you mark my words."

"But I don't even like him," Edna said.

"That's what you think," Miss Aimée winked.

"He doesn't like me either," Edna said opening the door and trying to keep a good distance between her and Miss Aimée in case any of the roaches felt like taking a leap. Miss Aimée laughed.

"Why are you laughing?" Edna asked.

"I'm laughing because they say love is blind. Why do you think he's writing all those letters and showing them to you for?"

"I don't know," Edna said.

"Then you're pretty stupid." Miss Aimée smoothed the wrinkles on her face and scratched her head again. The dogs had stopped pacing the minute the door was opened, and they stood frozen, staring at Edna. They began to growl again, and a couple of cats jumped onto one of the higher stacks of junk. The eyes of the animals reflected in the candles.

"Well, thanks," Edna said.

"Hold it," Miss Aimée insisted.

"What for?"

"Well, look, honey, I was saying when you first came in here that I feel there is really something nice about you. I really like you. The first time I saw you, I said, 'This is a terrific girl. This girl isn't selfish. She's come here because she wants to help somebody, and there's so few people like that on earth.' But . . . what's your first name?"

"Edna."

"Oh yes, Edna. You're going to need help every week from me."

"I couldn't afford it," Edna explained, moving quickly onto the porch. She took deep breaths of the fresh night air to clean out her lungs from the stink in Miss Aimée's house.

"No, this is going to be free," Miss Aimée said.

"Free?"

"Yes," Miss Aimée said, her eyes lighting up and her mouth breaking into a smile of great compassion. "Edna, you're a chosen person, and you've been sent to do the work of God. I know God would want me to help you for free."

Edna stared at Miss Aimée, disbelievingly. "Do you mean that?"

"Of course I mean it," Miss Aimée said seriously. "But what you need is the Candle Novena."

"What's a Candle Novena?"

"Every week for thirteen weeks I need to light one of those candles in there for you and that boy. Then everything will really work out all right. And for ten minutes, every night, I've got to say a prayer for you. It's a very sacred ritual, and a lot of work for me, but I don't mind doing it for you."

"No thank you," Edna said. She couldn't believe how kind Miss Aimée was.

"It's free, honey, you've got nothing to lose."

Edna paused a minute. "Well, if you insist," Edna said, starting down the porch steps and feeling strange at the sight of the giant hand in front of the house. But by now, even the hand seemed commonplace next to the haunting image of a librarian going to her mother's grave to bury a book.

"Like I said, my prayers will be free," Miss Aimée continued to explain. "But the candles cost five dollars apiece, and I know you wouldn't want me paying for them—I'm just a poor woman—so every week, all you have to do is stop by and drop off five dollars."

"I'll think about it," Edna said.

"You really need candles," Miss Aimée said definitively.

Edna saw her bus coming from far down Richmond Avenue so she used it as an excuse to break into a run towards the bus stop. "Thank you," Edna called out as the same couple of kids came racing along the sidewalk again yelling "Pew, pew, pew, pew!"

Chapter 17 /

Marsh decided he would simply not think about Edna Shinglebox. It was a mistake. He trusted her; he told her things he hadn't told anybody else. She was just as big a phony and megalomaniac as everyone else on earth. Now he'd have to find somebody else to help him. But the horrible thing was that he knew time was running out.

Marsh sank down in his seat during the morning homeroom period while attendance was being taken. There was an assembly program going on and his homeroom wasn't going, so that left them with an hour to kill. The only good thing about it was that it meant all the other periods would be ten minutes shorter. He was drawing a doodle of Miss Ripper, the homeroom teacher, who looked exactly like a mature Saint Bernard. Miss Ripper said everybody was supposed to do schoolwork and not sit around talking. The assembly program announced for the day was supposed to be some kind of General Motors thing where they came in with a jet motor that made a loud noise and thought they were really cool by hooking some kid up to a Van der Graaf generator to make his hair shoot out all over so he'd look like a human porcupine doused with electrons. GM came every year and did the same kind of gimmick. His father had warned him about all that kind of brainwashing, and he was glad his homeroom wasn't going to the assembly. Besides, he wanted to work on another hate list.

This morning's hate list went like this: (1) I hate GM. (2) I hate AT&T. (3) I hate Edna Shinglebox because she doesn't want to help me and Paranoid Pete. (4) I hate that Mary Poppins is a junkie. (5) I hate that I was such a bad judge of character and thought that Edna Shinglebox was okay. (6) I hate all companies that put big doses of sugar in their products, because it makes babies get hooked on cookies. (7) I hate girls that go around writing Holland on their books and give you a cute little smile because we're supposed to know that Holland stands for Hoping Our Love Lasts And Never Dies. (8) I hate Edna Shinglebox because she's anti-raccoon. (9) I hate Lady Godiva because she wore a fall. (10) I hate Edna Shinglebox because I told her too much. P.S. I also hate all big industries because you end up having a situation with thousands of stockholders who just collect dividends and watch the Dow Index go up and down, and pay a group of cold-blooded executives to make decisions which are detrimental to the environment, because all executives care about is making money and not losing their jobs. In fact, that's all that stockholders care about; making money.

Marsh had just finished his last hate of the list, and was deep into contemplation when the front door of the classroom opened and Edna Shinglebox came in on a pass. He watched her go to Miss Ripper who nodded yes to something, and he was very disturbed when he saw Edna coming down his row.

"Miss Ripper said I could talk to you for a few minutes," Edna said.

Before Marsh could say anything, Edna had swung onto the seat with him, and the only urge he had was to shove her right off the seat and knock her on the floor.

"I want to apologize to you," Edna said.

"For what?"

"For what I said."

Marsh practically pounced on her. "Look, I made a mistake trusting you; that's my tough luck. I should have listened to you when you told me you were a big social cripple."

"I'm not a social cripple."

"Hah!"

"Don't hah me," Edna said. "I came in here to tell you I was sorry, but you're nothing but a big crybaby."

"Look, get off my case," Marsh said so loudly a lot of kids in the classroom turned around. Even Miss Ripper looked up so quickly that her jowls expanded, making her look like she had a keg of brandy strapped under her chin. Marsh noticed that Edna looked like she was going to cry. She turned her eyes away from him and looked downwards.

"Marsh," she said softly, "I'm sorry. I want to be your friend."

For a minute Marsh believed her. He even thought about putting his arm around her and giving her a hug, but he couldn't trust her anymore. And even if he wanted to, he couldn't stop his mouth from shooting off. There was a part of him that really despised her for the things she had said in the lunchroom. He was not a liar. "Your problem is when you were a kid, all you ever got for Christmas was mental blocks."

"I want to be your friend," Edna repeated quietly, this time lifting her gaze and looking into his eyes.

Marsh felt like he'd hooked into a tender spot and he couldn't stop himself from digging in further. "You know, when it comes to psychology, I'm a couple of thousand light-years ahead of you. You couldn't make a new friend if your life depended on it. You've got depression written all over your face with a Magic Marker. Everybody says you look snobbish, and those who don't think you're snobbish say you're a big bore."

"How would you know?" Edna asked him. "Nobody talks to you either."

"You wish!" Marsh said. "Your problem is you don't communicate effectively, because you're all screwed up. You're self-conscious, screwed up, and out of it." Marsh noticed tears forming in Edna's eyes. A few of them began to run down her face. He felt terrible, because he didn't really want to hurt her, but it was much too late for that; she'd already seen his list of hate which he'd left smack out on the desk.

"Is that what you do?" Edna asked.

"What?"

"Sit around, writing how many ways you hate me?"

Marsh refused to answer, and Edna just sat there looking at the list. There was a long pause, then Edna turned to him again. This time she looked like she had been shot through the heart by a thirty-eight magnum, dumdum bullet. She looked ready to die, and he felt her hand touching his hand under the desk; her fingers crawled around his, and before he knew what had happened, she was actually holding his hand. He wanted his fingers to respond, to curl around hers, but he felt paralyzed. Instead, his hand remained motionless and he thought of the expression *mano muerto*, which was something he'd read about how some guys pretend to have a dead hand so they can get cheap feels. In this case, he only thought of the expression because his hand really felt dead. Finally she let go of him and got up out of the seat. She stood in the aisle next to him, looking down, waiting for him to say something. A few of the kids in front of his desk turned and looked; they knew something strange was going on. Even Miss Ripper was staring. Then Edna just moved slowly back up the aisle, opened the door and was gone.

Marsh was the first one to arrive at Meizner's class, fifth period. Everyone except Edna Shinglebox arrived before the late bell, and Marsh felt relieved that at least she had the decency not to show up, but two minutes after the late bell, the door opened and in Edna came. He knew at least she was pretending he didn't exist, and he did the same right back to her. Mr. Meizner had decided to do an exercise the class had done several times before. The class was divided into two sides, and kids could earn points for their team by how honestly they expressed their feelings. If you told something so-so, you got one point, and if you were really shocking, you got ten points. The way it

ended up today, it was with Marsh on Team A together with Doris and Elaine Bach and Snooks; Edna
was on Team B with Jo, Jacqueline Potts and Mario
Lugati. The whole thing ended up being a bore, and
the only one that earned more than six points was
Mario Lugati who confessed that he wanted to blow
up the Chase Manhattan Bank branch at 2 Fifth Avenue because he thought the security was good and
low, but such nice people worked there. Marsh had
confessed he was having a sensuous affair with a
minister's daughter. Snooks confessed he was wearing his mother's perfume. At the end of the mass
confessional, Jacqueline Potts had the big news of the
day when she announced that she was going to have
a party, and that all the kids in GTE were invited. She
was going to have it Saturday night, but she said she
had to move it to Sunday because her parents weren't
going away until Sunday morning, and Butch Ontock
thought it would be better to have the party when her
parents weren't around. She also warned everybody
if they called the house because they forgot the address or something during the week, not to let on that
there was a party going on, because her mother and
father weren't going to know about it. It was just
supposed to be the members of GTE and if anyone
wanted to bring a date they could. Plus, Butch Ontock
was inviting a teenage evangelist that he and a few
guys from the football team had met when they
played a game up in Massachusetts. Apparently, the
teenage evangelist ran a commune, and all of his dis-
ciples in the commune thought he was God. The commune was supposed to have their own rock band and

everything. This teenage evangelist, who was simply known as God Boy was supposed to be so terrific, that Butch Ontock thought he would be more popular than Christ by 1990. God Boy was supposed to really know how to run an Experience so people could feel God and the Spirit of the Universe. He was also supposed to be able to summon up the music of the spheres with his rock group. And Jacqueline said God Boy had been on "Eyewitness News" the year before because he had published a new cookbook on different ways of preparing fertility beans. Everyone in GTE was so excited about the party they buzzed all the way to the door; all except Edna, of course. Marsh's mind was already planning to bring a very lovely, kind and sweet girl to Jacqueline's party. And the one thing he did know, was that it wasn't going to be Edna Shinglebox.

Chapter 18 /

The Friday before the party, Edna was working in the *Crow's Nest* office with Jacqueline. Miss Conlin, the faculty advisor for the newspaper, was running around like a chicken with her head cut off. But the thing Edna really liked about Miss Conlin was that she had a lot of experience in the real world. She'd spent years on a big newspaper, so when she talked about journalism, she knew what she was talking about. Besides, Miss Conlin was always taking a course at the Columbia Graduate School of Journalism. Halfway through the period, Miss Conlin told the girls she was going to cut out because she was going to a play that night in Manhattan, and she asked Edna to sneak into the main office and punch her out on the time clock so she wouldn't be docked for any pay. Edna or Jacqueline did that for Miss Conlin at least three times every week so it was nothing new.

When Miss Conlin left the office, Edna took over doing Jacqueline's gossip column so Jacqueline could finish working on her party list.

"My mother and father are going to kill me when they find out on Monday," Jacqueline said.

"Why do they have to find out?" Edna asked.

"Oh, even if I get the place cleaned up before they get back I have neighbors around me that squeal about everything I do."

"Maybe you should just tell your mother and father and get it over with."

"If I tell them, that's the end of the party. They've never once let me give a decent party in their precious glass house." Jacqueline was wearing Butch Ontock's Varsity jacket and she pulled it closer around her. It was warm in the office and it seemed so strange to see someone wearing a coat.

"Butch is making me buy beer and cigarettes," Jacqueline said.

At first, Edna was going to keep her mouth shut, but then she decided that would be old Edna. She felt like saying something, so she was going to say something. "You don't sound like you really want to give this party," Edna said.

"I don't," Jacqueline admitted.

"Then why are you doing it?"

"Because Butch wants a party."

"Suppose you just told Butch that you didn't want to give a party. I mean, your house isn't the best place to give a party; it has a lot of valuable things in it and it has a lot of glass windows, and you know how kids always get drunk at parties. I think you're taking a big risk, especially with the whole football team invited."

"If I called it off now, Butch would drop me."

"Not if he really liked you, he wouldn't. Besides, you don't even know who this God Boy is. He'll probably come down with a few of his friends, and for all you know, they might be crooks."

Jacqueline looked disturbed at what Edna was saying. "If you don't mind," Jacqueline said with a certain coldness to her voice, "I think we'd better talk about something else. I'm giving the party. I hope you'll come, and I hope you'll have a good time, and that's it."

"Sure," Edna agreed. "It's just that I thought I should tell you what I thought."

Edna returned her attention to the slips that she'd gotten out of the Gossip Box. "What girl in Study 503 thinks she should have gotten the lead in *South Pacific*, and didn't get it because the daughter of some teacher in this school was shown favoritism?" "John F. uses crib sheets for dates." "If at first you don't succeed, cheat." "Help send a girl to Boys Town." "Report your loco police." "Legalize private murder —why should the government have all the fun."

Edna thought the gossip submissions were better than usual. As a rule, she hated the whole column. It always seemed to have the same names in it and the same problems and the same corny jokes. Her mind began to drift and she began to think of Miss Aimée again. She felt like telling Jacqueline that she'd gone to the witch's house, but she decided Jacqueline looked like she wasn't in such a good mood. Edna had several dreams about Miss Aimée. Both times she'd awakened because she dreamed a large cockroach had crawled into her mouth. They were horrible dreams because whenever she dreamed about a cockroach, it was usually the size of a small animal—actually, about the size of a raccoon, for that matter.

Carrying around a raccoon in your pocket was the clearest example of misplaced love Edna had ever heard of. She'd read once about how families shouldn't even have dogs because most of the time everybody in the family goes around hugging the dog and hating each other. If there was no dog around, they'd have to hug each other. In a sense, Edna realized she was jealous of Marsh and his raccoon. Although, deep down, she decided she wouldn't care if Marsh eloped with the raccoon. Maybe the raccoon was a female, and they could live happily ever after as Mr. and Mrs. Marsh Raccoon Mellow; God knows it would make the gossip column.

Suddenly Edna was very angry, because she felt tears running down her face and she had promised herself she would not do that anymore. And it was just as bad as ever because she didn't know why she was crying. She told herself maybe it had something to do with seeing herself on a hate list. He hates me, she finally thought very clearly. That boy hates me so much he takes the time to itemize the ways. Some poets write things like "How do I love thee? Let me count the ways. . . ." Why couldn't I be an inspiration for a poem like that? Edna thought. I must really be some kind of a freak to encourage boys to sit around writing things about how many ways they hate me. "Loneliness is when there's a quiet voice inside telling you you need the touch of another human being." She remembered those words from the television show with that nasty hostess. "A feeling of despair and a secret we are ashamed to admit to our friends." Edna began to believe maybe there was something despicable about her; maybe she should be dead. Edna looked up to see what Jacqueline was doing. Jacqueline was still involved with her party preparation list. Then Edna looked towards the window. They were three stories above the ground, and if Edna wanted to, she could just walk over, open the window, and throw herself right out. She could try to aim herself so she'd fall straight down, with her head heading for the concrete. If she wanted to, she could wait for next period when Jacqueline wouldn't be there. She'd be alone in the office, and then Edna could tape her legs together, so when they found her, she wouldn't embarrass anyone because her legs were in an irregular position. She could just shove herself backwards out the window, but she'd have to be careful not to push herself so hard that she'd do a complete flip; that way she might break only her legs. It would have to be perfect so that her skull would shatter, and her brains would splatter all over the courtyard of Curtis Lee High.

Of course, Edna wasn't taking that daydream very seriously. Sometimes it was fun to sit around and plan your death. It was more like something she would daydream about in days gone by. Now, if anybody was going to be shoved out a window, she thought, it would be better if it was Marsh. The trouble with killing Marsh, was that he'd probably enjoy it. "Girls frequently plead with me and my father to love them." Hah! Edna had to let out a laugh at that one.

"What are you laughing at?" Jacqueline asked.

"One of the gossip items."

"What?"

Edna scanned the slips in front of her quickly, trying to find one that was really funny. "Herman Melville eats blubber."

"That is funny," Jacqueline laughed. Jacqueline picked up her party list and turned to Edna. "The way I figure it, there's going to be about thirty."

"Is that all?" Edna asked.

"Isn't that enough?"

"Yeah, it's enough, but I thought you said Butch invited the whole football team, and then you said a lot of the kids could bring dates if they wanted."

"Yeah."

"Well, I'd figure about forty, then."

"I guess you're right. Are you coming with Marsh?" Jacqueline asked.

"No."

"I thought the two of you were an item."

"That's a joke!"

"Too bad. He's good-looking."

"You're kidding!"

"No, I mean it," Jacqueline said. "I think you'd make a good couple."

Edna brushed her face and realized there had still been a tear on her cheek. She was afraid Jacqueline had noticed. As she wiped the tear away, she remembered the time during the Say-Hello-To-A-Face session that she had felt a tear on Marsh's cheek. Then she found herself peeking out of the corner of one eye to make sure Jacqueline wasn't looking at her. And when she looked at Jacqueline, she wished that, like Jacqueline, she had somebody's jacket to wear. Edna didn't think it had to be a team jacket; there was something nice about the thought of having a boy's coat around her shoulders. She wondered how she'd feel wearing Marsh's Levi's jacket, even if he left the three feathers taped on the shoulder. Or she'd even be happy with his plain, old corduroy jacket that he sometimes wore. In fact, the more she thought about it, the more she understood the meaning of wearing a boy's jacket. The jacket would retain some of the boy's spirit; some of his warmth. And it seemed as though it would be wonderful to have that kind of protection going for her. Maybe I do like a boy, Edna said to herself. She thought about that for a long while to see if she really meant it. Maybe I like a boy, maybe I like some boy, maybe there *is* a boy. But the last time she thought about it, the sentence didn't end, and a big BUT was tacked on at the end of the thought. And after the BUT, came . . . He doesn't like me. That thought hurt her, but she told herself that there were a lot of other boys in the world, and the next one who might come her way might even be normal. Maybe she'd be lucky enough to find a boy who didn't keep his father in a cremation urn under his bed. That did seem to be above and beyond the call of duty. In fact, when she thought about it clearly, that was so way-out, it was absurd; it was sad and it was funny, and it was weird, all bound together. And somewhere, at that moment, she heard the tinkle of a piano; it was like Gertrude the Ghost was somewhere in her head playing "Laughing on the Outside (Crying on the Inside)." Maybe that's what life as a teenager was supposed to be; always the two emotions going on at the same time, and on top of that, the kid was supposed to do everything his parents,

/   *180*

teachers and sociologists said. Maybe if she grew up to be famous and rich, all that would change. Maybe that was the only answer to ever changing that condition; being like Marsh's parents and her own parents didn't seem to solve anything. Maybe the only way you didn't end up with a whole life filled with laughing on the outside, and your heart cracking on the inside was if you were famous like all those people hanging on the walls in Marsh's room. Maybe you had to be famous like Black Beauty, or Jesus Christ, or John F. Kennedy. Maybe you had to be Freud or Trigger. And just as her mind was spinning along, remembering all those faces on the walls of his room, something dawned on Edna. Everyone hanging on the walls of Marsh's room was dead. That was what they all had in common; in fact, that was the only thing they all had in common. Everyone wasn't even of the same species; there were humans and horses. The only common denominator, was that all of them were dead. That was the secret hanging on his walls. Marsh Mellow had a photographic morgue. From that point of view, the cremation urn was in absolutely the right place. It seemed as if there was a giant secret hanging over everything about Marsh. The pictures were only part of it, and so was the urn. There was still the rocket, the giant rocket he said his father had bought him at a firework stand that had a giant eucalyptus tree next to it in South Carolina. There was a secret in the letters that he had written, pretending that they were from Paranoid Pete. There was a secret in the nuthouse. There was a secret in everything, in that rocket that was capable of hurtling into the sky and exploding into an American flag. There was something about the whole, crazy mess that seemed to involve a plan; and some of the parts were just starting to fit together. Maybe she was giving up too soon, Edna thought. Maybe learning how to love someone, and learning how to let someone like you back was more complicated than she had thought. Maybe fiction always had a way of simplifying things. Love wasn't like a comic book, or the way novelists threw it down in a book. "You filthy dirty little pig" she could remember Schizo Suzy's voice screaming out at her. The words were clearer now that she wasn't running to save her life. And just then, Edna's neck jerked for a moment and she felt guilty again. Somehow she sensed she was involved in something that was more than Marsh's problem. She was coming face-to-face with something close to her, and if she continued running, maybe one day she'd have to do something like the librarian who had to go to her mother's grave and bury a book. Edna felt like a ton of guilt was crushing her, and she suspected it was guilt that was pressing down on Marsh, and making him do the things he did. What if they could tell each other why they were so guilty? Maybe that would be part of the secret, Edna thought. Maybe that was the part about Miss Aimée that wasn't a crock. Miss Aimée, like everybody else in life is probably half truthful. Maybe Miss Aimée had been right when she told Edna she would end up with this crazy boy. And at that moment, Edna felt like a thousand volts of electricity had been passed through her body. She realized that if she did love Marsh, if she *could* love that particular boy, that her main competition was a dead man.

Chapter 19 /

Edna was the first one to arrive Sunday night. Jacqueline had asked her to come over a little early to make
a few bowls of onion dip, and put out paper cups for
the half-gallon bottles of Almadén Red Mountain
claret wine. After that, there were a lot of rolls to
slice because Butch said all the guys wanted veal-
cutlet grinders. Jo, from GTE, had been over most of
the day frying the cutlets, and she also helped Jacqueline create a big pot of Buitoni spaghetti sauce jazzed
up with extra doses of oregano. Everything had to be
put out on a large buffet table because Butch insisted
that everybody be able to make their own grinders.
Edna thought that was a little crazy, because she
could just see all the kids ripping through those cutlets like there was no tomorrow.

Edna wanted to be in the house before anyone
else anyway. She knew it'd be easier on her meeting
a couple of people at a time rather than if she came
late and had to face the whole party with one fell
swoop. Besides, she was feeling very nervous, and
was thankful she had a good reason to get out of
her own house while Mrs. Shinglebox had been making dinner. It had kept her mother out of Edna's hair
except for the last few minutes when Mrs. Shin-

glebox chased Edna around the living room with a comb. Then she insisted Edna borrow her Guatemalan shawl so that it would set off Edna's deep blue slacks and delicate matching blouse. Edna fought the shawl violently until she caught a glimpse of herself in the hall mirror.

"See," Mrs. Shinglebox said. "It makes you funky without being too funky."

"You're right, Mom," Edna said, slightly annoyed. It used to burn her up when her mother was wrong, and sometimes it burned her up even more when her mother was right. Mrs. Shinglebox pulled Edna into the dining room and spun her around in front of Mr. Shinglebox.

"Doesn't she look just like Ann-Margret?" Mrs. Shinglebox kept harping. Then, somehow, Edna managed to get out the front door with her ego still intact. She grabbed the 111 bus to the bottom of Emerson Hill. From there, it had been a long walk up to the Pottses' house.

Jacqueline's house was very famous on Staten Island because it looked like it was something out of a James Bond movie, even though it had been built over twenty-five years ago. People always called it the Glass House because it was mainly glass, and it was four stories high so there was no missing it the way it stuck out on top of the hill. Everybody said nice things about the house now, like how contemporary it was, but when it was first built, it was considered so ugly that the architect had to leave town because everybody canceled their building contracts with him. The poor guy ended up out in California where he became famous and made a fortune building movie stars' homes and Malibu condominiums. Edna loved the house, and a lot of other people were still very impressed by it. Even her mother had done cartwheels when she heard that her daughter was going to a party there. Mrs. Shinglebox thought it would have to be a very high-class society party with only the finest young ladies and gentlemen. Edna had a good laugh about that, and she didn't bother to explain to Mrs. Shinglebox there was only going to be a few jerks from GTE; some even bigger jerks from the football team, and a couple of religious nuts from Marblehead, Massachusetts, one of whom thought he was God.

Jacqueline had been on the phone when Edna first arrived at the house. She had waved at Edna to run around and take a look at the house, which was exactly what Edna wanted to do. There was a nice rustic fence around the hillside property, and since the glass house went straight up there was a lot of room for an enormous, kidney-shaped, heated swimming pool. The pool was steaming like a lobster pot. And right next to it was a Riviera whirlpool which was some kind of contraption about three feet deep that eight people could sit in at a time, and hot water bubbled and whirled when a switch was thrown. Jacqueline said it was great for hangovers, and that one night she and Butch fell asleep in it and came out looking like prunes. On the first floor of the house was a spacious kitchen-dining area with a red-brick fireplace. The kitchen section had all kinds of modern appliances including two microwave ovens, and a centrifugal juicer. The big feature on the second floor was a huge living room with a massive, white-brick fireplace. And the decor was phantasmagoric. It had wall-to-wall carpeting that was so thick, Edna felt like she was walking through snowdrifts. And a whole wall was crammed with stereo equipment and control knobs. There were fat, overstuffed sofas and chairs and paintings on the walls of children leaping through fields of poppies, and old ladies in gowns, dancing at balls with men who wore wigs. There was one picture in particular Edna liked; it was an oil painting of a nude young boy who looked like he lived in the eighteenth century and had a lot of problems. Huge, sliding glass doors filled one whole wall of the living room, and led out onto a terrace which was cantilevered over the pool below. A terrific exterior stairway led down to one side of the pool where there was an immaculately trimmed lawn that sloped down so sharply, Edna hadn't the faintest idea how a gardener managed to mow it.

The third floor of the house had four regular-type bedrooms, one of which was Jacqueline's. And there was the maid's quarters, and a den that looked like Mr. Potts did a lot of work and manipulating there. Edna found out that Mr. Potts had made his money in some field called Creative Advertising; in fact, most of his loot came from a fish account where he came up with a promotional campaign based on a slogan that went "Remember, an anchovy is only a sardine that knows Sales Psychology." The den also had a projection television that let you see television on a screen that was six feet high and five feet wide. Then on the fourth floor of the house, there was the master bedroom suite that looked like something Bacchus would enjoy. Mirrors were all over the place. There was a great, circular bed that rotated when you turned a switch. There were automatic drapes, closets with automated hangers that whirled around, and another huge wall of glass with electric eyes that opened the large doors onto the deck. The fourth-floor deck also hung right over the swimming pool, which Edna thought was particularly neat because if someone was a sleepwalker, at least if they fell over the edge, they still had a chance to land in the pool. The bathroom in the master suite was fantastic. It had a raised bathtub, with faucets made of dragons' heads, and a toilet with a no-noise flush. For that matter, there were bathrooms all over the house, plus lots of closets, storage space, and an impressive laundry room. On the right side of the house, on the first floor, was a whole playroom with pinball machines, table tennis, a pool table, and just beyond that, through another set of doors, there was a trampoline on the lawn under a tree. It was obvious that if you bounced hard enough on the trampoline, you could grab the lowest branch of a huge oak tree which hovered above. And as Edna had gone through the house, even though she had to admit it was elegant and opulent, she felt sad. She knew she'd love to have a house just like it, but she finally figured out that she didn't know whether she'd be very happy in it if she had to live in it all alone. That was something that had crossed her mind a number of times; even if she was the richest girl in the world, she figured she'd still be pretty miserable unless she had somebody to share things with. And beneath that layer of sadness, she knew there was something else still gnawing at her, and that was a dream she'd had the night before. It was a dream with a lot of morbid visions in it about death and aging. She remembered one part of the dream very clearly, and that was the part where she'd given birth to a baby, and the first thing she did was to run and hold the baby up for her mother's approval. "It's my baby! It's my baby!" Edna had said in the dream. And her mother only stared at her. Edna realized that she had waited too long to have a baby because in this dream, her mother was already dying from some horrible disease. Then there was another part in the same dream—it probably had come first, but she couldn't be sure. It was a part where a boy had fallen in love with her and chased her down a spiral staircase trying to give her a hypo. Edna knew that a lot of the dream had to do with her anxiety about going to the party. She had bad dreams before every social event. After all, she knew she believed consciously and unconsciously that the possibilities for disaster were always endless. Somebody might slip LSD into the punch, or they might feed her a magic mushroom. She didn't know how to handle wine and cigarettes, no less magic mushrooms. She heard there had been a party the year before where Mary Bobbin ate a dried root at a party, and then tried to climb the Verrazano-Narrows Bridge. But Edna knew there was still even a third level of sadness and fear connected with this particular party. In the middle of her tour, Edna went back to the empty living room and sat in a luxurious, black-leather chair. She tried to stop herself from worrying about what would happen during the party. She took out a note she had written that morning to see if it still said all the things she wanted to say to Marsh. She'd written it on a piece of engraved stationery that an aunt of hers had given her the Christmas before. She hoped the big lettering on the top of the paper wouldn't seem too pretentious to Marsh: FROM THE DESK OF EDNA SHINGLEBOX. The thought crossed her mind that she might be put off if she got a note from someone with that kind of heading. Her eyes scanned her letter quickly: *Dear Marsh, I'm writing this because it's the only way I know to tell you what I want to tell you, especially the way you were to me in your homeroom with Miss Ripper and all the kids watching. I've always had trouble letting a person know my true feelings because I am a coward, and ashamed to let a person know I like them. Please excuse my handwriting and grammar because I'm not perfect in English. What I want you to know is how I feel deep down about you, and then you can do whatever you want, but at least I will have been honest with a person for the first time in my life. I hope that tonight, after you read this, you'll like me very much. What I'm afraid of is that you don't like me, and that I bore you, and that you think I have no feelings for you. I had this dream that we'll become wonderful friends and be able to tell each other the worst and the best things about ourselves and will still be friends. The thing I want more than anything is to be truthful with you; I want to tell you my true feelings, which is some-*

thing I never did with anyone in my life. And I want you to do the same with me. Okay? What are you thinking now? What are you feeling? What are you hoping? What are you afraid of? Am I way off base? All I have been able to think about is how much I want us to be friends, and how much I need your friendship. I am sad and lonely. Please forgive me for saying that, but it's true. I came to the party tonight only to see you and pray that you'll come over to me after you read this letter. If you don't, I'll understand. If you want me to help you with your father, I will. I'll try the best I know how. I hurt inside when I think of what you must be going through! I'm sorry I don't have the guts to tell you all these things to your face, but I think you know that some things are easier to write in letters. Regards, Edna.

Then Edna had folded the paper back up and put it in her pocket. She'd gone downstairs and had been thankful that there was a lot of work to do.

Jacqueline now was busy taking cigarettes out of packages and arranging them in brandy glasses. "Butch said I had to supply Marlboros."

"He's really got a little nerve, doesn't he," Edna said. "Aren't you afraid, having so many kids come over to this knockout of a house?"

Jacqueline sounded a little worried. "I figure most of them will stay on the first floor or play leapfrog around the pool or something. Besides, the food and wine is down here."

"Why don't you just tell them, no kids upstairs."

"I went through all this with Butch. He says it's

rude. If you invite people to your house, you're supposed to let them go through it, wherever they want."

"I wouldn't," Edna said.

By eight o'clock, most of the kids from GTE had arrived. That made Edna realize everyone in that class was socially retarded. Actually, everyone from the class was there except Marsh, and they all looked quite spiffy. Jacqueline appointed Jo in charge of the stereo system. The turntable was on the second floor in the living room with all the gadgets, and Jo had to be shown how to work the switches that put the music on speakers all over the place, including speakers for the pool. Mario Lugati had arrived with Doris and Elaine Bach; that was sort of nice, Edna thought. Edna had suspected Mario was getting to like Doris, because on the day when it was her turn in GTE to be thrown up in the air, it was only Mario who said that everyone should stop trying to make her head hit the ceiling. Besides, it was rather well known that both Doris and Elaine had finally stopped wetting their beds. Since Meizner's class, a whole lot of things had changed. There'd been a lot of improvements in personality focus, as Mr. Meizner used to say. Jo seemed to get more like a boy, but by the same token, she also seemed happier. She was strutting around changing records wearing an army jump suit, and if nothing else, she looked distinctive. Also, she was the only one who was really nice to Elaine Bach. Sometimes Jo would walk through the halls holding Elaine's hand, but nobody said anything because Jo had become Curtis Lee High's shot-put champion. Snooks arrived with a boy from McGee High School. And both he and his friend looked pretty shook-up because a gang of boys in Stapleton had chased them, calling them names. There were a few other minor skirmishes and emotional upsets, but after a couple of glasses of wine, everybody seemed to be having a nice time and staying in the kitchen area. Snooks finally recovered enough to deliver his rendition of "I'm Looking Over a Four Leaf Clover" a cappella. Then, some kid from the football team arrived and things were awkward for a few minutes because he started shooting his mouth off about what a great house Jacqueline had to rip off. That's when a bunch of cars began pulling up. It seemed like there were more than nine cars arriving at once. Everybody was peeling rubber up the hill and sliding on gravel and showing off going around the bend. It looked like Emerson Hill had been turned into the Grand Prix road course with the Pottses' house as the finish line, and there were at least three or four kids in each car.

It didn't take Edna more than a minute to realize there was going to be a lot more than forty kids at the party; in fact there were already more than that and half the football team wasn't there yet. Butch was supposed to be leading the way for the kids from Marblehead, Massachusetts, and as it was, Edna knew only about half the kids there. Most of them weren't even on the football team. Some had been in one class with her or another; some she recognized only because some pictures had come into the *Crow's Nest*. Richard Kay, Vincent Rolio and Gilbert Barker came with Joan Canyon, Joan Hybred and Norlicka Tobinson; those three girls were known as the three easiest girls in the school, except for Norma Jean Stapleton. Then there was Ed Skahn who was the type any girl would love to run into, especially if she was driving and he was walking. He was with Greg Cutter, John Kenny and John Mell. Renée Rare arrived with Chris Phleghm whose father was an alcoholic district attorney. Chris Phleghm's brother, Nick, arrived with Bonnie Hilderstraw who always went to parties with her own record, and would dance "Slaughter on Tenth Avenue" at the drop of a hat. Betty Slagen and Tillie Roe came in together, and they said they had been invited by Billy Selmond who was on the football team. Some very freaky kid by the name of Hansen came in with Maureen Clapper, and they were both sporting matching riveted jeans which looked ridiculous. Then there was Lucille Bore who was so cranky you had to say things to her like "Tomorrow will be Monday, if it's all right with you." Marmaduke Jones came by himself, and as good as he was as a Junior Class politician, he was a complete bust trying to be the life of the party. Gert Ronkiwitz came in looking like she was still wearing her crown as last year's football queen. She had such an artificial laugh, Edna couldn't stand to be near her. Edna realized half of what she was thinking was only because she was so nervous keeping an eye on the front door for Marsh to come in. She wanted everything to go right. She'd have to decide just the exact moment to give him the letter she'd written. She'd wait until he'd had a glass of wine maybe, and then she'd just saunter over to him and press the letter in his hand. Maybe she'd whisper, "Please read this." Then she'd just turn quickly and go away. That would probably be the best approach. Maybe she'd go upstairs. She fantasized that Marsh would take the letter out by the pool, wanting to be alone while he read it. Maybe if she went to one of the decks on the second or the fourth floor, she could peer over and watch him reading it from above. She'd give him a few minutes, and if he didn't come upstairs looking for her, she'd come down. Maybe she should wait longer upstairs to make sure he'd come up, then they could be alone and talk. On the other hand, if he didn't see her downstairs, maybe he'd think she just left the party. She'd have to make sure that didn't happen. Or maybe she should just tell him, "Here, read this—I'll be waiting upstairs."

By nine o'clock there was a nice buzz to the party. The sliding glass doors on the first floor had to all be opened, and a lot of kids were straying out near the kidney-shaped pool. Richard Kay and about a half dozen others had gone upstairs just to take a look. They'd asked permission from Jacqueline and Jacqueline said it was okay. Then a few others went up, and somebody turned the stereo system all the way up until the entire living room was beginning to vibrate.

"We're going to need more sauce," Jacqueline moaned.

"I'll do it," Edna offered. Several of the other girls were willing to help too, except for Joan Canyon, Joan Hybred and Norlicka Tobinson who were already practically throwing their bodies at every guy on the football team.

"Great grinders," a lot of kids commented, as they

moved around the buffet table. Most of the boys were putting two and three veal cutlets on each grinder, and Maureen Clapper must have been drunk before she and Hansen arrived because it wasn't five minutes before she dropped her grinder in the swimming pool. That really burned Edna up. It just seemed a very revolting and careless thing to do. Edna used her annoyance at Maureen Clapper for energy to stir the big pot of sauce. Then she happened to glance out of the kitchen window, and there at last was Marsh. Edna felt her heart starting to dance on her diaphragm again. She was very excited, and she felt that tonight was going to be a wonderful evening. She could see Marsh was wearing the same outfit as the night he came to take her to the Magic Elephant. In fact, maybe that's why he's dressed that way, Edna thought. Just to remind me of that wonderful evening. Instinctively, Edna put her hand in her pocket to make sure her note was ready. At exactly that moment, Edna noticed that there was something attached to the end of Marsh's left hand. Edna almost passed out when she realized it was Norma Jean Stapleton. In fact, Edna was so startled, she froze, looking out the kitchen window.

"What's the matter?" Jacqueline asked, noticing Edna's stiff position.

"Nothing," Edna said.

Jacqueline leaned over to see what Edna was staring at. "Oh, my God," Jacqueline said. "When Norma Jean Stapleton comes to your house, you've got to fumigate it in the morning because she leaves cooties all over."

Edna buried her head in the sauce pot and began stirring like a madwoman. She hoped Jacqueline wouldn't notice her reaction, but it was too late.

"You *do* think he's groovy, don't you," Jacqueline said. Jacqueline winked, and then disappeared into the crowd with a fresh tray of sliced Italian bread. Out of the corner of her eye Edna saw Marsh and Norma Jean come into the kitchen and then stroll by hand in hand. They shot towards the buffet table like piranha going for a calf that had fallen into the Amazon River. They started fixing themselves grinders like there was no tomorrow. Edna knew very well Marsh had seen her, and she could hear him laughing extra-loud and artificially. Edna also noticed Raccoon's little head peeking in and out of Marsh's jacket pocket. She thought it was unforgivable that he had to drag that poor, cute, little innocent victim along. Edna also heard a lot of kids cracking their usual cracks about Norma Jean Stapleton. Like one kid said, "I didn't know this was going to be a pig party." That line always got a big laugh, because the worst thing that had ever happened to Norma Jean Stapleton was the time the tennis team decided to have a party where each guy had to bring the ugliest girl they could date. Nick Phleghm took Norma Jean, and his job was to arrive last and bring a live baby pig. He had told Norma Jean that the baby pig was a door prize and she didn't suspect anything until they arrived at the party. Norma was petting the baby pig, but after a minute all the girls took a look at each other and figured out what kind of party it was, especially when all the boys roared with laughter. Some of the girls broke down crying, including Norma Jean, who was supposed to have stood there with the baby pig in her arms until she was so pathetic, Nick Phleghm even felt sorry and took her home.

It seemed every time Edna looked up from the stove, Marsh was looking her way and slurping up his grinder. He'd also suddenly become animated and do something like stroke Norma Jean's hair, or pat her on the back, or let out another horselaugh as though Norma Jean Stapleton was the most sensational date in the world. Finally it seemed Marsh was waiting only to get Edna's attention, and when she'd look at him, Marsh would spring into action with his arm around Norma Jean, and finally he took her strolling out to the pool. Raccoon's head was still popping in and out, looking very bewildered. Edna felt the sad, big black eyes of the cute little furry ball were pleading with her for help. She didn't know whether Raccoon would even remember her; she'd never read anything about whether raccoons had good memories or not. But Edna had grown very fond of the animal. Edna told herself she shouldn't feel that way; it was probably just because the animal belonged to Marsh that she loved it. At that moment a van and a bus pulled up outside the glass house and all hell broke loose. Kids were running around saying "God Boy's here! God Boy's here!" Almost everybody ran out onto the front lawn like rats deserting a ship. The van had what looked like a hundred thousand dollars' worth of amplifiers and speakers, and the members of the band looked like they had the kind of mentality that would go to see toe dancers at a ballet and wonder why the management didn't hire taller girls. They all had long hair and hillbilly clothes, and they moved fast to get the equipment set up around the pool area. Butch Ontock came running up to Jacqueline to explain that God Boy had brought a busload of kids from his commune up in Marblehead. And from what Edna could see, it looked like most of that crew had gone the way of all flesh.

"I don't have enough grub!" Jacqueline yelled.

"Who cares," Butch said. "This crew is already stoned out of their minds." Butch ran back towards God Boy's bus.

A minute later, almost everyone was off the bus and a group of kids from the commune began lighting candles and walking like paraplegic geese towards the house.

"Oh my God," Edna heard Jacqueline groan as she ran back into the kitchen. "They've got a procession going on out there! A procession!"

Edna poured the batch of new sauce into what was left of the old batch on the buffet table, and went out on the lawn to watch God Boy make his entrance. The kids with the candles were parading in the front gate, and Butch Ontock and Greg Cutter were flanking a very tall boy who looked sort of plain and simple, but was wearing jeans and a phosphorescent, Renaissance-prince shirt. But as he got closer, Edna could see that this boy had the most beautiful smile Edna had ever seen in her life. It's like you would hardly notice him unless he smiled, but the minute you saw his smile you couldn't take your eyes off him. He smiled at all the kids who were lined up staring at him on the lawn, and Edna could tell they were all fascinated by him. It was a very weird phenomenon. There was something tremendously magnetic about this boy in the phosphorescent shirt—the way he moved, the way he carried his head—and the sound of his voice was angelically sincere. "Hello Brothers, hello Sisters," the boy said. He reached out and touched some of the kids as he moved by them, and at one point he gave Butch Ontock a big hug. Then he singled out Bonnie Hilderstraw and put his arm around her. She kissed him even though she'd never met him before. God Boy was saying other things, most of which Edna couldn't hear because she was on the outside edge of the crowd, but as he came closer and more light hit his face, Edna was aware of an enormous tension lurking beneath the slow, steady motion of his movement. "Tonight will be your night," God Boy said at one point, and then turned his head and repeated it. "Tonight will be your night." Edna hadn't the faintest idea of what he was talking about, and she was sure no one else did either. But it was all very moving and spiritual, and there was no doubt that there was something very special about this boy. A few kids shook his hand and called him God Boy, but he corrected them and asked them to just call him Michael. "We're all children of God," he said.

Scurrying back to the house, Edna happened to glance up to the second floor and saw Marsh and Norma Jean Stapleton leaning over the second-floor railing of the deck. Marsh was staring down at Edna, but the moment Edna looked up, Marsh put his arm around Norma Jean quickly. Seeing that made Edna feel miserable. She actually even felt a pain near her heart. She hurried back into the house and the first thing she did was pull out the letter she had written to Marsh and rip it up. She threw the pieces of the letter into the garbage compactor and pressed a switch. There was the loud crashing of broken bottles and she was glad that the thoughts she had written down were now crushed into garbage. Within another couple of minutes the crew from Massachusetts had moved in and taken over the entire kitchen.

"What are they doing?" Jacqueline demanded to know.

Butch started feeding Jacqueline a big line and put his arm around her and led her off to quiet her down. But Jacqueline kept repeating it. "What are they doing? What do they think they're doing here?" Edna had to admit that the girls from the commune seemed to really know what they were doing, even if they were opening up all the kitchen closets. They looked like they were getting ready to eat Jacqueline's family out of house and home. In another minute, steaks were being cooked, roasts were being defrosted; they just laced into everything. Edna decided to get away from the whole matter, and besides, she was pretty exhausted from all the work she'd done. She decided to go upstairs to the living room, not because Marsh was there, but just because she felt like it. She even took a glass of wine with her. As she was going up the stairs, there was a deafening blast from the band which was all hooked up at the pool. Jo had to shut off the stereo system, although it didn't really matter because the amplifying system the band had brought with them was capable of drowning out everything. From the living-room windows Edna could see a lot of the kids had started dancing down by the pool and it was suddenly apparent that the kids from Massachusetts had everything under control. A huge, wrought-iron candelabra had been brought in from the van and ended up being the destination of all the lighted candles the kids had carried in the procession. One by one, each kid had put a lighted candle in the candelabra until there were more than thirty candles. They tried to keep it upstairs in the living room, but Jacqueline screamed because there was so much wax dripping. She made them take it and put it down in the kitchen. And the light from the candles was so bright that the electric lights in the kitchen were shut off. Edna noticed there seemed to be three main bodyguards that stayed close to God Boy. They looked like teenage versions of Little Caesar, Public Enemy Number One and Scarface. She'd noticed them first sizing up the kitchen and outdoor area, and then deciding that it wasn't suitable for their leader. So now they were upstairs and had taken over the living room.

"What about the wax," Jacqueline was running around complaining. "What about all the wax down there? It's getting all over the tiles."

"It comes right off with hot water." One of the girls from the commune was telling her not to worry.

God Boy was led to a place of honor on the living-room terrace. A sofa had been dragged out so he'd be comfortable, and kids began to sit at his feet, including a whole slew of girls who had brought him wine, food, and for some reason, three bags of Taco chips. Edna was afraid to go near God Boy, so she just stayed on the fringe, behind the glass doors. She was also very aware of the fact that Marsh and Norma Jean Stapleton were still at the other corner of the terrace. Marsh looked like he was still having the time of his life, or at least playing at having the time of his life. But Edna also thought Norma Jean Stapleton looked like she was getting a little bored. Every time Marsh would hug and handle her, Norma Jean seemed to be quite uninterested and was twisting and turning to look at a lot of other boys who were in the room. Sometimes she would just stare at another boy even while Marsh was laughing and talking to her. Edna was also aware that Marsh was still looking over and checking to make certain that Edna was still looking. At that point, he reached into his pocket and Edna was furious to see him lift Raccoon up into the air. There was no doubt he was deliberately waving the animal to make Edna even more outraged. There was a lot of smoke from cigarettes, there was the blaring noise of the band; poor Raccoon was not having a good time, and Edna could see it in the poor animal's eyes. Maybe Marsh was immune to Raccoon's feelings, but Edna certainly wasn't. Then he put Raccoon back in his pocket and gave Norma Jean a big squeeze and a long kiss. As far as Edna was concerned, that was even worse, putting Raccoon back in his pocket, because with him pressing Norma Jean up to him, Raccoon was probably getting squashed. That was one thing Edna could not stand by and let happen. She didn't care what Marsh thought of her, she didn't care if Marsh and Norma Jean decided to elope and run off to Ethiopia, she had a right to look after that raccoon and she was going to do it.

Edna walked briskly across the entire terrace, and she noticed how shocked Marsh looked at her approach.

"Excuse me," Edna said, fighting to keep her voice calm and controlled. "Marsh, if you'd like me to hold Raccoon, I don't mind. I think he'd be more comfortable and I could take him out on the lawn and let him play." Norma Jean just stared at Edna and put a stupid grin on her mouth.

"No thanks," Marsh said. "Raccoon's just fine in my pocket. Don't you go worrying about it."

"Marsh," Edna said, "it's very stuffy here, it's very noisy, and you're crushing him in your pocket." Edna tried to sound factual. She wanted Marsh to know that she was really interested in the animal's welfare and that she wasn't over there to make any trouble for him and Norma Jean or anybody else.

"Are you Edna Shinglebox?" Norma Jean asked, curling her upper lip and beginning to breathe through her mouth.

"Yes," Edna said. "I know who you are."

"I'll bet you do," Norma Jean said. "And I know who you are. You're the girl who goes through life pushing doors marked pull."

Edna ignored Norma Jean's crack and continued at Marsh. "Give me him before you hurt him." Edna reached towards Marsh's jacket where two little cute dark eyes were staring out at her. Marsh pushed her hand away and Norma Jean moved so that she stood between Edna and Marsh. It was as though Norma Jean suddenly switched all the energy she usually devoted towards undulating her body into quick, nasty words.

"Why don't you just beat it," Norma Jean said, and then turned her back and gave Marsh a big soul kiss right in front of Edna. Norma Jean kept the kiss going until Edna felt embarrassed and stupid, and finally couldn't do anything except walk away. She also felt her right arm lifting the glass of wine to her lips. She took a big swig and then headed straight for the terrace stairs. As she came down the stairs there was a very weirdo boy from Marblehead who was at the bottom watching her. Edna pretended she didn't notice him staring. Just then, Marmaduke Jones and Betty Slagen were thrown in the pool with their clothes on. Everyone was laughing and hooting, and Edna just pushed right by the weirdo. To the right, she could see the commune girls still marauding through the kitchen. Now they were opening up everything from the Ritz crackers to the Apple Jacks, and it was obvious that some of the guys had found Mr. Potts' liquor supply because several boys were running by, chug-a-lugging out of fifths of Chivas Regal and Johnny Walker Black. It looked to Edna as if the whole party was getting a little out of hand, but she also noticed that Jacqueline seemed to have given up trying to stop things. She saw her and Butch walking over towards the trampoline and Butch was smothering her with kisses. And she also saw them turn around abruptly and then start up the terrace stairs. When Edna was farther out by the pool, she saw Butch and Jacqueline in one of the upstairs bedrooms. That was one thing bad about the glass house. You could see everybody in every part of it, just like it was a great big ant colony, unless somebody would close the drapes.

Edna spotted an empty table out at the end of the pool, and she decided she'd go sit down and just watch the madhouse. By now there were over sixty kids around the pool and she could see at least that many running around through the glass house. She could also see that Marsh was still watching her from the second-floor terrace.

Then the weirdo boy from the commune who had been staring at her when she came down the stairs plopped uninvited into the chair next to Edna. This boy was so weird, because he looked like a Cro-Magnon boy, and he wore a vest made of soda-bottle tops. In fact, he looked like one of those boys that would have an extra chromosome, the kind of mutation that makes some boys be more like miniature criminals.

"Some pad, huh?" the kid said, taking a deep drag on what was the thickest stick of grass Edna had ever seen. "Want a toke?"

"No thanks." Edna didn't even know what a toke was, but she didn't want one.

The boy looked her over carefully; finally he spoke again. "Has anyone ever told you that you look like the kind of girl who lives in constant fear that your last breath will be a hiccough and you won't be able to say excuse me?"

"No," Edna said, sipping her wine. "Nobody ever told me that." She glanced up towards the living-room terrace and could see that Marsh was watching everything she did. She also noticed that whenever Marsh was certain Edna was looking, Marsh would start pawing Norma Jean, and Norma Jean in turn was beginning to look more bored than ever. Now she was even waving to other guys behind Marsh's back.

"I don't usually go to parties like this," Edna explained.

"Look, I just didn't want you to think I was Bogarting my joint."

"I don't know what you're talking about."

The boy leaned forward on one knee and studied Edna like she was a paramecium. "You look like I just asked you to chew a 5 Day deodorant pad."

"No kidding," Edna said. "You look like you just *did* chew a 5 Day deodorant pad."

"Are you a stewardess?" the weirdo asked.

"No."

"You look like a stewardess I met at a Mazola Party."

Edna thought that one over. She also noticed that the more the boy was talking to her, the more Marsh seemed to be leaning over the railing watching her. She decided maybe she had something going here, so she decided to make it look really good. Edna moved her chair closer to the boy, and then she swung back her head and let out a laugh as though she were having a great time and chatting with the most interesting boy in the world. Marsh was so far away, he wouldn't be able to focus on just what a crazy weirdo this boy really was. "Your tongue is so long," Edna said with a wonderful smile. "I'll bet you can seal envelopes five minutes after you've put them in the mailbox."

"Look, silly puss," the weirdo said. "I just finished six months in the slammer." He took another deep puff on the cigarette and bent over, putting his head between his legs. "They call me the Baseball Kid because I'm thrown out at home so much. Get it? Ha, ha!"

"Oh, I get it," Edna said. "And I bet you think that Beethoven's Fifth is a bottle."

Edna flashed him an even sweeter smile, and burst into bigger laughter as though she were really having the time of her life. She noticed Marsh was straining to see everything. Marsh had even started a very animated hugging of Norma Jean at one point, but what he didn't know was that Norma Jean was holding another boy's hand behind his back. Then Edna noticed that Norma Jean said something to Marsh and excused herself, like she had to go to the bathroom or something. She left him on the terrace and disappeared upstairs. Edna could see through the glass windows that Norma Jean had gone up at least to the third floor, but if Edna's suspicions were right, she'd probably end up in the master bedroom suite because Greg Cutter, John Kenny and John Mell all scooted up the stairs right after her.

"My problem," the weirdo boy was saying to Edna, "is that I've followed the Ten Commandments all my life. It's just that I've never caught up to any of them. Get it? Ha, ha, ha!" He pushed his cigarette towards

Edna. "Here, suck on my giggle-weed."

"I said no thanks," Edna repeated with a huge smile that was hurting her cheeks. She then tossed her head again so that Marsh would think she was really having a ball. Then Edna saw that Marsh took Raccoon out of his jacket and started petting him. She knew Marsh was doing it just to burn her up.

"I'm talking to you," the weirdo boy said.

"I'm sorry," Edna said. "God forbid I shouldn't give you my total attention, you're such a fascinating person! Particularly with that vest made of pop-bottle tops."

"I asked you if you'd like to hit the moon."

Edna thought that was a particularly lovely invitation, although she hadn't the faintest idea of what it entailed. She also felt very guilty because actually, she was using this kid, and as weird as he was, she had no right to exploit him. She also decided it was deceitful. What happened to her whole new policy of being honest? "Look, I've got to tell you something," Edna said.

"What?" the weirdo asked, taking another deep breath and putting his head between his legs. "You want to try hyperventilating?"

Edna took a deep breath of fresh air and then decided this kid needed both barrels. She put a big smile on her face so Marsh would still think she was having a wonderful time, but she spoke rapidly and with a great deal of sincerity in spite of the phony smile. "I'm going to clue you in, kid, because I have a new honesty policy. Do you mind?"

"No, shoot," the kid said.

"I think you're sick," Edna said. "You look like something's the matter with you; like something's damaged your brain. I don't know what you've been on—cocaine or speed or whatever—but you look emaciated, you look like you don't eat right. Something's eating at your brain cells. And I think you could use a little medical help. I'm sitting here smiling at you, but I feel sorry for you. And I want to tell you, just looking at you makes me so sad and sick inside that I could break down crying, but I've got enough of my own problems and I can't take on your case. I also want you to know, half of the kids that came with you from your commune look just as sick as you are. I'm telling you this because I don't think what you're doing is a joke. I'm smiling at you, but I want you to know that I think you're killing yourself." Edna stood up and walked quickly away. She felt some tears rolling down her cheeks because what she said, she really believed. It made her sad to sit and talk to that weirdo. He was sick, and he looked like the kind of kid you'd find dead from an overdose. There'd been enough of them at her school, and it was no joke. She knew she could walk faster than he so she wasn't worried even if he came after her. All she heard was his voice yell out over the pool, "And let me tell you, you dog face, it's not nice to fool Mother Nature!" She wasn't even sure it was the weirdo's voice, but somehow she felt somebody had yelled it out, and that it applied to her, but she didn't care. Next to that kind of problem, she was on Easy Street. When Edna got to the kitchen, she saw Jacqueline running around like a chicken with its head cut off, putting newspapers on the floor all around the base of the huge candelabra. The candles were all still burning and the wax was falling all over the floor and Jacqueline wanted it to fall on the newspaper.

"Can I do anything?" Edna asked.

"Yeah, help me get some of this newspaper down. If I'm not able to get this wax off in the morning my family's going to kill me," Jacqueline said. "I didn't know there were going to be so many kids. I could really kill Butch, I really could. I could just kill him!"

"I know what you mean," Edna said. "I'm just crossing my fingers none of these freaks walk through the glass windows."

"Did you see Norma Jean?" Jacqueline said.

"What do you mean, did I see her? I saw her contorting on the terrace, and I saw her disappear upstairs," Edna replied.

Jacqueline bent down on her knees to spread out another set of newspapers. "They've got her in the bathtub on the fourth floor."

It took a moment for Edna to picture the sight, and then she knew what Jacqueline was talking about. "Is Marsh with her?"

"No," Jacqueline said. "But there's at least ten other guys in charge of the soap." Jacqueline made a dash for more newspaper when Edna was aware of the fact that the band had stopped playing. Someone was speaking into a microphone, and Edna walked outside to see what was going on. Everyone had stopped dancing at the pool and was staring up at the living-room terrace. She couldn't see Marsh, but the focus of attention was God Boy who was at the edge of the terrace, addressing the crowd over a microphone. Everyone seemed absolutely captivated by his beautiful smile, and now it was clear that he also had a deep, hypnotic voice. "To see the Spirit of the Universe," God Boy was saying, "you must use the Inner Eye which is the miracle that comes to you only if you believe in yourself."

Edna moved farther out towards the pool so she could watch the whole scene and yet not be trapped in the middle of it.

"You are all protecting yourself, guarding yourself," God Boy continued. "And I can feel it even though many of us have never met before this evening. What I want to ask of you now is to make my visit with you have a meaning you will never forget. It is the voice within your soul that I wish to hear sing. I wish to hear a song sung that has never been heard in the world before. I want you all to think of this song—a song that has never been on earth. I want you to hear it played in your mind, and I want you to bring it into being with every dream of hope in your heart. This song will be faint at first, but as you listen to me, I want you to feel it grow. In the silence of this night, in the light of this great glass tower, beneath which we gather, I want you to let this very private song have its birth and let it flow until it fills your hearts. And now I want you to hum this song you hear. Hum your own song and send it skyward." Edna felt something strange happening. She felt goose bumps run down her arms as the sound of humming began to grow around her. All the kids from the commune who were really into what God

Boy was talking about started the whole thing off and then several kids from Curtis Lee High joined in, and within minutes, practically everybody was humming and swaying, including mobs of kids on the living-room terrace and the fourth-floor terrace. Edna even noticed Billy Selmond and Lucille Bore humming, and they usually never went along with anything at a party. Then suddenly there was the sound of a fight breaking out on the fourth-floor terrace. There was screaming and yelling, and God Boy never once looked up or broke his concentration until the thing was settled. Whatever the commotion was, Edna swore she heard Marsh yelling at the top of his lungs. And a minute later, a couple of the commune girls were ushering Norma Jean Stapleton down from the fourth floor. It looked to Edna as if Norma Jean was buttoning up her blouse. And while all of this was going on, most of the kids just stood swaying and humming like they were waiting for some momentary interruption by a demon to pass. There was another small commotion on the fourth-floor terrace and Edna saw Scarface and Public Enemy Number One shoving Marsh to the edge of the terrace. It didn't look like they were going to throw him over or anything like that, it was more like they were detaining him. At that moment, Butch Ontock was leading Jacqueline by Edna. "What happened?" Edna asked. Jacqueline made a grimace. "Marsh caught Norma Jean in the bathtub."

"Silence!" God Boy demanded. His voice shot into the microphone and reverberated as if all the tension that one sensed lurking beneath his exterior was ready to explode. The mob went silent and everyone hung on his next word. "Sing," he said. And in a moment the humming had started again, and it was as though the disruption had never occurred. "You'll see only love. You will feel only truth. You will think only goodness," God Boy said ritualistically. "Raise your arms to the planets; raise them up to the stars and let your song rise. Let the great cerebrum of the Universe demonstrate his love for you tonight. Let him send another song to your ears in return, and let there be harmony in your bodies. Let the Great Eye of the Sky caress you. Let the Eternal Wind brush past your heart. Tonight you will not be afraid to do the beautiful things you think. A miracle is going to happen in your lives. Louder!" God Boy started to raise his voice fanatically. "Louder! And now I want your song to pervade this beautiful home and this beautiful lawn. Let it consume this entire, magnificent hilltop. And now I want everyone to move slowly around the pool, and as you move I want you to believe that you are being guided by the blazing light of love."

Edna couldn't help thinking that Mr. Meizner could really take some lessons from God Boy.

Edna decided she had better start moving, because everyone else was and if she didn't, she'd stick out like a boulder in a stream. Some of the kids from the commune had begun to act like ushers. It was a very subtle process but Edna couldn't help thinking of the commune kids being collie dogs moving a herd of sheep. They made some of the kids move clockwise around the pool, and others counterclockwise so that constantly there seemed to be faces passing each other. The band began to blast out some strange, electronic background, but God Boy's voice rose over it all. "Walk proudly! Transmit your song. Listen and be ready for your song to blend with the music of someone else here tonight. Feel all your songs as they're coming together. As you move, be ready to receive the love-look of anyone who passes."

Edna noticed the faces of the kids flowing by her, and she thought they looked hypnotized. In fact, it made her think of the *Invasion of the Body Snatchers*, which was one of her mother's favorite movies.

"Let your eyes explode," God Boy called into the microphone. "Let your eyes explode with love! I want you to touch your Brothers and Sisters as you pass each other. Reach out your hand and touch each other!"

Edna tried to avoid all the hands that were flying out like bats in a cave, but eventually, some of the kids were getting through. She didn't know what to do. If she went running out of the crowd, which is what she felt like, it would look funny. This must be what "going along with the crowd" means, Edna told herself. And she almost laughed out loud.

"Touch each other like you're supposed to do in the real world," God Boy continued. "Touch each other with your songs and with your epidermis, with every extremity. Touch each other's shoulders. Everyone! Touch your body! Tell your Brother and Sister that they are young and beautiful and that you sing your song for them. If your clothes are in your way, take them off. Don't be ashamed, because in the eyes of

God the human body is a beautiful thing."

Edna didn't hear another word God Boy was bellowing, because half the kids around her actually started taking their clothes off. To be blunt about it, she had to admit that the girls from the commune were nude in two shakes of a lamb's tail. In another minute, so was half the football team. Some kids were jumping in the pool and others were just hugging each other like they were doing a polka. And the band began to play stupendous, crashing chords. The whole scene began to look like a triple-X surfing epoch. Edna tried to back away from the pool and found there were a lot of nudeniks already running around the hill. Most of them looked stoned, and they were into this thing of rolling down the hill and then running back up the hill like a pack of really weird Jack and Jills. The only thing Edna could think of doing was to get back to the house and then escape out the front door. But as she got near the stairs to the second-floor terrace, Norma Jean Stapleton came skipping down, naked as a jaybird. She was prancing along, holding hands with Greg Cutter and Chris Phleghm, and they all jumped into the whirlpool and threw the switch. The whirlpool was bubbling like crazy but it really got out of hand when Maureen Clapper jumped in with a box of Ivory soap. At that moment Edna heard a scream from the fourth-floor terrace and she looked up just in time to see Marsh wild, and looking very drunk. He took off his jacket, threw it behind him, and jumped out into the air. Edna cried out instinctively as he fell the four stories, landing into the pool with a tremendous cannonball. She was sure he must have killed himself, and she ran to the edge of the pool. At the same time, another level of her mind knew that Raccoon was probably still in the jacket that he had thrown off on the top deck. Maybe it was stupid of her to think of an animal when a human being might have just been killed, but Edna couldn't help it. Edna reached the pool just as Marsh surfaced and she realized he was very much alive because he was still screaming. He pulled himself up out of the pool and did a flying leap into the whirlpool where he started punching Greg and Chris. A few of his punches went wild and Norma Jean got socked on the jaw. Everybody was pushing and shoving now around the pool, and Edna lost sight of the action for a minute. She didn't quite know how it happened, but somehow Greg Cutter and Chris Phleghm had pulled Marsh up out of the whirlpool and were shoving him towards the house. Greg Cutter was punching him in the stomach and Marsh looked like he was going to be mutilated until he picked up a lawn chair. Marsh started spinning in a circle like he was some kind of rotary blade, and he was so busy spinning, trying to hit everything near him, that Edna knew Marsh didn't see Nick Phleghm pick up a potted tree.

"Duck!" Edna screamed.

Marsh dropped to his stomach just in time, and the potted tree sailed over his head. The crashing noise of glass breaking was earsplitting as the pot sailed through a set of glass doors, knocking over the candelabra with all its burning candles. The candles tumbled out onto the newspapers which were still spread all over the floor and it didn't take a second before the newspapers were on fire. Some of the commune girls in the kitchen ran to try to stamp out the fire. One girl even tried pouring the pot of spaghetti sauce on the flames, and another girl came running forward with a coffeepot of water. It was already too late because the kitchen drapes began to burn and the drapes went up like they had been soaked in kerosene. Marsh and Greg Cutter were still going at it when Norma Jean was trying to pull them apart. She was screaming, "Fire! Fire!" And the only reason they stopped was because the flames had gotten so big, there was a paralyzing moment of disbelief that the house was actually in flames. Some of the kids didn't know what to do at first, and laughed. But then the situation became very real. The kitchen had so many cracker boxes and tablecloths on the buffet table, that in another half minute it was clear nobody was going to be able to do anything except run for his life. A lot of kids came running down the stairs from the second-floor terrace. The flames had begun to lick their way out of the first-floor doorways, and the second-floor terrace began to burn. There were a lot of girls who reacted by bursting into tears. Most of the boys were so stoned, they were just running back and forth around the house yelling "The house is burning down! The house is burning down!" By the time Edna saw Marsh again, he was lying on his stomach at the far end of the pool and throwing cold water on his face. A trickle of blood was running down his brow from what looked like a very small cut. Before Edna could stop Marsh, he was up on his feet again and taking off after Chris Phleghm. Chris didn't know what hit him as Marsh rammed him with his head.

"He's crazy!" Chris yelled, starting to run away. "This freak is crazy!"

Marsh still tried to grab Chris, but stumbled over one of the kids who was running in circles on the lawn screaming "The house is burning down! The house is burning down!" By this time, Edna had to agree that anyone who was calling out that particular phrase was giving a fairly accurate description of what was going on, because the flames were already well up into the second floor. Suddenly she remembered something and elbowed her way to Marsh. She grabbed him by the arm so tight he couldn't shake her loose.

"Raccoon!" she shrieked.

She saw Marsh turn stark white at the word. "Where's Raccoon?" Edna screamed again, trying to shake him sober. Marsh pushed Edna away and went running back towards the house.

"Maybe somebody brought him down," Edna yelled after him. She managed to grab Marsh again.

"Let go of me!" Marsh cried. "Let go of me!" He shoved her again, and ran towards the flames.

Edna yelled to a group of kids near the house. "Don't let him go in! Stop him!"

The kids heard her and spun just in time to see what Marsh was doing. They reacted instinctively, and it took five guys to hold Marsh and pull him away from the burning staircase. There was no way he could have gotten up to the second-floor terrace, because it was already burning, and there seemed to be an up-draft pulling the fingers of the flames as high as the fourth-floor wooden deck. The only thing Edna could think of doing was to run around to the side of the house and see if she saw any motion on the upper deck. She hoped Raccoon had already been carried out or crawled down the side of the house. Maybe he jumped—anything. Maybe someone had brought him down with them and let him go in the woods. Edna shielded her eyes from the light of the flames and then started to move farther away from the house, along the wooded section near the trampoline. She looked up at the fourth-floor terrace, and what she saw froze her heart. There was a small, furry head with two, frightened, tiny black eyes staring down at her. "Jump, Raccoon, jump!" Edna screamed so loudly she thought her vocal chords would snap. "Jump!" The fire roared so loudly she knew the poor animal would never hear her, and if he did, how could he understand her! There was another rush of flames, and Edna saw the animal back away from the edge of the terrace. Through the slats of wood on the deck, Edna glimpsed the small silhouette of his body. The silhouette moved to the center of the platform, ran in a circle for a moment and then stopped. Flames surrounded the deck in the same way Edna had once seen a boy burn a tick to death. He'd taken the insect off a dog and placed it in the middle of a piece of newspaper, and then lit the edges. The tick had tried to escape, but when it realized there was no way out, it seemed resigned and waited for the flames to explode its body.

Chapter 20 /

Marsh knew Raccoon had to be somewhere in the woods below the house. He felt terrible, because he knew how frightened the animal would be and it was all his fault. The fire would have scared him, all the screaming, the cars roaring away from the house. There was a terrible noise when the commune bus almost crashed into the hook-and-ladder fire engine that got caught on one of the turns near the top of the hill. Two other fire engines were coming up another side, and their sirens were shrieking enough to scare anyone. Two cop cars were already on the scene. Just then, John Mell and Bonnie Hilderstraw came running past Marsh. They were still putting on their clothes.

"Have you seen a raccoon?" Marsh asked. They just kept running. Joan Canyon and Maureen Clapper were racing down another path and he called to them. "Have you seen a raccoon?"

"No," Maureen yelled back, without turning around.

Then he saw Edna. She was walking away from the house, down a path. She looked like she was some kind of a stunned robot in a science-fiction movie. Her eyes seemed glued to the ground, defeated. Not that she was looking for anything, more like she was ready to disintegrate. He called to her and she looked up for a moment, then she just kept walking. He could see her face and it seemed shiny and wet; it looked like she'd been crying, but maybe she'd only been splashed by the pool water. By now the entire house was ablaze and it was as if Edna were illuminated by a spotlight. He caught up to her. "Hey, did you see Raccoon?"

Marsh had to jump to avoid getting kicked by Edna. Her foot swung out again and again, and she tried to punch him on the shoulder. It was then obvious to him that she was crying. She stared at him a minute as though she wanted to kill him, and then she just turned and started running down the path.

"What's the matter?" Marsh yelled after her.

It took him a minute to catch up to her, and this time he grabbed her. "I asked you if you saw Raccoon!" he yelled. Now he was angry. She could at least answer, but instead she tried to kick him again. This time she missed and fell down on the ground. Marsh couldn't figure her out. Maybe she'd gotten stoned with that weirdo kid she was talking with by the pool. All he wanted was to know if she saw Raccoon. The one thing he knew for sure was that nothing bad had happened to the animal because he had a lot of smarts and he would have known how to get out of that house before anyone else. He would have crawled right out of the jacket and down the side of the house. It didn't matter if the house was half glass or not, raccoons had special paws with fingers, and they could grab on to anything. "I asked you if you saw Raccoon!" Marsh yelled at her. He was furious when she wouldn't answer and only began to push herself away from him. Finally, she tripped again and then just stopped fighting.

"He ran into the woods," Edna said. She pointed off to the side and burst into tears again. Mechanically she got up off the ground and started walking away from him again.

"Wait!" Marsh called after her, but Edna just kept heading down the hill.

Marsh looked in the direction where she had pointed. He ran through the wooded area calling for the animal. He even looked up in the trees, straining his voice to make it louder than the firemen and the roar of the fire. At one point he saw Jacqueline Potts being taken across the lawn by what looked like a couple of neighbors. She looked like a basket case. In one part of the woods he met the Phleghm brothers again, and they were so drunk they were walking into trees. He asked them to help him look for Raccoon and they told him he was nuts. He began to get worried then and ran faster and faster through the yards and the thickets around other houses just below the Pottses' house. He was badly ripped by rosebushes, and once he tripped over a stone, banging his knee into a garden post. At least Edna had seen Raccoon running into the woods, and that was the important thing to him. If a hundred drunken, stoned kids could get out of a burning shack, it was a sure thing that Raccoon had made it. Some girl had probably even picked him up and knew he belonged to Marsh. She probably would call his house, or bring Raccoon to school tomorrow. Everybody knew Raccoon was his. In fact, probably right this minute, he knew Raccoon could be up a tree, watching him. Raccoon was probably laughing, watching Marsh run around like a yo-yo calling "Raccoon, Raccoon!" Raccoon was probably on a big oak branch having a good belly laugh.

In another few minutes Marsh was exhausted and realized his body was beginning to shake from his cold, wet clothes. Somehow he sensed there was no point in looking much longer. Raccoon was obviously fine, and that was that. They'd have to just be separated for a few hours, and the best thing he could do for Raccoon would be to clear out of there, because if the police caught Marsh, he knew he'd get in a lot of trouble over the fire. As it was now, probably the only thing anyone would squeal was that one of the Phleghm brothers threw a tree through the window. He knew it would only be a matter of an hour or so before they were on the Phleghm kids' trail—divide and conquer, that's the way the cops worked, and Marsh knew it. They'd grill a half dozen kids and every one of them would screw up each other's alibis. By the end of that night, they'd pin the rap on someone.

Marsh still called for Raccoon all the way to his car. Finally, he got into the car and was thankful, for once, that his mother had bought such a small thing; it was easy to turn around, and in a minute he was headed back down the hill. Half the guys that had the bigger cars were still trapped. A lot of them were stoned and had blocked each other, and when the cops and fire engines had arrived, they finished the job. There were at least five cop cars by now, and Marsh passed another one as he drove down the hill. The main thing he hoped was that he'd see Edna walking along the road. He figured she wouldn't get in anyone's car, because most of the kids that had cars were stoned. But there was the chance that maybe she did like that weirdo boy she was talking to; maybe she got in his car—if he had had one. Marsh didn't understand how she could have spent so much time talking to such a freak.

Marsh drove so fast his car almost went over the side of the hill at one bend, but he braked just in time. He knew Edna might almost be at the bottom of the hill by now, particularly if she took one of the paths that went straight down instead of the curving road. He came around one house that had a lot of glass set in the windows that looked like spiderwebs and he thought he saw her on the side of the road, but it turned out to be one of the commune girls who was staggering, clutching a stack of records and a portable radio. She obviously had ripped them off from the party. Then he passed Richard Kay and Vincent Rolio at the next bend, and they were just jumping up and down like they had gone insane. He stopped the car at the bottom of the hill expecting to see Edna at one of the bus stops, but she was nowhere to be seen. He figured maybe the 113 bus had come along and she'd already gotten on it. But that didn't worry him because he could head it off in a minute or two. He was just about to step on the gas when a figure emerged from a cluster of huge rhododendron bushes. He knew Edna had seen him, but she turned sharply and started walking quickly down Richmond Road. Marsh floored the accelerator and then hit the brake so he skidded to a stop right next to her. In a flash he had the window rolled down.

"Get in," he said, flinging the door open.

He half expected her to pick up a rock and throw it at him, but she just stopped in her tracks.

"I said get in," he repeated. She was still motionless when he threw his shift into park and got out of the car. He was surprised that she went meekly with him. He helped her into the front seat and slammed the door. "Are you all right?" he asked. Edna wouldn't say anything.

Marsh drove slowly along Richmond Road. Another fire engine and a police car came roaring by from the opposite direction. "Look, I'm sorry," Marsh said. "I'm sorry about the house." Maybe that was what was bugging Edna. Maybe she thought he was the cause of the house burning down. "I couldn't find Raccoon, and I looked all over. I'm glad you saw him so at least I know he's okay." Edna still wouldn't look at him, but kept staring straight ahead.

"Oh, he's okay," she said bitterly.

"You're probably happy," Marsh said. "You wanted him to go back to the woods."

Edna shuddered. It seemed almost as though she was growling and all he heard was the last part of what she said. "You're a double s.o.b."

Marsh was so glad to hear any sound emerge from Edna's mouth, he didn't pay any attention to exactly what the words were. The thought had crossed his mind that she'd gone into trauma or something and lost her power of speech. Anything could have happened, he didn't know. "I didn't want to get into that fight," Marsh said. "It wasn't my fault."

"Nothing's ever your fault," Edna said.

"Right. I had a date, and when you have a date you've got to be courteous and all that kind of stuff."

"That was some date," Edna said, drying her face with a Kleenex she'd pulled out of her pocketbook. She blew her nose. "They ought to call you Liberty Bell, because you're half cracked."

"Look, I only took her because you flaked out on me."

"I did what?" Edna asked.

Marsh was going to keep hitting her with the same tone, but somehow he realized he'd better lower his voice. "I can't do it alone."

"You can't do what alone?" Edna practically screamed at him.

That killed all conversation in the car for at least five minutes. Marsh was aware of Edna staring at him and he was also aware that he was grinding his teeth. He was angry that he couldn't stop himself from doing it. Finally he took a deep breath and said quietly, "Pete called." He looked at Edna and saw she was staring at him with such a sharp gaze that he had to swing his eyes back onto the road and keep them there. Finally Edna looked straight ahead and he was glad to have her burning gaze lifted off him.

"And what did he say?" Edna asked.

He sensed a tension in her voice like she was getting ready to hit him again. "You'll think I'm only lying if I tell you," Marsh said. "So why don't we just skip it. I know you're not interested, so just pretend I never said anything. My problem's got nothing to do with you. You just look out for yourself." They drove along in silence for another minute. Finally Edna spoke.

"I won't think you're lying," Edna said in a monotone.

"Yes you will."

"No I won't," Edna insisted quietly.

Marsh waited another moment and then cleared his voice. He knew this part of the story was going to have to come eventually. There wouldn't be any way to avoid it. He knew that once he said the words, that everything might get out of control and begin tumbling, like rocks down a hill. There'd be no turning back. The word *destiny* flashed across his mind, and he felt as though for the first time in his life he knew what that word meant. Not that he knew what his exact destiny was, but that he knew there was such a thing as the inevitable. The words rolled into his mind as if he had actually been programmed to say them. "They'll be cutting a piece of Pete's brain out in seventy-two hours," Marsh said.

He was aware of Edna's head turning slowly towards him. He knew she was studying him carefully.

"I don't care," Edna said precisely. "I don't care at all." And then she found herself screaming at him. "You raccoon-killer! You raccoon-killer!"

Marsh couldn't help himself. He swung the back of his hand out towards Edna and it collided with her face. The slap was so hard, she was thrown against the side of the car. She tried to open the door of the car, but Marsh slammed on the brake, skidding to the side of the road. He grabbed her arm before she could open the door, and he slapped her again and again. She screamed and threw her arm up to stop his hand, but even as he was doing it, he was aware of something very strange. He was aware that Edna Shinglebox wasn't crying.

Suddenly he stopped striking out at her. At the same time, he saw she no longer was trying to escape from the car. He felt instantly and deeply ashamed; not only because of what he had done to her, but because he was aware that he was crying. He slowly lowered his head onto her shoulder and held on to her. "Come with me," Marsh heard himself beg. "Oh, God, please come with me. Please goddam help me."

Chapter 21 /

"My, you're home early," Mrs. Shinglebox said with a slight touch of disappointment in her voice. "Did you have a nice time?"

"It was okay," Edna said. What was she going to say, that she came home a little on the early side because the house burned down? That would trigger her mother into two hours of questions and throw a big solid-steel wrench into Edna's plans.

"Did you meet any boys?" Mrs. Shinglebox asked, zooming straight to the heart of the matter.

"A few," Edna said, trying to act as nonchalant and calm as possible. Edna clung to the shadows in the downstairs hallway so that her mother couldn't see she had been crying. Besides, for all Edna knew, she might have a black-and-blue mark on her face, and that would alert her mother's detective instincts to a point beyond control. Edna strolled into the kitchen and poured herself a glass of milk. She figured she had better do all the things she usually did when she came home after a night out.

"Were there any debutants there?" Mrs. Shinglebox inquired.

"A couple," Edna called out. The thought struck

Edna, as she sipped her milk, that indeed her recent decision to be more truthful about her own life and feelings had made her into quite a little liar to her parents. Maybe there should be a whole, special category for lies told to parents. It was sort of a type of compulsory prevarication necessary to protect mothers and fathers from going berserk. Curtis Lee High might even do well to teach a course in creative fibbing. After all, Edna was only being considerate of her mother. Her mother really wouldn't sleep very well knowing that the party had turned into a conflagration, and that a boy wanted her to split for California to help spring his fictitious paranoid father from a lunatic asylum before a lobotomy was to be performed.

"Was that Marsh's car you got out of?" Mrs. Shinglebox asked, as she barged into the kitchen to fix a plate of cookies for Edna.

"Yes."

"I'm so glad you're talking to him!" Mrs. Shinglebox exclaimed. "It's so wrong to judge a book by its cover. After all, if I had done that, your father would never be your father."

Edna kept herself in rapid motion so that her mother could never quite nail her under a light. Edna tossed her hair, she swung her head back and stretched out her jaw as she sipped her milk, she whirled to take a cookie, she darted back out into the hall as though she'd forgotten something in the hall closet. The thing Edna was very glad about was that her father had already moved away from the color set which was kept in the living room, up to the bedroom which had a smaller black-and-white set.

"I'll bet the inside of that house is exquisite," Mrs. Shinglebox queried.

"That it is," Edna assured her. Edna decided she'd set up her excuse for the morning. "I told Jacqueline I'd go over in the morning to help her clean up."

"That's nice," Mrs. Shinglebox said. "But aren't you going to school?"

"School?"

"Tomorrow's Monday, dear."

"Oh, *school*," Edna remembered. Her inventive mind did double time. "That's why I said early. See, I'll go over before school; just for a half hour or so. Help vacuum the rugs. All the girls agreed to pitch in and help out."

"I thought they would have hired help," Mrs. Shinglebox said suspiciously.

"Oh, they do," Edna said. "A lovely couple, but they went home to Mexico for a special holiday."

"I didn't know there was a holiday in Mexico at this time of year."

"Oh yes. It's called The Feast of Our Lady of Guadalupe."

"What a wonderful family the Pottses must be," Mrs. Shinglebox said, following Edna upstairs.

Edna waited until she was in a very dark shadow before she whirled around and gave her mother a quick kiss good night. "See you tomorrow, Mom," Edna said, waving.

"Marsh is such a lovely boy," Mrs. Shinglebox said as Edna closed the door of her room. The sound of the television in her mother's room crept through the walls, and Edna heard her mother call out one last thing.

"We're watching a movie about hostile vegetables!" Then Edna heard her mother go into her own room.

Edna breathed a sigh of massive relief and sat on the edge of her bed. She rubbed the side of her face where Marsh had hit her. She still had time to think things over, and of that she was thankful. Marsh would have to drive all the way back to his house and change his clothes; Edna knew that would take him at least a half hour. Edna lay back on her bed, still wearing her clothes. She rolled around for a few minutes so the bed would look like it had been slept in, then she stopped squirming and just lay on her back, staring at the ceiling. She felt like a character in a short story she had to read for an English class when she was a freshman. The first part of the story had been very boring because it went into detail about all the kinds of junk this man had in his room. Edna had always hated long, descriptive passages in stories because she simply didn't find objects as interesting as people. The whole thing about the story was that this man was sitting absolutely still, watching an open window where his cat was trying to catch a bird. The big problem with a cat trying to catch a bird on his windowsill was that there happened to also be a heavy flowerpot on the windowsill, and if the cat wasn't careful, it was sure to knock the pot off the windowsill, and the pot would go crashing down, probably on some poor person's head who would happen to be walking by on the sidewalk five stories below. The whole story was about this man sitting absolutely still, and what he was thinking. The man thought if he drove the cat or the birds away, that wouldn't solve the danger, because they'd only return. He also thought that if he moved the pot, his stupid servant would just go and put it back on the windowsill. So after thinking about the situation for a long while, the man decided there was nothing he could do except postpone the tragedy; therefore he did nothing. As Edna remembered the story, she realized that in a sense, she was in the same situation. She felt as though no matter what she did, there was a certain tragedy that had to happen involving Marsh and her. She thought, if this tragedy has to happen, then it might just as well happen tonight.

Edna messed up her pillow some more, and then wrote a note. She left it on her pillow. *Dear Mom and Pop, I woke up early and went over to help Jacqueline clean up. You were still sleeping. See you later. Love, Edna.* Maybe her mother would fall for it, and even if she tried to check it out by calling the Pottses' house, there wouldn't be any answer because there was no longer a Pottses' house. And somehow Edna believed that she would be back by the next afternoon regardless of all the things Marsh said that had to be done. Edna had listened to his whole plan in the car. Marsh said now they had less than seventy-two hours to get to California. Then there was his elaborate explanation of how they would fire the giant American flag rocket near the eucalyptus tree that his father had described as being outside his nuthouse window. There were huge leaps in logic as Marsh had outlined his plan, but Edna never questioned them. Marsh said once his father knew they were outside that Paranoid Pete could make a break for it. Pete would probably bribe a guard or an orderly, Marsh explained. He said his father had told him on the phone that, thank God, everybody at the asylum was as corrupt as the rest of the world and he felt he could bribe his way out the door. At one point when Marsh was rattling on, Edna was going to stop him. She wondered what he would do if she told him that he was all screwed up, that she wasn't going to go along with the plan. But while Marsh was spinning out one preposterous detail after another, Edna found her thoughts drifting to Miss Aimée. Miss Aimée had told her certain things—and that if Edna only knew how to use them she could help Marsh. Edna instinctively felt that what Marsh was doing by babbling on about his incredible modus operandi, was that he was pronouncing that he was near the breaking point. Edna sensed that if she didn't help him tonight, she never could. She let him get it all out, see how far he would really go.

Edna took her small suitcase out of the closet. This was the first time it was going to be used for anything more than a pajama party. She packed her toothbrush, some toothpaste and only one set of clean clothes. She picked the clothes that would be suitable if she were to go to school the next day. Her mother had an uncanny sense about going through her laundry and wardrobe. Her mother's eyes were so sharp she could spot a missing Q-Tip, and maybe it'd take her a day or two, but eventually she'd ask Edna if she had a mastoid. Marsh said it took forty-four hours to drive straight through without stopping, to California, and that he and Edna could make it just in time. Edna knew it was a physical impossibility for Marsh to do all that driving. When she left him, he already looked ready to collapse, and she decided he'd probably conk out sometime before dawn. She'd let him sleep a few hours in the car, and then she'd wake him up and he'd have to realize that they would never make California in time. Actually, it seemed as though Marsh had built in so many impossible elements, that what Marsh had really done was to put himself into the position of having to admit the truth about everything to Edna. The worst thing that could happen, Edna thought, was that Marsh would want to keep on going and Edna would have to call home and tell her mother and father what she was up to. They'd go a little berserk on the phone, but she had a feeling they'd be able to handle it and let her see it through because, ultimately, Marsh was going to have to face up to things. Even if they arrived in Los Angeles, there would not be any such nuthouse. And no matter how many American flag firework rockets they shot off near eucalyptus trees, Paranoid Pete was not going to show up. Genies might come out of lamps, but dead men don't get out of urns.

Edna sat in the dark at her window and waited. She watched the street until she saw the green-and-white Mazda pull up under the designated streetlight. Edna turned her lamp on and off as a signal. She then opened the window of her room. She'd already tied a piece of nylon fishing line around the handle of her suitcase. She swung the suitcase out the window and lowered it as though she were letting down a crab trap. When the suitcase was safely on the ground, she cut the string. She put her nightgown on over her clothes, then she tiptoed out of her room. The television was still going in her parents' room and she was thankful because a few of the stairs made very loud squeaks. If her mother did come out of her room and see her, Edna would tell her she was just going down for more cookies. A minute later, Edna was safe outside the front door. She ran around to the side of the house to where the suitcase was on the ground. She took off her nightgown and put it inside the suitcase. With the string trailing from the handle of the suitcase, Edna moved across the lawn towards the waiting car.

Chapter 22 /

Edna felt a tightening in her throat as Marsh paid the toll on the Outerbridge Crossing. The car climbed the great arching roadway above the Arthur Kill and when she saw the lights of New Jersey stretched out in front of her she felt as though she was leaving more than her home behind her. She'd be back, maybe in an hour, maybe it would be a day; at the most, she'd be home in a week. But she knew she was never going to be the same person again. A truck carrying sheets of metal preceded them across the bridge and the jangle reminded Edna of the sound of Gertrude the Ghost playing the piano. Where was a Harvey Wallbanger now that she needed one, she thought.

For the first time since she'd known Marsh, he was particularly silent and nervous. He kept rearranging himself in his blue, patched-denim jacket, and he had changed out of his wet multi-colored boots into a pair of Hush Puppies. "Love doesn't exist anymore the way it used to in the great classics like *Summer of '42*," Edna remembered him telling her once. He was sure right about that! Edna tried starting a conversation, but Marsh growled that he had to concentrate on the road. By the time they drove onto the New Jersey

Turnpike it had started to rain and he was forced to hunch forward to see the road. Every so often they'd pass a huge, lighted sign warning that the speed limit was fifty miles an hour and there were other smaller signs saying: "Speeders Lose Licenses."

"At least you don't have to worry about losing your license," Edna said, but Marsh was not amused. Edna let a few minutes go by and then she decided she'd better try a few things to see just where Marsh's mind was at the moment.

"You drive very good," Edna said. "Who taught you?"

"Pete."

"Great. My father wouldn't let me touch our car."

"Pete had to teach me so I could drive us home whenever he tied one on."

The thought of Marsh's father stumbling drunk and being plowed into by a bus flashed across Edna's mind. She wondered if Marsh might not be remembering the same thing, or did he have some special way of shutting off that memory. Edna would feel horrible if she ever saw her father drunk. She could imagine Mr. Shinglebox potted at his florist shop. She couldn't imagine what it must be like to see your father killed right in front of you. How much did Marsh see? Was it a bus that just knocked Pete down and ran over his body? Or did it hit him with such force that it threw him high up into the air, then broke his neck or something when he hit the pavement? It was so awful to think about, Edna decided not to think about it; she blocked it right out of her mind. Actually, she realized she blocked it out just like she had blocked out Raccoon's death. The picture of that animal staring over the edge of the terrace with the flames tearing into his fur was something she couldn't bear to fully visualize again. It hurt so much, she had to pretend it never happened. Maybe that was the only way anybody could deal with anything like that. Pretend it never happened. And if what a human being had seen was sufficiently abominable, then maybe it was the magic of the mind to protect that human being so totally by making the person not know the thing had ever really happened. And it wasn't that Edna hadn't been thinking of Jacqueline the whole evening; what the kids had done to her, what had happened to the house, Butch Ontock, the shotgun Jacqueline had mentioned once in the *Crow's Nest* office. Her mother's Valiums. There was only just so much sorrow Edna could bear thinking about in one night.

Edna turned around to make certain her suitcase was on the backseat. It was the first time she had noticed Marsh's suitcase. It seemed so large.

"Did you bring much?" Edna asked.

"Nope."

Edna's eyes lingered on his suitcase for a moment. She had a feeling that there was something more than clothes inside of it. The rain was coming down harder now, and Marsh had to slow down. He leaned still farther to see through the flapping of the windshield wipers. There weren't many cars on the turnpike, and it was now almost one o'clock in the morning. They'd passed several service stations and the names of them seemed especially eerie: James Fenimore Cooper Service Area; Woodrow Wilson Service Area; Joyce

Kilmer Service Area. Edna had never realized how historical the New Jersey Turnpike's service areas were. It reminded her of the decor in Marsh's bedroom. The New Jersey Turnpike service stations all seemed to be like one long lineup of dead men.

Finally they passed the Camden and Pennsylvania Turnpike exits. Marsh said they were going to take the southern route which they'd pick up right outside of Washington, D.C. At this time of year he said sometimes there were terrible ice storms on the north route. His father had taught him that much and they had taken the southern route last time. Everybody, just everybody in the world was supposed to know the southern route was the only route to take at this time of the year.

"Your father was pretty smart, wasn't he?" Edna offered, leaping at the chance to twist the conversation around to his father again.

"He wasn't retarded," Marsh said in a way that sort of cut that topic short. Edna realized after a few other attempts at conversation that there seemed to be an understanding between her and Marsh that everything she mentioned had an undercurrent of "Hey, let's get down to brass tacks"; and every response he made seemed to be "Oh no you don't." The only time Marsh said more than one sentence in a row was when they passed Philadelphia and Marsh said the best time he ever had in school was when he went with his General Science class on a field trip to the Franklin Institute. He said the whole class got on a bus that picked them up at school, and they had a teacher who looked like a nervous chicken, and the class was really the dregs of the earth. He said one kid in the back of the bus was passing around grass like it was going out of style, and the kid was having an imaginary conversation with his grandmother that had everyone howling. Then the other highlights were at the museum where one kid threw an apple at a movie screen that was showing the life story of Louis Pasteur. And a little later, when all the kids got bored and went out front to a fountain and started jumping around in it. Marsh said some kid by the name of Heap stole rolls of toilet paper from bathrooms in the museum and all the kids soaked wads of it in the fountain and threw them at the side of the building.

About a half hour later Marsh and Edna drove off the New Jersey Turnpike and onto another turnpike marked for Washington, D.C. They stopped at a service area called The Maryland House and had ice-cream cones. Edna bought a box of butter crunch, and while they were filling the car up with gas, Edna decided to make up a story just to see how Marsh would react to it.

"Some lady I know died in the washroom here," Edna said. "She was on her way back from a Miami Beach bus tour and she was doing a lot of cha-cha dancing and things like that, and they say she just got off the bus here with the whole crowd and keeled over. That was a few years ago."

Marsh started the car and didn't say anything.

"Yeah, she'd done a lot of other things too. She went waterskiing, and I think kite flying, something like that. Put too much of a strain on herself."

Marsh put on the radio and played it so loud it hurt

Edna's ears. Edna realized she'd better just shut up and eat her butter crunch.

She was still eating butter crunch when they saw a sign saying: Washington, D.C. 20 Miles. By now it was almost four o'clock in the morning and she could see Marsh really looked ready to pass out. Edna had managed to doze off for what seemed about a half hour at one point, but she woke up when Marsh had to swerve the car suddenly. Edna was having a dream about the car being wrapped around a telephone pole, but it turned out that Marsh had simply let the right tires dip off the turnpike onto a soft shoulder for a moment.

"Maybe you ought to pull over and sleep," Edna said, putting on her seat belt for the first time.

"I took a couple of NoDoz."

"Well, I don't think they're working."

"Well I do," Marsh said nastily.

Edna began to calculate the timing again. She realized it had taken them over four hours to get outside Washington, so working backwards, if she wanted to walk in the front door of her house as though she'd only been at school, that would mean they had about eleven hours to do what had to be done without her having to make a phone call to her parents telling them what was really going on. The tricky part about the eleven hours, she knew, was that four and a half were already used up for the return trip, and that's if they were to turn around right this minute. That left only about six hours to play with, and every minute they went forward, would mean an extra minute they would need to get back. In other words, every hour forward would need another hour to get back, and that wasn't even allowing for Marsh to get some sleep. Edna realized that if something was going to happen, it would have to happen soon or she wasn't going to get away with anything. My God, she thought, Edna Shinglebox, *professional runaway.* She remembered her mother sitting on her bed and her head began to jerk. "We think you're very beautiful," Mrs. Shinglebox had said. "The butcher thinks you are too. What a wonderful, sensitive daughter." Edna wondered how wonderful and sensitive the butcher would think she was when Mrs. Shinglebox told him she was a fugitive. Edna looked at Marsh and let out a scream at the top of her lungs.

"What's the matter?" Marsh jerked up in his seat.

"Your eyes were closed!" Edna said furiously.

"They were not."

"Nobody drives fifty miles an hour while I'm in the car with their eyes closed! You need sleep."

"I'll take another NoDoz."

"You need more than a NoDoz. You need a transfusion!" Edna realized her new job would be not to watch the road, but to watch Marsh's eyes to make sure the lids didn't lower. "At least let's stop for coffee," Edna insisted, but Marsh just ignored her.

It was still drizzling when Marsh made a wrong turn and drove onto a highway that circled Washington. Edna knew it was the wrong turn, because every twenty minutes or so she'd see the same signs all over again. She didn't bother saying anything, because she wanted to know just how long it would take for Marsh to realize that he was in some kind of huge traffic pattern around Washington, D.C. She thought he'd catch on the third time they passed one huge sign that said "To Alexandria." Finally Marsh pulled the car over to the side of the highway. He yanked a map out of the glove compartment, looked it over, and then sped back onto the circle highway. At least his anger seemed to wake him up a little, but then she noticed he had taken his shoes off.

"It's against the law to drive without shoes," Edna said.

"What are you going to do? Make a citizen's arrest?" he snapped at her.

"Don't be sarcastic."

"You could just roll down your window and start yelling 'Hey everybody, this guy in here is driving in his socks!' "

Edna realized she was getting tired and cranky herself. She was going to apologize, but she hardly got the first word out when he shot her a look of rage. Then he suddenly swung the car wheel and they went flying off an exit marked "Capitol District." Edna looked at the teenage maniac next to her and she had a good laugh remembering what her father had said: "One of these days a boy will come along and take one look at you and see all the beautiful things I see, and you'll never get rid of him." She began to pray that her father was wrong about the never getting rid of him part.

For several miles there were just a lot of small houses with trees, and then there were a few miles of construction and the road narrowed to a single lane. There was still no traffic, so it didn't matter. But a lot of the houses along this section began to look like real slums. They looked worse than anything Edna had ever seen on Staten Island. The car went into a long underpass, and when it emerged it seemed to Edna as though they were in a totally different world. Suddenly everything looked all spruced up. The Capitol Building was lit up on the left, and every block or two seemed to have a famous monument on it. The easiest one to recognize was the tall, needle tower which was the Washington Monument. And after that, there was a beautiful rectangular building with pillars, and they didn't know what that was until they had driven half-way around it and saw the statue of Lincoln sitting in a huge stone chair.

Marsh slowed the Mazda and looked from side to side as they drove through what looked like a deserted city. Again Edna got the feeling she was in a morgue. There were memorials all over the place; big marble buildings erected to the memory of the very famous and the very dead. It all seemed like just one more extension of Marsh's bedroom and the New Jersey Turnpike. All some kind of mass memorial. And the thought crossed Edna's mind that if many more famous people died, it wouldn't take long before the whole earth would become just one big monument. "In my day, all we did was sit still and look like a well-groomed corpse," Edna remembered her mother had said. If only Mama could see me now, Edna thought.

"This place has wall-to-wall crooks," Marsh said. "They only commute into the offices in the daytime, then they decide who's going to live and who's going to die, who's going to get the graft and the payola and the political appointments—and then they clear out so that the minorities don't shoot them at night. Everybody's out for themselves. Everybody's a killer."

Edna let that remark float in the air for a moment. She didn't want to change Marsh from his subject, but she thought he was going a little bit too far.

"Some people are nice," she said blandly.

"Nobody's nice."

"What about George Washington?"

"He was a phony."

"What do you mean, he was a phony?"

"He wore wigs and wooden false teeth."

"You're crazy."

"I am not crazy. He also went around buying and selling slaves, and the only thing he was the real father of was real-estate rip-offs."

"Would you mind not driving so fast," Edna said, her patience really running out.

"Just shut up," Marsh said. His tone was so mean, Edna was about ready to just throw in the sponge. Instead, she decided she'd count to ten and check to make sure her seat belt was secure. She felt better after counting to ten, so she decided to count to a hundred. By this time she seemed to be back in control again.

"Maybe it takes a long time to be honest," Edna said as Marsh raced the car around a turn and onto a main road along the edge of the city. There was a river on one side, and vast stretches of lawns and parkland dotted with other huge monuments bathed in spotlights. Edna saw a historical marker proclaiming that the river was the Potomac, and a minute later she noticed next to the highway an isolated cluster of curved apartments. There was a large canopy on which, in large letters, were the words "The Watergate." Edna thought Marsh didn't notice the building, but suddenly he rolled down his window and started screaming out "Crooks! Crooks! Crooks!" Then he rolled the window back up and slammed his foot back down on the accelerator. "Liars!" Marsh said through his teeth.

"Please don't drive so fast," Edna pleaded. The words were no sooner out of her mouth, than the car lunged forward with greater speed. Marsh was driving so fast he ended up on a kind of loop and for a minute it was like they were driving on the Indianapolis Speedway. Finally, the road straightened out again, and they were flying back along the edge of the Potomac. Edna watched the river until it seemed to blur from the speed. She cleared her throat and decided she'd better speak up now or forever hold her peace. Her voice was soft, but frightened. "You're a liar too, you know," she said.

Marsh didn't answer. His laser-beam eyes seemed glued on the roadway ahead and he gave the car more gas until the rear wheels began to slide from side to side.

"You're trying to kill us both," Edna said. "I know about your father, Marsh. I'm sorry. I'm very sorry."

Edna was still looking at Marsh as the car began to skid sharply to the right. By the time she looked out the front windshield, the car was already flying up over the curb. Instinctively, she put her left hand up to the roof, and her right hand braced against the dashboard. It felt so strange, because in the second she had to react, she still found herself with enough time to realize she was going to be in a crash. The car went forward, out of control, and plowed onto the riverbank. The next thing Edna was aware of was that she was turning over and over and over, and she waited for the whirling of the earth and sky to stop and for her to die. Then she felt the motion slow and her car door flew open. The motion slowed even more, and she was sure the car would roll until she was crushed. Then the motion seemed to stop for a second and reverse ever so slightly. She didn't even remember releasing the seat belt, but she must have because she had swung from an upside-down position and was crawling out the door. A second later she was aware of being on her feet and walking, dazed, near the edge of the river. The car had finished rolling a few feet from a low, stone wall and she was aware of the water beyond and of a wind striking her in the face. She felt her head to see if she was bleeding, but she saw no blood. It was so weird because she was in shock, and yet she *knew* she was in shock. Then another set of instincts became manifest and she rushed back towards the car. There was a trace of smoke coming from the front of the smashed, upside-down car and immediately her eyes spotted the rear window. It had miraculously popped out in one piece and was lying on the ground.

"Marsh!" Edna yelled. "It's going to blow up!" Edna didn't know whether Marsh was dead or alive, but she screamed several times, and then she saw Marsh pull himself out of the rear window.

"What happened?" Marsh mumbled, getting up on his feet and spinning in a circle. Edna grabbed him by the arm and led him away from the car. Looking over her shoulder, she couldn't believe they had survived the pile of twisted metal. She knew it had turned over at least a couple of times, and the whole thing had felt like some awful ride at an amusement park. She tried to talk again, but couldn't find her voice. She somehow knew they were both in shock. She cried out when Marsh ran back to the car. She was aware that she was yelling over and over something about how the car might catch on fire, that the gas tank would explode. But in a second Marsh had grabbed his suitcase and came running back. It seemed like such a strange thing to do, Edna thought, to be in shock and crawl out of a wreck and then in a minute go running back after a measly suitcase.

"Yours is crushed behind your seat," Marsh said. "I couldn't get it out."

"I don't care," Edna said.

The next thing Edna was aware of was the two of them sitting against the river wall a good distance from the car. The car didn't even look like a car anymore and it was obvious that it wasn't going to be good for anything except a junk heap. And then there came the sound of a police siren. It was very faint and very far away. She didn't see how anyone could have reported the accident because there was nothing but deserted park grounds and monuments. Watergate seemed so far down the river, but even if somebody was up on one of the balconies she didn't think they would have even noticed. It was still so dark out. She knew anybody with any sense would be sleeping.

"Let's get out of here," Marsh said. He stood up clutching his suitcase.

"Maybe we've got broken bones," Edna said.

"We'd know about it if we did."

"Not necessarily. Maybe we need an ambulance," Edna muttered, and she thought even further . . . maybe what they needed was their families and some help and some food and some sleep. She was aware of herself muttering, and she couldn't stop as they hurried along the river road until they reached the first bridge that led over the river. With every step she took, the more she wanted to say, "Let's go home. Let's get off this merry-go-round. Let's just give up and do something like nice normal kids. Let's go to school; let me go to work on the *Crow's Nest*; let me go home and watch television; anything." And then she had this absolutely absurd thought of going to a drugstore and buying a postcard with a scenic view of Washington and sending it to her history teacher. And maybe she'd send one to Miss Conlin. Edna knew it was absolutely bizarre that her mind would think of doing such things while in the middle of a disaster.

"What are you stopping for?" Marsh asked.

This wee little voice inside of Edna was chattering again. The little voice wanted to tell Marsh that she wasn't going to go any farther. This was it. It was great fun, but it was just one of those things. Edna watched Marsh walk out on the bridge. He went to the first lamplight and then leaned over to look at the river below, then he looked back at Edna as though he were puzzled at her behavior. For a moment she thought she was dreaming. What she saw made a chill run through every cell of her skin. It was as though she were looking at a movie: Take One: A boy alone on a bridge with a suitcase; beautiful, ornate lampposts glowing and stretching across a river that gleamed in the night. And in the background, the destination of all, were the massive black-and-gold gates of a huge cemetery. For a moment Edna's neck twitched, but then she thought she heard the laugh of a witch and decided to walk forward.

Chapter 23 /

Edna caught up to Marsh near the center of the bridge; he'd stopped again. She noticed there was a rather large rip in the side of the suitcase and Edna's attention was drawn to the flash of something metal. She looked closer at the tear in his suitcase, and in the light from one of the bridge lamps she knew it was the corner of a shiny bronze urn. Edna knew they weren't alone on the bridge. In fact, for a moment she thought she was starring in a movie called *Let's Kill Jennifer* which had a promotional ad about a girl being in a rowboat with a skeleton's hand coming up out of the water to get her.

The urn made a clinking sound on the cement when Marsh set the suitcase down. Edna could see the urn was straining at the tear in the suitcase and it looked as if when Marsh would move it again, the urn might probably roll right out onto the roadway. Instinctively, Edna bent down and pulled the corner of the urn until it slid out of the hole in the suitcase. It was partially wrapped in a T-shirt that said Kiss Me Quick on it. Quickly, and as if it was the most natural thing in the world, she put the urn up on the railing of the bridge and then leaned over to look down at the water with Marsh. Edna thought he looked like he was still in shock.

"I think we'd make better time if you didn't have to lug this along," Edna said.

Marsh looked up for a moment. She knew he saw the urn, but he didn't react. Then he returned his gaze back down to the water.

"We should get rid of it here," Edna said. She waited a minute, but there was still no reaction from Marsh. "Don't you think so?" Edna asked.

Marsh still didn't say anything, so Edna just let him think things over a minute. Then she decided to move the urn an inch forward towards the edge of the cement railing. She waited another minute and when Marsh didn't say anything she pushed it still farther so that now almost half of the urn protruded over the railing. She saw Marsh glance at it out of the corner of his eye, so she was certain that he knew what she was up to. The sound of the police siren became louder and Edna waited as long as she could. Finally she just gave the urn a good shove and it went flying out falling down towards the water. The urn hit the river with a big splash and it started to sink as the current swept it rapidly under the bridge. Marsh ran to the other side and Edna was right behind him. There was nothing to see except the reflections of The Watergate and the streetlamps on the tips of the waves. Not far away on the riverbank they saw the flashing dome of the police car stop at the wrecked Mazda.

"Come on," Marsh said. He started to move as fast as he could with the suitcase and Edna had no trouble keeping up with him. Another siren screamed through the night and it seemed like there was no place to hide. There were a lot of road reconstruction sites, and anything that moved on either side of the river could be seen if somebody cared to look. The police would certainly know the car was still hot and steaming. When Marsh and Edna reached the other side of the river, there were only the giant gates of the cemetery and a few small buildings. There was really nothing much to hide behind and the cemetery fence was so high and endless Edna could only think about the joke of how cemeteries are the most popular places in the world because people are dying to get into them.

They made it to the dark side of one of the small buildings. Edna peeked out from one corner to see what the police were doing on the other side of the river. It looked as if they had gotten tired of examining the wreck and now they were scanning the riverbanks. At that moment her eye caught a large sign near the building that had a map of the cemetery and a timetable announcing the departure of tours. Edna almost keeled over when she realized what cemetery it was. And the idea that there were little tour buses to take the public around to see graves was horrifying. The sirens began to scream again and Edna could see the police cars moving along the far side of the river. In a minute they would be at the bridge.

"What now?" Edna asked. She turned and saw Marsh was already hobbling along with the suitcase towards the monstrous cemetery gates. She realized he had spotted one section where it looked like a person might slide through the bars, but until she saw him disappear, she figured the only way they'd fit through there would be to be greased with butter. She got to the bars in time to help Marsh through with the suitcase. Socks and underwear were still dropping out of the tear.

"You're dropping stuff," Edna yelled as she turned sideways and shoved herself through the bars. One of the police cars, its searchlight flashing, was crossing the bridge. Edna kept close behind Marsh as they ran up the first slope of the cemetery and she only turned around once when she realized the police car had stopped at the middle of the bridge. She heard the sound of a car door slamming and she realized the cops had found the T-shirt and God knows what else that had dropped out of the suitcase. Even though she was running through acres and acres of graves, it did seem a little wild that the cops at that moment were probably trying to fit things together, and Lord only knew what they'd think of the Kiss Me Quick T-shirt.

Edna thought they had run at least a half mile up through graves before Marsh finally stopped. There were miles and miles of graves on both sides of them, all with the exact same small white stone announcing the name of the soldier buried below it. Rows and rows, thousands and thousands of dead sons and fathers and men who had gone off to the wars and been shipped home dead. Now the river seemed far away, and she was sure the police would never find them as long as they stayed in the cemetery. There were too many trees, and boulders and knolls and special monuments to hide behind. There was even an open grave they had passed with an apparatus for lowering a casket; a big mound of fresh dirt was just waiting nearby.

Marsh was sitting on the grass between two graves. His suitcase was at his feet and he was staring at the gaping hole in its side. Edna looked at him and knew something had gone wrong. She'd thought she had been so smart on the bridge. She thought it was just the right thing, but now she felt it had been a mistake. She'd been hoping that some kind of magic would happen, that the melancholy prince would suddenly be free. The urn would sink to the bottom of the river and the prince would look up and think Edna Shinglebox was a princess and they'd go off to a discotheque or something and live happily ever after. She sat on the grass next to him which meant part of her was resting on a grave. She patted the grass apologetically and then felt an enormous sense of depression. She didn't know whether she was coming or going. Maybe the cops should come along and lock the two of them up in a nuthouse. She was thinking one black thought after another when her eye caught the sight of a small light flickering behind some bushes about a hundred yards down the hill on the left. The light reminded her of Miss Aimée's sign shining in the night. For a moment Edna's depression gave way to anger. She was angry at herself because she felt she had all the answers right in front of her and she still didn't know how to put them together. And after the anger Edna was consumed by guilt. Maybe she didn't feel as guilty as that librarian who didn't know how to handle the death of her mother, but maybe almost as guilty. There was something that seemed to click in about the way Miss Aimée had handled that; it was as though Miss Aimée had some kind of gypsy instinct that presided over her gyp tactics—the candles, all that other garbage, were phony. But there was something about what she had told the librarian that seemed to hold something very profound and true. Edna imagined the librarian walking up to the edge of her mother's grave. She pictured the librarian getting down on her knees and digging up the earth and sliding her book into a small hole, and then covering up the book with dirt. The great symbolic act, Miss Aimée had said—*the symbolic act*. But there was more to it. The librarian had to say the words. She was the one that had to tell Miss Aimée what was true about her mother. Those were the two conditions, and maybe that's what had gone wrong with the urn. Marsh still hadn't said anything. When the cremation urn had been between them on the bridge he didn't say anything; he didn't even do anything. It was Edna who had thrown it into the river. Maybe that was the mistake, Edna thought. If Marsh had done it, maybe that would have been the symbolic act.

The light she had been looking at began to flicker even more and she realized it wasn't just the branches of the bushes moving in the wind in front of the light. She suddenly realized she had been staring at a torch.

Edna slowly got up off the ground; she picked up the suitcase and started walking towards the torch. "Come on," she said to Marsh.

They had to walk around to the front of the area in

order to reach the paved path. A huge resplendent marble platform lay in a half-moon shape at the base of this grave. The top of the grave itself was covered with irregular Cape Cod granite stones and protected by a small, black, chain fence. The torch burned near the center of the stones and illuminated the name of the man buried beneath. *John Fitzgerald Kennedy.*

Marsh mumbled something.

"Did you say anything?" Edna asked.

Marsh was silent for a long while; finally he spoke. "He wasn't so bad, but they blew half his head off."

Edna decided not to say anything at first. She waited until she thought it was the right moment, and then she said, "He was probably a pretty good father too. Don't you think?"

"Maybe," Marsh said.

Edna burst into tears and just stood next to Marsh staring at the burning torch. She was furious with herself for breaking down because she knew she mustn't; she had to pull back, hang in there a little longer until all the pieces came together. A moment later she managed to stop the tears.

"Do you have anything to tell me?" she asked.

Marsh didn't answer. Edna waited a minute, then she picked up the suitcase again and walked to the curved, marble patio. She set the suitcase down on the marble rim and noticed there were words carved into the stone. Some of the quotes were terrific and she didn't even know the president had ever said them. The one beneath where she had set the suitcase was the only quotation she'd ever heard before: "And so my fellow Americans ask not what your country can

do for you, ask what you can do for your country."
She turned for a moment; she wanted to point it out
for Marsh. She decided not to. If he said anything,
he'd probably just say something cynical that he
didn't mean like that some hired speech writer had
probably cooked it up and JFK was just getting all the
credit now. Marsh walked over to her and picked up
the suitcase.

"Let's get out of here," he said.

He yanked the suitcase handle so hard, it was as if
he was angry with it—and the entire side of the suitcase gave way. His junk spilled out all over the marble patio. Marsh gave the suitcase a kick and just sat
down with his back against the marble railing. Edna
surveyed the junk. There were some ball-point pens,
a Max men's hair dryer, a paperback called *God's
Smuggler* and a few more socks and shirts, as well
as a sweater. Also, there was a long, flat cardboard
box Edna had seen twice before.

"Do you mind if I open the box?" Edna asked. She
didn't even wait for an answer, but just lifted the top
and put it to one side. The rocket lay in the bottom of
the box like a man in a coffin. The instructions were
still wrapped around the body of the rocket with a
rubber band. Slowly, she lifted the rocket out of the
box and stood it upright. She noticed Marsh was staring at the rocket, and just the way he looked, she
knew what had to happen. She took the sheet of instructions off the rocket and moved the rest of
Marsh's junk away from the area. The sheet of instructions was really stupid, because all it had written
all over it was WARNING, WARNING, WARNING

and that a person needed a match to light the fuse. She read it twice to see if she missed anything and then she tore the paper in half. One of the halves she turned over to the blank side and put it in Marsh's hand along with his ball-point pen. "I want you to write something," Edna said, not asking *would* he, or *could* he, or *please*, or anything like that. It was simply an order. "We're going to write down whatever we hate most in the world. Just one thing; one most terrible thing!"

"Forget it," Marsh said. He started to walk away and Edna didn't know what to do. Then he stopped near the stairs and looked back. While he looked at her she took the other half of the paper, picked up the pen and wrote something very quickly. She knew she wasn't saying it the way she might if she had more time. All she could do was at least get the thought down. *I hate not being able to tell you I want to touch you.* She walked rapidly to Marsh before she could change her mind, and pressed the piece of paper into his hand. Then she hurried back to the rocket. She kept her back to Marsh and this time she counted until she couldn't bear it any longer. All she knew was that in a minute, in a second, she'd have to turn around and look at the first boy to whom she had told something that was so important to her it made her hurt inside. She expected him to be gone, but when she turned around he was sitting on the marble wall, writing. Whatever he wrote, he crossed out. Then he wrote again, and this time he came over to Edna and gave her the paper. She looked down, and the familiar handwriting shouted up at her: *I hate that my father is dead.* Edna didn't look at Marsh; instead, she rummaged through the pile of his junk looking for the rubber band that had held the instructions on the rocket. When she found it, she took their two pieces of paper and attached them to the body of the rocket.

"I need a match," she said.

"I don't have any."

Edna didn't waste a second. She ripped off the back cover of the paperback and rolled it into a tight little wand; she headed for the torch. She stepped over the low chain and then bent far over, putting the end of the cardboard into the flame. She hurried back to Marsh, cupping the flame from the wind. She was about to light the fuse when her hands stopped suddenly.

"Get over here!" she yelled.

Marsh moved slowly towards her.

"Hurry up," Edna ordered.

Marsh waited until the flame was close to burning Edna's fingers, and then he grabbed the cardboard and brought the flame to the end of the fuse. The fuse began to spit sparks and Edna didn't have to be told to get away. Edna and Marsh ran to the end of the marble patio and out onto the lawn. They were still running when they heard the whistling sound and saw the reflection of light on the tombstones in front of them. They stopped and turned to look back. The blast-off was over and the first stage shot high up into the night sky. A trail of sparks showed the rocket climbing hundreds of feet before the second stage exploded sending a blinding set of red and white streaks across the heavens. Edna and Marsh bent their heads back as far as they could, and Edna knew, as she watched the sky, that she was seeing the spectacular end of a ghost. In an instant there was the explosion of the last stage of the rocket, and then, at last, there were the stars set in their proper place.

Format by Kohar Alexanian
Set in 11 pt. Century Expanded
Composed, printed and bound by The Haddon Craftsmen, Inc.
HARPER & ROW, PUBLISHERS, INCORPORATED